The Start of Something Big

Tales from Grace Chapel Inn

The
Start of
Something
Big

Sunni Jeffers

Guideposts
CARMEL, NEW YORK

Acknowledgments

All Scripture quotations are taken from
The Holy Bible, New International Version. Copyright © 1973,
1978, 1984 International Bible Society. Used by permission
of Zondervan Bible Publishers.

www.guideposts.org
1-800-431-2344
Guideposts Books & Inspirational Media Division
Series Editors: Regina Hersey and Leo Grant
Cover art by Edgar Jerins
Cover design by Wendy Bass
Interior design by Cindy LaBreacht
Typeset by Nancy Tardi
Printed in the United States of America

 # Acknowledgments

Special thanks to my husband Jim, who patiently reads every word and offers excellent insights; to Karen Solem for opening doors; and to my writing sisters at Coeur d'Alene.

—Sunni Jeffers

Chapter One

Jane Howard pushed with her foot just hard enough to start the swing swaying gently as she sat on the elegant Victorian front porch of Grace Chapel Inn and sipped lemonade. She watched sunny-yellow daylilies and raspberry-red peonies bob daintily on their stems as honey bees crawled deep into their blossoms, gathered pollen, then buzzed off to other blooms.

Jane's sisters—her partners in the inn—Louise Howard Smith and Alice Howard, sat on the nearby wicker chairs, talking quietly. Wendell, the inn cat, snoozed in a third chair. The warm sun, sweet scents and soft voices brought back images of childhood, when Jane would sit on a colorful braided rug, cutting out clothes for her paper dolls while her older sisters sat and talked. She chuckled at the memory. They had seemed so ancient to her then, all of fifteen and twelve years her senior, and they had discussed grown-up things while she created pretend worlds for her paper figures. That must be . . . over forty years ago. Goodness. How could that be? But, yes, Louise's short, neat silvery hair attested to the passage of years, and Alice's countenance bore the soft gentleness of years of kindness and compassion that she showered on her friends and her patients at the hospital.

Jane closed her eyes so she could listen to the sounds of nature more intently. The clear, sweet flutelike song of an oriole made her heart sing. "*Hmmm.* Beautiful," she said.

"What's beautiful?" Louise inquired.

Jane opened her eyes. "Sorry. I didn't mean to interrupt you. I was listening to the oriole and thinking what a glorious day this is. I can't remember a prettier June day."

"That's exactly what Vera said when we walked this morning," Alice said. "The sky is such a startling, clear blue."

"Yes," Jane said, "it makes me feel—oh, I don't know—expectant. Sounds silly, I suppose, but I feel like something special, something exciting is about to happen."

"When Viola and I had lunch at the Coffee Shop, Fred was there. He told us that he's forecasting excellent weather for the next month," Louise said. Fred Humbert owned Fred's Hardware and had gained local distinction as an expert weather prognosticator. "Our esteemed mayor overheard Fred's prediction. Lloyd called it a good omen for the Fourth of July festivities."

"Omen, *shmomen.* It's nothing of the kind," Alice said. "It is an answer to prayer. Our trip is less than a month away, and I have prayed every day for excellent weather. I do believe the good Lord has heard my prayers. And I take that as a sign that He will work out all the details to make this a memorable time for the ANGELs."

Alice was the leader of a church group of middle-school girls known as the ANGELs. Periodically she would take some of the older girls on a special trip.

"I can't think of anything bigger or more daring than taking five teenage girls to New York City for a week. Has Vera decided whether she is going with you?" Jane asked.

"Not yet. She said she would let me know this week. She wants to go, but she usually helps Fred in the hardware store during her summer breaks from teaching. They do a lot of cleaning and reorganizing, and the store tends to be busy over the Fourth of July holiday. She is a little concerned this year though. Business is quite slow since that Do-It-Yourself Warehouse opened in Potterston."

"I'd think the townspeople would support a local business. Fred works so hard and helps so many people in Acorn Hill, he deserves their loyalty." Louise said.

The front door creaked open, and Ethel Buckley poked her head around the edge. "There you are." She stepped out of the inn onto the porch. "I came in through the back door. I wondered where you all had disappeared to."

"Come sit down, Aunt Ethel," Louise invited. "We can get another glass for you."

"Oh, I wouldn't want to put you to any trouble . . ."

Jane rose from the swing and moved toward the door. "No trouble. I'll just get a glass and be right back."

Ethel lived in the carriage house behind the inn. She always had a purpose for coming over and rarely refused refreshment.

"Well, if you insist. Thank you, dear."

Before Jane stepped through the doorway, she saw Ethel reach for a butter cookie. When she came back, Ethel was still standing. She remained standing even after Jane handed her a glass of lemonade and sat back down on the swing.

"I didn't want to tell my good news until you returned, Jane, but I can barely contain myself," Ethel said, putting her hand over her heart as if she were out of breath or suffering a palpitation. She looked perfectly healthy, though, and Jane thought her red hair looked a shade brighter today, whether from the sun shining on it or a touch-up at the Clip 'n' Curl. Ethel drummed her cheek with glossy peach fingernails and looked at each of them, waiting for someone to pick up on her cue. Aunt Ethel loved drama and took every opportunity to stage a scene.

"What is it, Auntie?" Alice asked.

"I just received a telephone call from my darling daughter

Francine." She took a deep breath, as if to still her heart. Jane might have been concerned, but their aunt did everything with a theatrical flair.

"Francine is coming for a visit!"

"That's wonderful news," Louise said. "It'll be so good to see her. When is she coming?"

"She's coming for the week of the Fourth of July. Honestly, I wonder how she can break away from all she does. She's squeezing this visit in between several charity events that she's involved in." Ethel set her glass on the table and wrung her hands. "This visit came up so suddenly. I don't know if I can be ready in time."

Jane took a sip of lemonade to hide her smile. The drama was extreme even for Ethel.

"That's the week I'm taking the ANGELs to New York City," Alice said. "I hope Francine stays long enough for me to see her when I get back. What do you need to do, Aunt Ethel? Perhaps we can help you get ready."

"Oh, I couldn't impose."

"We'd be happy to help," Jane said. "We want Francine to enjoy her visit too."

Ethel turned to Jane. "You did such a lovely job of decorating the inn. If you really want to help, perhaps you would give me some advice on a few small changes to the carriage house. I want everything to be perfect. Not that I couldn't decorate by myself. I do have a certain eye for design. However, you are young, like Francine, and perhaps could suggest some changes more to her liking. Nothing major, mind you."

This time Jane let her grin bloom in full. "Young." Yes, she and Francine were a mere fifty. And Ethel wasn't that old. Somewhere in her midseventies, Jane believed, although Ethel, who usually couldn't keep a secret, never divulged her age. "I'd be delighted to help."

"Wonderful, dear. Could you come over this afternoon so we can begin formulating plans?"

Jane caught sympathetic looks from her sisters. There went her plans to work on her jewelry that she supplied to Sylvia's Buttons and Nellie's dress shop. She swallowed a sigh and gave her aunt a smile. "Just give me time to clean up our dishes, and I'll come over."

"You go on ahead," Alice said. "I'll take care of the glasses and plates."

"Well, all right then."

Ethel beamed, and Jane had a sinking feeling that the decorating could involve something much bigger than a few changes. Ethel was every bit as opinionated as Louise was, and remodeling the inn had brought Jane to several show-downs with her oldest sister. But then, Jane loved to decorate and she loved a challenge. She tried to cheer herself. *This could be fun*, she thought.

As she stood in the small living room with her aunt several minutes later, Jane surveyed the subdued pastels, the old-fashioned maple furniture and the overstuffed armchair that Jane remembered from her childhood visits to Aunt Ethel and Uncle Bob's farm. She loved that chair and couldn't imagine replacing it, although it was far from modern. It had been reupholstered a few years ago. Perhaps new throw pillows would help to dress up the living room. Knickknacks and family pictures covered every square inch of available space. They needed to go. Not altogether, but the look had to be simplified.

Jane wondered how welcome her ideas would be. Even though she'd asked, Ethel rarely sought advice. Jane knew that she must exercise restraint.

"What kind of changes do you have in mind, Aunt Ethel?"

"I want to make things look more modern. It won't take much, however, it could use some touches, if you know what I mean."

"Well, yes, but you don't want to decorate just to please Francine. After all, you have to live with the decor."

"Oh, Francine has excellent taste. I would like anything she would like."

"I've never been to Francine's house. What style does she prefer?"

"Her home is very elegant. She entertains a great deal, you know. Geoffrey's position in the law firm requires a lot of socializing. Francine hired an interior decorator, and I'm sure she spent a great deal of money on all the formal furnishings. The wallpaper in her dining room is raw silk."

"Do you want to add formal touches to your decor?" Jane asked, thinking that would be hard to do in the small, countrified architecture of the carriage house. Jane loved the charming little home, but it still had the ambiance of a converted carriage barn.

"Only a few. Just enough to give my home a little class. Francine's house is a bit too formal for Acorn Hill. But I don't want her to think that my home needs improvements. Not that she'd dream of being critical, but Francine is used to nice things, you know."

"I'm sure Francine appreciates the charm of the carriage house. It is a historic structure, after all. But I can see your dilemma. We don't have much time. Perhaps we should make a list of the most pressing tasks."

"Yes, I thought of that. I started a list." Ethel retrieved a sheet of notepaper from the maple desk in one corner of the living room and handed it to Jane.

To-Do List

1. Guest room:
    a. Paint or wallpaper
    b. New drapes
    c. New bedspread and pillows
2. New drapes in living room
3. Decorating touches

Jane's mind churned with possibilities as she read the precise handwriting. Ethel wanted formal touches. Jane didn't care much for formal styles, but she could pull it off. Besides, the final choices were up to Ethel, and she wouldn't hesitate to voice her opinion. Jane thought the old maple furniture needed a facelift. She remembered when those same pieces occupied Ethel and Bob's farmhouse when she was a child, and the furniture had seemed old then. "Where shall we start?"

"The guest room. Come and see what you think." Ethel opened the French doors to the small room that doubled as a guest room and office. It occupied the space that at one time had been the horse stalls. By the time Jane was born, the horses had long since been replaced by an automobile, and the stables had been transformed into living quarters for various people whom her father temporarily housed until they could get back on their feet.

Jane looked around. The room was plain. It had an ornately carved Murphy bed attached to the wall that looked like a wardrobe when closed. Jane had always loved that old bed. "We could add a glaze to the walls to give it a special look, and perhaps a wallpaper border would dress it up. I have time if you'd like to go to Fred's Hardware and see what's available. That would give us a start."

"Wonderful. Let's go now."

Jane and Ethel walked to Fred's Hardware. Only one car was parked in front of the store. Inside, Jane was surprised by the absence of customers. Alice had said Fred's business was slow, but the aisles were deserted. It seemed almost eerie, until Jane heard voices. Fred was talking with another man, and their voices grew louder as they moved to the front of the store. She couldn't help overhearing.

"I have the parts to fix that lock. It wouldn't take long. I could do it tonight after the store closes," Fred Humbert said.

"I don't want to fix the old thing. I want a new one like this ad shows."

Jane didn't recognize the gruff voice of the man talking to Fred.

"I don't carry that lock, Luther. It isn't good quality. It'll be falling apart in a year."

Ah, that explains it, Jane thought. Luther Grose, Byrdie Hutchinson's brother-in-law, was a habitual grouch. He didn't live in town, but he and his wife often visited Byrdie.

"Just because something is new and made overseas doesn't make it junk," Luther said.

"I never said that. But this particular lockset isn't brass. It's flimsy. I'm telling you, it's not worth buying. If you don't want to fix the old one, I have some good quality locksets that aren't too expensive."

Jane glanced at Ethel, who was listening intently to the men's conversation. Jane felt as if they were eavesdropping, but what could they do? They couldn't sneak out and pretend they didn't hear. The men were between them and the doorway. Besides, she and Ethel were legitimate customers. Ethel's eyes were wide and alive with interest and indignation. *Oh dear,* Jane thought, *this is going to be all over town by evening.*

"Your locks are twice as expensive as the ones at Do-It-Yourself Warehouse. And they have four times your merchandise," the man said. "Unless you match their prices, I'm taking my business to Potterston from now on."

"Do what you have to do, Luther. When that lock breaks, you come in here, and I'll get you a good one."

Luther stomped out. The door *whooshed* shut behind him. Fred let out a heavy sigh. He stepped in front of the paint aisle and saw them.

"Afternoon, Ethel . . . Jane. I'm sorry about that."

"What is this Do-It-Yourself Warehouse, Fred?" Ethel asked.

"It's a big chain store that gives deep discounts. They buy in huge quantities, then sell at low prices." Fred shook his head. "I can't compete."

"The residents of Acorn Hill are loyal," Jane said. "They won't fall for that."

Ethel nodded in agreement. "That Luther Grose is a troublemaker. Everyone knows that."

"Luther isn't the only one, I'm afraid," Fred said. "Business has been unusually slow for this time of year. People are planting gardens and starting summer projects, but they aren't buying their supplies here."

"Well, we are, aren't we, Aunt Ethel? We came to look at paint samples, particularly glazes or wall treatments. Aunt Ethel is interested in making a few changes to the carriage house."

"You ladies take all the color cards you want. If you find a color you think you want, I can mix up a sample for you. You can borrow those wallpaper books, too, if you'd like. And there are several books with decorating ideas. Just bring them back when you're finished."

"Thanks, Fred. We'll do that. And don't worry. Things will work out," Jane said, although she didn't have a clue how Fred could do battle with the corporate Goliath in Potterston.

Jane and Ethel left with decorating books in their arms and determination in their steps. At least they could give Fred some business.

Jane set serving dishes of beef stroganoff and noodles on the kitchen table and sat down. It was her night to say grace. She bowed her head. "Lord, we thank You for our many blessings, particularly this food and the beautiful weather. Thank You for our friends and for each other. And please help Fred's business. He works so hard, and it just isn't fair that a big business can come in and lure his customers away. Lord, make people around here see that they should be loyal to one another in Acorn Hill. In Jesus' name we pray. Amen."

Jane opened her eyes and looked at her sisters. Fred's dilemma weighed heavily on her mind. "You were right about that big hardware warehouse in Potterston, Alice. Aunt Ethel and I went to Fred's, and it was like a tomb. All except for Luther Grose, that is. He's really a disagreeable man."

"He's a bit gruff," Alice said, "but he helps Byrdie, so we mustn't judge him too harshly. Is that why you prayed for Fred?"

"You always find something good in everyone. Maybe Luther was having a bad day, but that's no excuse for what he said." Jane leaned forward. "He practically accused Fred of overcharging people, and he said he's taking his business to that new store. Fred seemed so discouraged. He told Aunt Ethel and me that he can't compete and that business has slowed since the big store opened. It makes me so angry. These big chains come into an area and drive the small local merchants out of business."

"Do you think the problem is that serious?" Louise asked.

"I'm afraid so. It's not fair, and I intend to do something about it."

"What can you do?"

"I don't know, but I can't just sit here and let them destroy Fred's business."

"That happened in Philadelphia with music stores," Louise said. "Some stores closed, but others adjusted the way they did business and actually prospered. I think the large store's advertising increased public awareness of their products."

"What did they do differently?" Alice asked.

"They specialized in older and hard-to-find music. The big stores carry the most popular items."

Jane shook her head. "Fred carries merchandise for home improvements and building materials. That's his main business. I don't see how he can change that. How can he go head-to-head with this big company?"

"I don't know," Louise said, "but we'll pray for him. Fred's a good man. He helps everyone in town. I'm sure people will remember that and support him."

"I certainly hope you're right," Jane said.

"I'll talk to Vera when we walk tomorrow morning," Alice said. "Maybe she'll have an idea how we can help."

"Good. We all want to help," Louise said. "Now, please pass the stroganoff. It smells delicious, and I'm hungry."

"Sorry." Jane picked up the casserole dish and passed it to her sister. Her own stomach growled. She smiled. "I was so intent on Fred's problem, I forgot that I was hungry." She took a hot biscuit and passed the cloth-draped breadbasket to Alice. "Speaking of hungry, are the ANGELs still raising money for your trip, Alice?" Jane asked.

"Yes, but what does that have to do with being hungry?"

"Maybe they could have a bake sale outside Fred's Hardware. That might attract people, and then they would go inside and buy something. I'd help them."

"They had a very successful bake sale two weeks ago," Alice said.

"They could have another one. Everyone likes to eat," Jane said.

"True. All right. I'll see what Vera thinks. If she's interested, I'll ask the ANGELs."

Chapter Two

A lice reached both hands high over her head, stretching as she walked to meet Vera first thing the next morning. She loved summers because Vera didn't have to teach school and they could walk more frequently. The sun warmed the morning air and coaxed the pansies to open their sleepy heads to the light. Alice hummed a hymn as she walked. Vera was doing some stretching exercises on her front lawn when Alice arrived.

"Beautiful day, isn't it?" Vera said, greeting Alice with a smile.

"Glorious! Ready to walk?"

"Oh yes, and I need it this morning," Vera said. "Fred is down in the dumps, so breakfast wasn't very cheery."

"Poor Fred. That isn't like him. It's because of that big hardware store opening in Potterston, isn't it?"

"I'm afraid so. It's only been open a week, but Fred has already seen a marked drop in business, and he had words with Luther Grose yesterday."

"I heard. Jane and Ethel were in the store when it happened."

"Oh dear. Fred didn't tell me that. Ethel probably has the story all over town already."

"Most likely. I'm sorry, Vera. I'm sure she will encourage people to support Fred."

"He doesn't want sympathy. And it's not just the money. He wants people to come to the store because he gives good service and good advice, and because he wants to help people. He tries to keep his prices reasonable, but with competition like this—especially their special sale items—people might question his integrity, like Luther did."

"Fred has a fine reputation, and I'm sure the townspeople will remember that when the initial interest in the new store wears off."

"I hope so."

"We're praying for Fred. The Lord always provides."

"Thank you, Alice. You're always such a comfort to me. I do believe these walks keep me sane as well as in shape."

Alice laughed. "Me too."

"I know better than that. You stay in shape bending and lifting and running up and down the halls at the hospital."

As they walked, Vera fell into preoccupied silence. Alice suspected Fred's business problems were weighing heavily on her friend's mind. After a quick loop around town, they arrived back at Vera's house.

Vera took a deep breath, then turned to face Alice. "You're not even winded. It's not fair. Alice . . ." Vera's voice trailed off and a frown creased her forehead.

"What is it? I can see something's bothering you. How can I help?"

"You are such a good friend to me. It makes me feel all the more guilty." Vera reached out toward Alice. "I . . . I can't go to New York City with you. I'm sorry. I know you were counting on me to help you with the girls, and I feel terrible leaving you in the lurch, but I need to stay and help Fred."

"Of course you do. I wouldn't dream of having you leave

Fred when he needs you. Don't worry about it. I'd love to have you come with us, but I can find someone else."

Vera smiled, clearly relieved. "Fred doesn't know that he needs me. And I don't know what I can do to help him, but I can straighten shelves and help him decorate for the Fourth of July.

"Don't laugh," she said at Alice's raised eyebrow. "You know I hate housework, but working in the store is different, and I see people I don't see during the school year. The store is always busy during holiday weekends, so perhaps we can do some kind of promotion that will spur business."

"I'm not laughing, and I wish I could be here to help you. Perhaps Jane and Louise can pass out flyers or something. They asked me to find out how they can help. Which reminds me, Jane suggested that the ANGELs could have a bake sale in front of your store. That'd help with their trip and might draw customers into the store. What do you think?"

"Bless Jane and Louise. Just knowing we have such supportive friends gives us great encouragement. The girls are certainly welcome to have a bake sale in front of the store, whether it brings us customers or not."

Jane made a trip to Time for Tea for a special blend that she'd ordered. Afterward, she stopped at Nine Lives Bookstore for some light summer reading.

Jane pushed open the beveled-glass door. The bell overhead tinkled, warning Harry, the big orange-marmalade cat that was sleeping in the sunshine streaming through the glass. He moved just in time to avoid Jane's foot. Jane knew to step cautiously, however. A few of Viola's eight or ten cats—Jane was never sure just how many—always roamed the bookstore aisles. Viola came out of the back room, the long, tulip-bedecked scarf at her neck flowing behind her. She smiled brightly.

"Hello, Jane. How nice to see you."

"Hello, Viola. Did you get in that book I asked for?"

"You must be a mind reader. I received it in a delivery this morning."

"Oh good. I need something to read while I sit out on the porch. The weather is so glorious, I don't want to stay inside."

"Everyone seems to feel that way, and it's great for business. I have a display of summer reading over by the window if you're interested in looking for something else. Why don't you browse while I get your book from the back room."

"All right." Jane wandered over to the window. Florence Simpson was standing by a shelf, flipping through the pages of a large volume.

"Hello, Florence," Jane said. "Nice day, isn't it?"

"Too warm. You grow herbs, don't you?"

"Yes. I cook with a lot of herbs, and I can't always find them fresh in the stores." Jane saw *Herbal Remedies* in the title of the book Florence was holding. "Are you interested in growing herbs?"

"Not particularly. But I would like to try some of these natural remedies."

"Let me know what you need. I might be able to give you some of them."

"Perhaps I'll buy this book," Florence said. "I don't trust all the pills the doctors prescribe these days."

Jane looked at the display table. A book with a beautiful garden on the cover caught her eye. It contained a collection of Emily Dickinson's poems. She picked it up, opened it and read out loud:

> From Cocoon forth a Butterfly
> As Lady from her Door
> Emerged—a Summer Afternoon—
> Repairing Everywhere . . . .

"Oh, this is lovely! I must have it," Jane said as Viola came through from the back.

The door opened, the bell tinkled and Norbert Meinhard, the postman, came in with an armful of letters and flyers. He said "Good day, ladies," in his usual cheerful way, handed Viola a stack of mail and turned to leave.

Viola started to set the stack on the counter. "What is this?" she demanded in an unusually harsh voice. "I don't want junk mail. Especially not this." She held up a glossy flyer covered with bright red and blue graphics.

"Sorry, Viola. I'm just paid to deliver the mail, not sort it. And I can't throw out mail with paid postage, whether I like it or not."

"I know, Norbert, but this makes me bilious."

Jane nearly choked. Viola was outspoken, but her choice of words evinced such odd pictures. "What in the world is so terrible, Viola?"

"This advertisement for that . . . that Do-It-Yourself Warehouse," Viola said, spitting out the name as if it tasted truly vile. Viola waved the offending ad in the air.

Jane agreed with her sentiments.

Norbert beat a hasty retreat. The bell tinkled and the door shut behind him with a resounding thud. Jane took the ad from Viola and looked at the front page.

GRAND OPENING SALE appeared in large letters across the top of the page, just under the store name. Amid bright pictures of assorted hardware, flowering plants, patio furniture and barbecues, bold words and starbursts announced, FREE MERCHANDISE, FREE FOOD, DOOR PRIZES and TEN PERCENT OFF WITH NEW CREDIT ACCOUNT.

"This is terrible," Jane said. "Fred can't compete against this."

"It won't be easy. I know what he's facing. I had a fight on my hands when the book superstore opened in Potterston. I get upset every time another chain store moves into the area.

It isn't fair to the small businesses that serve the communities." Viola shook her head. "Fortunately, I have a more discerning clientele."

Jane tightened her jaw and stood straighter. "I can't stand this. I have to do something."

"What will you do?"

"I don't know, but I'll think of something. Perhaps we could stage a protest, marching out in front of the store with signs. If we could attract the local media, who knows? Maybe we could make the evening news on television. Perhaps I can convince the Potterston newspaper to carry a story about big business squeezing out small businesses. There must be something."

"I admire your sentiments, but I'm afraid you'll discover that the newspapers and television stations won't cooperate. The big chain stores buy a lot of advertising."

"That's unfair. Fred can't afford to run big ads. May I have that flyer?"

"Certainly. What do you intend to do with it?"

"Oh, I don't know, but I'll go check out the store and see what we're up against. Perhaps they don't offer good service or they carry inferior merchandise."

Jane had forgotten that Florence was in the store until she came up to the counter. "Good for you, Jane Howard. You give them a piece of your mind. You speak for the whole town, you know. If you need a letter-writing campaign, you just let me know. We'll show that big store that we don't tolerate bullies around here. It's time someone stood up to these big companies."

Viola shook her head. "Good luck, but I'm afraid it won't do any good. In my experience, big corporations don't give a fig what happens to local businesses. All they care about is their profit margins."

"I hope you're wrong," Jane said. She paid for her purchases and left.

Alice rarely shopped for clothes. Her needs were few. She wore her nurse's uniform to work, and at home slacks or jeans and a shirt were another uniform of sorts. Neither, however, would be appropriate for her trip to New York.

When she entered Nellie's dress shop, the owner, Nellie Carter, looked up. "Hello Alice, how nice to see you." Nellie had the flair and youth to make any outfit look attractive. She always looked like a fashion advertisement for her merchandise. In her early thirties, Nellie had established a successful business in Acorn Hill.

Color-coordinated clothing hung on racks around the room, and outfits with accessories were arranged on the walls like works of art, giving the store a bright, cheerful air. "How may I help you?"

"I'm going on a trip in three weeks, and I need something to wear. Something nice enough to attend a play, but practical, that I can wear sightseeing. Do you have anything like that?"

Nellie stepped out from behind the counter. Her bluish-green pinstriped dress buttoned down the front with big white buttons. Jane would know the name of that shade of blue and that straight, collared-dress style, but Alice didn't have a clue what it was called. She should have brought Jane along.

"I have several wonderful travel outfits. Do you have a favorite color?" Nellie asked as she went to a display rack.

Alice chuckled. "Not really. I usually wear white or my standard blue jeans and blouses. What do you suggest?"

"With your wonderful ginger hair and sunny complexion, this kiwi green would be perfect or this geranium. The blend between orange and coral is perfect for your coloring."

Alice eyed the racks of clothes dubiously. "You don't think they're a little too bright for me?"

"Not at all. They'll highlight the red in your hair and bring a little color to your complexion. I have a wonderful new blush that would give your cheeks a touch of color too."

"Oh, I don't think so. I don't wear makeup very often. Just a little lipstick once in awhile. And I was thinking of something more subdued. Just something comfortable and simple."

"Where are you going?"

"I'm taking some of the ANGELs from church to New York City for a week."

"You're taking teenage girls to New York City? Goodness, you're brave. I'd be afraid to walk down the street. Aren't you concerned about the crime?"

"No more so than when I go to work in Potterston. People are people no matter where you go, and besides, we don't need to be afraid. Psalm ninety-one says, 'If you make the Most High your dwelling . . . no harm will befall you. . . . For he will command his angels concerning you to guard you in all your ways'" (Psalm 91:9–11). Alice sighed contentedly. "I love picturing the angels that surround us."

"That is a comforting thought, but I'd still be afraid to go to New York. Rebekah Goldberg, my buyer in New York, has been asking me to come visit the showrooms in the garment district. She does a great job recommending fashions for the store, but looking at catalogs and Internet images isn't the same as seeing the outfits on models and feeling the fabrics. Rebekah offered to give me a personal tour and to introduce me to the suppliers. I would love to take her up on her offer . . ." Nellie's eyes shined at the thought, but the sparkle quickly disappeared. "But I wouldn't dare go by myself."

Watching Nellie's emotions flash from longing to defeat, Alice realized God had a greater purpose for her at Nellie's than buying clothes. In her excitement, she took hold of Nellie's hand.

"This is amazing. I need an adult to go to New York with me and help chaperone the girls. Vera Humbert was going to go, but she had to cancel. I've been praying for the Lord to provide someone to go with us. Nellie, I believe you are the answer to my prayers. You'd be doing me a tremendous favor, and you can take a day to tour the garment district with your buyer."

"Oh no, I couldn't do that. I can't leave the store, and besides, instead of helping you chaperone, you would be taking care of me."

"I know God's hand when I see it working. Please, pray about the trip and consider it."

Nellie looked doubtful but said, "All right, I'll pray about it, but I don't see how it's possible."

Alice smiled. "With God, all things are possible. Now, help me pick out an outfit to try on. Maybe you should make it two. I'll need more than one for a whole week. Something that won't wrinkle."

Nellie took an outfit off a rack full of green clothing and held it up. The color made Alice think of green apples and springtime. The lightweight knit fabric had a simple cardigan jacket with flowers embroidered around the cuffs, a white scoop-necked T-shirt trimmed in green and coral, and a pair of pull-on pants with pockets and elastic waistband. It even had a matching skirt. Nellie held the skirt and jacket up in front of Alice so she could see it in the full-length mirror. Alice was surprised how well the outfit went with her skin and hair. She couldn't help smiling.

"Yes," Nellie said, "this will be wonderful. Go try it on, while I pick out a couple more outfits for you to try. I'll bring them to the dressing room."

Alice had a hard time deciding on just two outfits, but she didn't need more. Where would she ever wear them in Acorn Hill? She had to admit, they were very practical and easy to wash. And best of all, helping her pick out the clothes seemed to encourage Nellie. *Please, Lord, give her the courage to say yes,* Alice prayed silently as she paid for her purchases.

"Here you are," Nellie said, handing Alice her change. "Say, I heard that Jane is going to Potterston to speak to the manager of that big new hardware store about unfair competition."

"Where did you hear that?"

"At the Coffee Shop. Everyone was talking about it. We're all upset about a big store moving in and undercutting Fred's business. Jane's so brave. I could never do something like that. Will you please let her know we're all behind her? We're all vulnerable, you know."

"Yes, I'll tell her. Thank you, Nellie. You've been a big help," she said as Nellie handed her the bag of clothes. "And don't forget to pray about the trip."

"All right. When do you need an answer?"

"If you could let me know by next week, we can begin making plans. I already made reservations at a wonderful hotel operated by an order of nuns for women travelers. They have top security and strict curfews, and it's not far from the garment district. I know you're going to have a splendid time."

"*If* I decide to go."

"*When* you decide to go. I'll talk to you next week. Oh, Nellie, I'm very excited about this."

Before Nellie could protest, Alice sailed out the door with her purchases. *Please, Lord, take away her fear and fill her with hope and excitement for this trip. Amen.*

Chapter Three

Jane didn't give herself time to consider her actions. She needed to find out more about this big chain store. Perhaps she could reason with the manager about the negative impact of the superstore's discount promotions on small businesses in rural communities like Acorn Hill.

All the way to Potterston, Jane rehearsed what she intended to say. She'd be firm. Unsmiling. Businesslike. The more she thought about the big hardware conglomerate crushing poor Fred, the more determined she became.

She had to park at the far end of the crowded parking lot. As she strode toward the entrance, she clenched the flyer she had taken from Viola. Outside, several young men in bright blue company T-shirts and ball caps manned barbecue grills and gave away free hot dogs. Jane could smell the enticing food all the way from her car. One large, shiny stainless-steel barbecue grill had a sign on it for a drawing. A young woman in coveralls and a bright yellow hard hat offered Jane a flat carpenter's pencil with the store name and logo on it, and an entry form for the drawing. Jane shook her head at the woman and resolutely entered the store.

A greeter smiled and offered her a brochure with special coupons, good for the grand-opening sale only. Jane said, "No, thank you. Where can I find the manager?"

The greeter pointed toward a sign that read *Customer Service*. That wasn't the answer Jane wanted, but she dutifully headed for the service desk. Half a dozen people stood in line in front of her. The wait increased her tension. By the time she reached the front of the line and faced the smiling customer-service manager, Jane felt ready to boil over. Taking a deep breath, she said a prayer for patience. Anger wouldn't help, and this poor employee had no control over his greedy employer.

"Good afternoon. How may I help you?" the congenial, middle-aged man asked.

"I wish to speak to the store manager. Could you get him for me, please?" She smiled, but her mouth felt stiff and her hands were shaking. She was sure her expression was more of a grimace.

"Perhaps I can help you." The man gave her an inquiring smile.

"I think not. This is a matter of . . ." Of what? Jane didn't know what would constitute a serious enough matter to gain her an audience with the manager, but she didn't let that stop her mission. "This concerns harmful advertising. I'm sure your manager will want to speak to me before this becomes a public matter." She stood straight, folded her arms and looked as stern as possible. She didn't know if the Potterston newspaper would be interested in a story about the plight of a small business—Viola certainly didn't think so—but Carlene Moss, the editor of the *Acorn Nutshell*, would cooperate. And Jane could start a campaign of letters to newspaper editors and the television stations.

"If you'll step to the side, I'll have someone escort you to the manager." The man raised a hand to summon someone.

"Thank you," she said.

The man waited on the next customer, his smile firmly back in place. A moment later, a young man appeared, spoke to the customer-service manager, then asked Jane to follow him. He didn't speak but led her to the rear of the store. The manager was standing in an aisle of plumbing fixtures, his back to Jane, talking to a group of people. Jane's guide started to interrupt them, but Jane stopped him.

"I'll wait until he's done," she said quietly. She didn't want to create a scene. "Thank you for showing me the way. You don't have to wait."

"That's all right. I'll stay with you," he said, and she supposed the customer-service manager had warned him not to leave her. Maybe he thought she might attack the manager. She almost smiled.

The conversation between the manager and the group was clearly drawing to a close. Jane heard one of the women say, "We really appreciate your generosity. With your donation of materials, we should be able to complete the new wing of the youth center."

"We are glad to be part of your project. Do-It-Yourself Warehouse tries to be a leader in community service, and we encourage our employees to volunteer."

The man had a deep, pleasant voice, and Jane couldn't take exception to his community spirit, assuming he really meant what he said.

"If you need people to pound nails, paint walls or install fixtures, let me know," he continued. "We give our employees comp time for volunteer projects."

He sounded sincere. With a store as large as this, he could do a lot of good in a community. Lucky Potterston. Just then, he turned, and Jane got a look at his face. His features matched his voice. Pleasant. Attractive. Kind of rugged, but nice. Manly. A bit younger than she was.

Hearing his conversation with the community group, she realized a protest would be useless. But what good did the chain's altruism do if the big company drove owners of small stores out of business?

Regardless, she couldn't blame this man for the

company's advertising policies. She supposed the sales flyers came from a big corporate office. Impersonal. From their fancy offices, they had no idea how their presence hurt a community. She felt a sinking sense of defeat. Fred helped the community of Acorn Hill all the time, but he didn't have the resources or people to make the kind of grand gestures a large corporation could make. That thought raised her ire, but she quickly realized her anger was illogical and misplaced. She couldn't fault a company for helping people.

The manager stood to the side as he spoke to his guests. "If you come with me," he said, "I'll introduce you to our lumber-department manager. He should have the items on your list ready to load."

He started forward, until he was right next to Jane.

"Excuse me, Mr. Loughlin," Jane's escort said. "This lady wants to talk to you. She has a concern."

"Thank you, Larry. Would you take my guests and introduce them to Steven, in the lumber department?"

"I'd be happy to, sir."

"Thank you." He turned to the group. "Please follow Larry. And let me know if I can be of any further help. Remember to call if you need volunteers."

Jane hadn't noticed the employee's name badge. Her bad manners embarrassed her. "Thank you, Larry," she said belatedly. He gave her a half smile as the others offered profuse thanks to Mr. Loughlin, and Jane began to wish she hadn't come. When the manager turned to her, towering over her, looking straight into her eyes, she wanted to sink through the floor. She clutched the rolled-up flyer that she held in her hands.

He smiled and extended his hand. "Todd Loughlin. How may I help you?"

Jane shook his hand and tried to smile. "Jane Howard, from Acorn Hill. I . . . uh . . . wanted to talk to you about your advertising."

He looked around. Several customers stood nearby, looking at fixtures. "Why don't we go to the employees' lounge,
where we can talk." He smiled down at her. "I'd suggest my
office, but my furniture just arrived, so it's a mess." He
extended his hand in the direction of the employees' lounge.
She suspected that his motives had nothing to do with her
comfort and everything to do with moving her away from
customers who might overhear her complaints, but she followed him without a comment.

They sat at a small table with bench seats. He offered her
a soda. She accepted an orange drink. He got one for himself
and sat down across from her.

"Now, what is your concern, Jane? I'm sorry our service
manager couldn't help you. What can I do for you?"

Suddenly, Jane's concerns seemed illogical. The big store
existed, and it wasn't going to disappear. Fred didn't stand a
chance. The reality hit her full force. She held her unopened
soda and stared down at the table. She had to rethink the
problem and come up with a creative strategy. She looked up.
He was watching her patiently, waiting to hear her problem.
What could he do? Nothing.

"I'm sorry to waste your time, Mr. Loughlin. On second
thought, you can't help me. I shouldn't have come." She
started to rise.

He raised his hand toward her. "Wait. You didn't ask to
speak to me for no reason. There must be some way I can
help. Please, sit down and tell me what's troubling you."

Jane glanced around, then looked into his eyes. Brown.
Warm and gentle. He seemed straightforward. Trustworthy.
"This room is just a small example of the problem. It is
almost as large as Fred's entire store."

"Fred? You said you were from Acorn Hill, didn't you?
Do you mean Fred's Hardware?"

That took her completely by surprise. "How do you
know about Fred's store?"

He smiled gently. "It's my job to know the competition."

"Competition? How can you call Fred's little store competition? That's just exactly the problem." Her indignation returned.

"Don't underestimate your local merchants. Is Fred the owner? Is he a friend of yours?"

"Yes, and your store is stealing his business."

Mr. Loughlin frowned. He suddenly looked intimidating. "We don't steal. We work hard to establish a good reputation, and we work within the community to help everyone, including our competitors. We study an area extensively to make sure the population can support an additional store before we open a warehouse. Potterston proved to be an ideal location. Statistics show that competition increases business for everyone. If your friend is a poor manager, his business might suffer, but that would happen with or without the Do-It-Yourself Warehouse."

"Fred is a good businessman," she protested. "He's honest and helpful and tries to keep his prices reasonable. That's why your store is such a threat. He doesn't have the huge buying power your store has. He can't even purchase merchandise at the prices that you sell it."

"Yes, I understand that problem, but there's another side to this equation. We cannot compete with the personal service a small hardware store can offer. You see, we're not head-to-head competitors. Small businesses have a niche that large corporate stores cannot fill. Fred should find that his business will survive and even prosper."

"I hope you're right, Mr. Loughlin . . ."

"Todd. Please, call me Todd."

"All right, Todd. Fred is active in helping our townspeople, and his business is an important part of our community."

"I was very impressed with Acorn Hill. In fact, I bought property not too far from there."

"Really? I'd have thought you'd buy near the store."

Todd chuckled softly. Jane felt herself relaxing. Such a pleasant laugh. Such a nice man. She thought Fred and Vera would like him too. He was a conundrum. She couldn't believe she'd actually come with every intention of blasting him. She shook her head.

"One of the big attractions of Potterston was the rural setting. You see, I came from Baltimore. We lived right in the city."

Jane glanced at his hand. No wedding ring. He caught her look and glanced down, then back at her face.

"Divorced," he said.

"I'm sorry. It's none of my business. I know that's painful."

"You too?"

"Yes. So, you were happy to get out of the city. That's how I felt too."

"Where did you move from?" he asked.

"San Francisco. But I grew up in Acorn Hill, so this was coming home for me."

"I feel like I've come home too. I love it here. I'm getting a late start, but I'm planning to put in a large garden."

"I love my garden."

"Vegetables or flowers?"

"Both. I'm a chef, so I grow a lot of my own herbs and produce. My sisters and I run Grace Chapel Inn. It's an old Victorian house built by my mother's family. I take care of the gardens too. I have a friend who owns the florist shop and nursery in Acorn Hill. He specializes in native plants. You must meet him. He loves to help local gardeners."

"Wonderful. I haven't met very many people yet. Too busy getting the store ready to open. I don't suppose . . ."

"Hi, Ms. Howard." A tall, lanky teenage boy stopped by their table. "Oh, excuse me, Mr. Loughlin. I didn't mean to interrupt."

"That's all right, Greg. You know Ms. Howard?"

Greg grinned. "Yes, sir. From church."

"It's nice to see you, Greg," Jane said. "Do you work here?"

"Yes, ma'am. It's a great place to work. I'm on my break now. I'll just get going. Wouldn't want to be late getting back to work." He smiled and walked away.

"Do you remember all of your employees by name?"

Todd chuckled. "I wish. Greg is very enthusiastic, and the customers love him. Hard not to notice him."

"His parents would be happy to hear that. I could see he was pleased that you remembered his name." Jane suspected Todd was a good employer.

A beeper went off, and Todd took a cell phone from his belt and answered it. He spoke for a moment, then hung up. "I've got to go. Duty calls."

"Well, I've taken up enough of your time. Thanks for letting me rant." Jane rose from her chair.

Todd stood as well, saying, "I'd like to talk some more. I need some gardening advice. Would you have dinner with me tomorrow night?"

His invitation startled Jane. "I don't know. I mean, we just met. And I, uh, came here to complain . . ."

"Please. We won't talk business. I need some gardening advice, and you obviously have knowledge of local plants. It'd be a big help to me."

"Well, I . . . all right," she responded hesitantly, accepting in spite of her misgivings.

"Good. Shall I pick you up?"

Pick me up? *Where everyone in Acorn Hill could see her going out with the manager of Fred's competitor?*

"I can meet you somewhere here in Potterston. That way I can do some shopping first."

"All right. There's a great new Italian place called Gillespie's a few blocks from here. Do you like Italian?"

"Love it. Six o'clock?"

"Great. I'll see you there, Jane." He smiled and left.

His smile stayed with her, all the way out of the store and all the way back to Acorn Hill. She looked for a mailbox with his name on it along the way, but she couldn't figure out which place belonged to him.

Todd Loughlin. Nice name. Nice man. Wonderful smile. And his voice still reverberated inside her head. Oh dear. She was attracted to the man who managed the Do-It-Yourself Warehouse. What would Alice and Louise think? What would Fred think? What had she done? If anyone found out that she was meeting the manager of that store socially, they'd label her a traitor.

An image of her ex-husband popped into her mind. She hadn't thought about Justin Hinton in months. Why now? Perhaps because she hadn't been so attracted to another man since she'd fallen for her husband . . . ex-husband. Justin had betrayed her, but that situation was nothing like this. She wasn't betraying her friends. In fact, talking to Todd Loughlin might give her some ideas on how to help Fred and Vera.

Chapter Four

The next evening, Jane was in the kitchen, putting the finishing touches on cold plates for Louise and Alice's dinner when Ethel tapped on the door and entered.

"That looks delicious," Ethel said.

"Would you like me to fix one for you too?"

"No, no. I have plans for dinner. Are you going out?"

"Yes. I have some shopping to do in Potterston."

"Oh, I do wish I could go with you. I want to look at bedspreads and curtains. Perhaps I could change my plans."

"Oh, I'm sorry, Aunt Ethel. I'm meeting a friend for dinner."

"I see." Ethel raised her eyebrows and gave her an inquiring look, waiting for more information, no doubt. Jane wasn't going to satisfy her aunt's curiosity. Of all people, Jane didn't want Ethel discovering her date with Todd. She hadn't even told Louise and Alice about it.

"Speaking of Potterston, I must say, I'm proud of you. I'm not surprised, though. After all, you are a Howard. We never shrink from a duty."

"What duty, Aunt Ethel? What are you talking about?"

"Why, your plan to confront that store manager in Potterston."

"How do you know about that?"

"Everyone in town knows about it, Jane, and I must say I'm disappointed that I had to hear it from Florence Simpson. You should have told me. I'm your aunt, after all." Ethel shook her head. "I'm sure it all happened in the heat of the moment, and I do applaud your sense of justice. The whole town is backing you. Florence wants to start a letter campaign, and I heard that Carlene Moss plans to write a guest editorial for the Potterston paper. If you want to lead a protest, I know at least a dozen people who would go with us and carry signs."

"Oh dear. I don't believe it'll come to that," Jane said. "Protesting isn't the answer."

"What is the answer, then?"

"I don't know." Jane wished she had not accepted Todd's dinner invitation. If anyone saw them, it would appear that she was fraternizing with the enemy.

Jane was wrapping tender crisp, cooked and chilled asparagus spears in thin pieces of prosciutto ham with cream cheese.

"Those look wonderful," Ethel said. "I do love fresh asparagus."

"I have extra. Let me give you some."

Jane added the asparagus spears to the plates of fruit medley, cold roast beef and cheese slices, and a small mound of cottage cheese with vegetable bits. She covered the two plates with plastic wrap and put them in the refrigerator for Louise and Alice. She took out several stalks of asparagus and put them in a plastic bag for Ethel.

"Thank you dear. Do you have a moment? I decided on a glaze."

"Oh good," Jane said, although that meant another trip to Fred's Hardware. Right now, she didn't want to face Fred Humbert. Especially since the whole town knew about her intention to talk to Todd. She placed a covered basket of fresh herb rolls on the table. They smelled heavenly, but she resisted the cook's prerogative to taste the food. Her stomach was churning as it was.

"So what did you decide on?" Jane asked.

"There's a perfectly lovely wall finish called plastic ragging in the book Fred loaned me. Do you think we could do that?"

"Yes. It's not hard. In fact, it will be fun." *And will get my mind off a certain store manager,* she thought. "Did you pick a color?"

"The illustration in the book is beautiful. They used a base of pale sea foam, which is a bluish-gray, and a glaze of soft celadon. It is very elegant and restful. If you happen to see any linens, please keep your eyes open for a bedroom ensemble in those colors. Perhaps something floral, but remember, it must be elegant."

"I'll keep that in mind." Jane smiled at her aunt, then washed her hands and removed her apron.

"I'd best be running along, then," Ethel said. "I need to change before Lloyd picks me up. Can we start painting tomorrow?"

"We'll need to purchase all our materials and equipment."

"I do hope Fred's Hardware has all the supplies we need," Ethel said. "I'd hate to have to go to that new store in Potterston."

"Certainly not." She was glad Aunt Ethel had turned to reach for the doorknob and wasn't paying attention to her. Jane was certain she looked guilty. "I may have some of the materials. Let me look tomorrow."

"That would be wonderful. Have a nice evening."

"Thank you, Auntie."

Jane fervently wished that she had not accepted a dinner date with a man she barely knew, a date that could be construed as a betrayal. She had picked up Craig Tracy's business card from Wild Things to give Todd. The referral would help him develop his garden, and then she could politely bow out and not see him again.

She hurried up the stairs to her room. She debated about what to wear and decided on a colorful floral peasant skirt and turquoise-blue blouse. She wore a pair of dangly beaded earrings that she had designed and pulled her hair up off her face with a favorite pair of mother-of-pearl hair combs. With a quick twirl in front of the mirror, she made sure nothing was amiss. Satisfied, she selected a sweater and took her purse and walked down the stairs.

The sounds of hesitant scales came from the open door of the parlor, where Louise was giving a piano lesson. Jane didn't see Alice, which suited her just fine. No explanations needed. She went into the kitchen and scrawled a note on a sheet of bright yellow, vegetable-bordered memo paper.

Dear Louise and Alice,

I'm headed to Potterston to shop and meet a friend for dinner. I left you dinner in the refrigerator. I shouldn't be late.

♥ Jane

Jane went out the kitchen door, relieved that she didn't have to face her sisters and their inevitable questions. Just as she opened her car door, Alice pulled in and parked next to her. Jane thought about making a fast escape, but that would seem odd, so she waited for her sister to get out of her car. She hated this feeling of being deceptive, although no one had asked where she was going. And she was no longer a child, having to clear everything she did with her older sisters or her father. What would Father say about this predicament? He wouldn't judge Todd because of his job. Neither should she or anyone else, she decided.

"Hi. I'm just on my way out. I left your dinner in the

refrigerator." She waited for the questions, but Alice just smiled.

"You are so thoughtful. You didn't need to fix our meal if you're going out. Louise and I can fend for ourselves, you know."

"I know. I wanted to. Well, I'll see you later." Jane slid into her car.

"Have a nice evening, Jane."

"I will," she said as she closed the door and started the engine. Alice stood watching her back up and pull out. Guilt assailed Jane again. *Oh, why did I agree to this date? Well, it isn't really a date . . . so what is it?*

Sooner or later, she would have to explain about Todd to her sisters. She knew from experience that she couldn't keep anything from them for very long.

She'd tell them that she was talking with the manager of the Do-It-Yourself Warehouse, trying to figure out a way to lessen the big store's effect on Fred's Hardware, when he was called away before they had finished their conversation. Dinner was an opportunity to finish that discussion.

I will be polite, but not too friendly, Jane told herself as she drove to Potterston. *I will make it clear that this is a one-time dinner. Todd is a friendly guy. And attractive too. He won't have any trouble making friends.*

Although Ethel's request for linens wasn't on her shopping list, Jane had allowed plenty of time before she was to meet Todd, so she stopped at a linen store. The large store carried everything from sheets, bedspreads and bath accessories to cookware, storage boxes, patio furniture and barbecue supplies. Looking at the lavish displays and large inventory, she wondered how any small business could compete with the big retail companies. She was almost relieved that she didn't find anything suitable for her aunt's guest room.

Jane stopped at the craft store that carried the supplies she needed for her jewelry and art. With the Fourth of July holiday coming, she wanted to make special patriotic jewelry for Sylvia Songer to stock at Sylvia's Buttons and Nellie Carter to stock at her dress shop. Both stores kept Jane busy.

Glancing at her watch as she stood in line to purchase her supplies, Jane saw that she had a few minutes to spare before she was to meet Todd Loughlin. She took a deep breath. Another two hours or so and she could put this episode behind her. She still hadn't figured out how to help Fred, but whatever she did would need to be more creative and productive than a protest against the Do-It-Yourself Warehouse.

She pulled into the restaurant parking lot and got out of her car, squaring her shoulders to give herself courage to go inside and meet the Do-It-Yourself Warehouse manager.

Todd was sitting on a bench inside the restaurant. When she entered, he rose and gave her a dazzling smile. He looked so handsome that her heart did a little flip. That reaction startled her. She hadn't been drawn to a good-looking man in a very long time. She blushed and felt flustered and hoped that he didn't notice, but he did, she was certain, as his smile broadened into a grin. The strong urge to turn and run hit her, but he stepped forward and reached out to her, taking her hand in a friendly gesture that totally discombobulated her, although he released it immediately.

"Jane. I'm so glad you came. I was sure you'd changed your mind."

"I wouldn't do that without letting you know."

He chuckled. "I kept telling myself that, but I wasn't so confident."

The hostess stepped forward and led them to a booth near the back. Jane took the seat facing away from the room. Not that she expected anyone to recognize her, but just in case.

Todd waited until she sat down before he slid into the bench across from her. He smiled at her.

"I believe I have put you in an awkward position," he said. "After I left you yesterday, I realized how it'd look to your friends to see us together. I wouldn't want to embarrass you or make you uncomfortable in any way."

His insight made her blush again. She smiled to cover her discomfort. "Thank you for understanding. In any other circumstance, I'm sure we could become friends, but you can see this is impossible. I can't consort with the enemy, you know," she said teasingly and hoped he wouldn't take offense. He didn't.

"I hope to convince you that I'm one of the good guys."

"Oh, I believe you. Otherwise, I wouldn't be here."

"Of course."

A waiter came and took their orders. When he left, Jane felt awkward and couldn't think of anything to say. Evidently, Todd felt the same, as he was silent. Jane cast about for something to talk about. *The weather. That's safe.*

"Hasn't the—" Jane began.

"The weather—" Todd said at the same time. They looked at each other, then laughed.

"This isn't a date, is it?" Jane said.

Todd smiled. "You're as uncomfortable with the thought as I am, aren't you?"

"Yes, I am," Jane admitted. She gave him a relieved smile.

"All right. This isn't a date, so we don't have to worry about impressing each other. Agreed?"

"Absolutely. And I can stop blushing."

"But you blush so charmingly."

"Oh please." She groaned. "Of course, you had to notice."

"Sorry. I have to admit, though, it did wonders for my ego. I've been nervous all afternoon."

"You? I can't believe that."

"Believe it," he said.

The conversation continued smoothly until their dinners arrived. The waiter set the plates in front of them, then left. Jane glanced at Todd, then picked up her fork.

"I know you attend church. Would you mind if I say a blessing?" he asked.

Jane put her fork down. "Please do." She bowed her head.

"Thank you, Lord, for this meal and for bringing a new friend into my life. Amen," Todd said very quietly, but just loud enough for Jane to hear.

Oh, help me, Lord. I'm in trouble here. I like this man. That can't be right, can it? And he loves You. I didn't count on that. What do I do now?

He smiled at her across the table, picked up his fork and took a bite of manicotti. "Wonderful. Sure beats my cooking. Now, I know we agree about the weather being beautiful. That was what you were going to say, wasn't it?"

"When tongue-tied, talk about the weather," she responded, grinning.

"Is it always this beautiful in June?"

"Always," she said. "The sun always shines. The wind never blows. It only rains at night. We never have mosquitoes, gnats, moths or tomato worms." Jane took a bite of her fettuccini and let the rich, creamy flavor and texture delight her taste buds. She usually preferred her own cooking, but this was exceptional, and the fresh-baked breadsticks were delicious. As she dipped a piece of one in the saucer of olive oil and balsamic vinegar, she hoped Alice and Louise were enjoying their dinner.

"I may be new to the area, but I am not that gullible. Although I have to admit, so far I love everything about Potterston. The weather, the people."

"Compared with San Francisco, this is heaven. Here we have four seasons, and we see the sun clearly, without the filters of fog or drizzle. Of course, I was fortunate enough to grow up here, so coming back was like stepping into a wonderful memory."

"I spent my whole life in the city, except for summer vacations at my uncle's farm in Connecticut. I loved those trips, but they were never long enough."

Jane asked him about his uncle's farm, and Todd regaled her with adventures that had impressed themselves on the memory of a young city boy in the wonderland of the country.

"I'd dream all winter about going to the farm. My uncle had a calf that became my pal. I practiced roping him and imagined being a rodeo cowboy. I fed the chickens and outwitted the hens to gather eggs for my aunt. She had a big old goose that chased me around the yard every chance it got." He laughed. "It was mean. I soon learned to make a big circle around the pond to avoid it."

Jane smiled at his stories. "What a great way to spend your summers. It sounds like you had a wonderful time."

"Yes, I did. And they took me to church with them. They went to an old-fashioned church with a steeple and a bell that rang out every hour and played a song on Sunday morning. And their church had an ice-cream social every summer. I took a turn cranking the handle and churning the ice cream. And the ladies all brought homemade pies. My mouth waters just thinking about those pies. I think that's why this move means so much to me. This area reminds me of those days. I plan to stay here permanently."

"I hope the area lives up to your expectations," Jane said. "A country home can be a lot of work."

"Don't I know it. The place I bought has an overgrown orchard, a brambly blackberry patch and encroaching woods. It has great potential, but it's a mess. So you see I need your expertise to help me resurrect the plants and trees. I don't know much about gardening, but I intend to learn."

"I'm not an expert, though I have learned quite a bit

since I returned home, and my friend Craig Tracy helps me. I brought his card." She reached for her purse and dug around for the Wild Things business card. She frowned. "*Hmm.* I know I brought his card. Now I can't find it."

"Could you introduce me? He's more likely to be helpful if he knows I'm your friend. Especially if he learns where I work."

Oh dear, now what shall I do? Jane wondered. *This isn't going the way I planned.*

"All right. I'll take you out to the Wild Things nursery. Craig can show you plants that work well in our climate and give you some tips on restoration." *And then I can step away from this . . . this whatever it is.*

"Wonderful. Would Tuesday be all right? That's my next day off."

"Yes." That would give her time to figure out what to do about Todd Loughlin.

"Where should we meet?"

"At the nursery at 9:00 A.M., if that's all right with you. Craig usually spends mornings out there."

"Great."

Jane gave him directions to the Wild Things nursery before they left the restaurant. He walked her to her car, took her key and opened her door for her. She started to get in the car, then turned to say good night. Todd had one hand on the top of the door, ready to close it, and the other on the car, encircling her as she looked up at him. The warmth in his gaze made her words dry up. Flustered, she looked down at the ground. He cleared his throat. She glanced up and realized he looked as flustered as she felt.

He handed her keys to her. "Thank you for your company. I look forward to seeing you again next week."

She smiled. "Thank you for a lovely dinner," she said. "I enjoyed talking with you." She thought she sounded stilted.

Jane slid onto the car seat. Todd closed her door and stood there as if waiting for her to do something. She could roll down the window and talk some more, or drive away. She opted for the latter, putting her key in the ignition and starting the car. He stepped back. She gave him a little wave, then put the car in reverse and backed out of the parking space.

Chapter Five

The Coffee Shop was more crowded than usual when Alice arrived a few minutes after noon on Monday. Fortunately, Nellie Carter already had a table near the back of the room. She waved when she spotted Alice.

Alice made her way back, greeting friends as she did. She sat on a chair across from Nellie.

"Goodness, what a crush," Alice said. "Everyone in town must be here."

"That's because June made blackberry pie," Nellie explained. "I asked Hope to save two pieces for us. With this crowd, it will go fast."

"Wonderful. I love June's pie."

June Carter was the owner of the Coffee Shop. While she purchased most of her baked goods from the Good Apple bakery, June considered blackberry pie her specialty.

Hope Collins came to take their orders. "Hi, Alice. I've got your pie set aside," she said with a wink. "Do you know if Jane talked to the manager at that new hardware store yet?"

"I don't know, Hope. She hasn't mentioned it."

"Well, you just tell her we're all rooting for her, okay? So, how are the trip plans coming?" Hope asked.

"Very well, thank you."

"Three of your girls washed my windows. They did a

great job. So nice to let all this wonderful sunshine in. I told June she should hire them to wash the Coffee Shop windows."

"That would be wonderful. Thanks, Hope."

"You bet. So what will you have? The special today is chef's salad. It's good," she told them.

They both ordered the special. Then Alice leaned toward Nellie, who was drawing invisible doodles on her placemat with her finger. "I was glad to see you in church yesterday."

Nellie looked up, and Alice could see the uncertainty in her eyes. Then Nellie took a deep breath.

"I thought I should go to church if I'm going to help you chaperone your girls. It only seems right."

Alice smiled clear from her heart. "It sounds like you've decided to go to New York with us. Is that right?"

"Yes." Nellie sat up very straight. "I followed your suggestion. I prayed. I can't tell you that I heard an answer, but I might not have a better opportunity to go and I know I'll never get the courage to go by myself. I asked Lorrie Zell if she could work while I'm gone. She helps part-time, but she's been very busy lately, so I figured if she said yes, it would be a sign that I should go. Well, she jumped at the chance."

"Wonderful, Nellie. I'm so happy. I know you won't regret this. I can't wait to tell the ANGELs. Would you like to come to our meeting Wednesday night and meet all of them? We'll be talking about our plans and putting together our itinerary."

"Yes, I can come. And I want to help. I'm very good at organizing. I can do research on the Internet and put together a list of items to take."

"Perfect." Talking about the trip made Alice's heart beat faster in anticipation. She was as excited as her ANGELs were. The girls had been planning for the trip and raising funds for months, putting on bake sales, raking yards, weeding gardens, washing windows and doing other menial jobs for the townspeople.

Hope brought their lunches. Nellie seemed to become more excited as they talked about various sites to visit in New York. After they ate their pie, Nellie pushed her plate aside. Her brow furrowed as she looked up at Alice.

"You are sure we'll be safe?"

Alice put as much reassurance into her smile as she could. "Yes. I've taken girls to the city before. And everyone at church will be praying for us while we're gone. We couldn't have better protection than that."

Nellie nodded. Alice wasn't sure she had succeeded in allaying Nellie's fears. Stepping out on faith and agreeing to go was a big leap for this young woman. She would have to keep Nellie focused on the positives. "We'll stay at the St. Julian Hotel for Women. I think I mentioned that an order of nuns runs the hotel for women travelers. They take excellent care of the ladies who stay there. They also operate a day care for low-income families. The girls are making little gifts for the children."

"Oh, what a sweet idea! I'd like to contribute too. I'll see what I can come up with." She glanced at her watch. "I'd better get back to the shop."

"Of course. I enjoyed having lunch with you." Alice stood, feeling somewhat awkward. She wished that she knew Nellie better, but they'd have time to become friends on the trip. Nellie spent most of her time at her dress shop and didn't seem to have close friends. Alice decided to change that. Nellie needed someone to pull her out of her shell. Alice reached out to squeeze Nellie's hand. "We are going to have a wonderful time. I promise."

Nellie stood and squared her shoulders, as if preparing for battle. "Yes. I believe we will." Her smile was a bit tentative, but Alice had to give her an *A* for effort. Nellie seemed determined to overcome her misgivings about the big city.

∞

Jane took extra care with dinner. Somehow, it gave her the courage to face her sisters. She arranged on salad plates fresh spinach from her garden topped with sliced almonds, diced apple, dried cranberries and thinly sliced sweet onion.

She debated keeping quiet about Todd. Craig wasn't likely to tell anyone about him, but not telling her sisters increased her feelings of guilt. Louise and Alice would be hurt if they heard about her meetings with Todd from anyone else.

Jane spread a white linen tablecloth on the kitchen table and arranged three place settings of their mother's Wedgwood china and pink crystal goblets. Several peony blossoms floated around a white candle in a shallow bowl in the center of the table. The formal table looked better than she'd expected in her eclectic kitchen, with its black-and-white checkerboard floor, paprika-colored cabinets and butcher-block counters. For tonight's dinner, she wanted the privacy of the kitchen and the comfort of her own domain to tell her sisters about Todd.

For dessert, a bowl of sliced strawberries sat in the refrigerator next to a bowl of fluffy whipped cream. A tray of flaky crescent rolls were browning in the oven. Jane glanced at her watch. Three minutes. She had told Louise and Alice dinner would be ready at five thirty. Her sisters were very punctual. She finished the salads with her citrus vinaigrette and garnished them with shaved curls of fresh Asiago cheese.

As she opened the oven to take out the rolls, the kitchen door swung open and Louise and Alice entered, laughing and talking as they came into the room. The talking ceased abruptly. Jane set the baking sheet on a cooling rack and turned toward them.

"What a lovely table, Jane. What is the occasion? Did I miss someone's birthday?" Louise asked.

"Not any of ours," Alice said. "And there are only three places set, so we aren't expecting company."

Jane carried a platter of the golden-roasted rosemary chicken and rice pilaf to the table. "We don't need a birthday or holiday to use the good china. I thought we needed a nice dinner to go with the magnificent weather."

"Oh, look at that chicken." Alice closed her eyes and inhaled. "It smells wonderful."

Jane removed her chef's apron, arranged the hot rolls in a basket and carried it to the table and sat down. Smiling at her sisters, she put her napkin in her lap and kept her hands there to keep her nerves from showing. "Alice, would you ask the blessing?"

"I would be delighted. But first, I have to share my good news. I am celebrating tonight. Nellie Carter has agreed to go with me to New York City as a chaperone."

"Nellie Carter? How on earth did that happen?" Jane asked.

After Alice gave her sisters the details, she smiled gently. "I prayed for someone to go with us, and God answered my prayer. Now I am counting on you, my dear sisters, to pray for us, as I know you will. I hope this will be a breakthrough of faith for Nellie."

"Of course we will pray. Nellie couldn't be venturing out with a better guide, Alice. I am sure the Lord is at work here," Louise said.

"I knew I could count on you," Alice said. She bowed her head. Louise and Jane did likewise.

"Heavenly Father, we are so grateful for our many blessings. Thank You for this food and the bounty of Jane's garden. Thank You for answering my prayers and sending Nellie to accompany me. Be with her and give her courage as the trip approaches. In Jesus' name. Amen."

"Amen," Jane said. *And please help me with my dilemma, Lord*, she added silently. She was happy for Alice and Nellie. Jane hoped God was listening to her own prayers as attentively as He listened to Alice's, but then Alice and Louise had been turning their problems over to the Lord for a long time. Jane's prayer habits were more recent.

As she carved the chicken and passed the platter, Jane decided to wait until dessert to tell her sisters about Todd. After all, she didn't want to spoil Alice's celebration.

Because of her nervousness, Jane could barely taste her meal.

"Delicious as usual, Jane," Alice said. "I never mastered gravy. Yours is so creamy and rich. Mother made gravy like this."

"Thank you."

"Yes, everything's perfect," Louise said. "Your meals are always a treat."

Jane poked at her meal while her sisters savored it. She knew she shouldn't feel guilty about her friendship with Todd. He was a very nice person.

She took their empty plates and her half-full plate to the sink. As she set a kettle of water for tea on the stove and prepared bowls of shortcake, she rehearsed what she would say. *I met this man . . . No . . . I have a new friend . . . No . . .*

She topped sliced shortbread with English custard sauce, sliced strawberries and dollops of whipped cream, then added a sprig of fresh mint as a garnish. Maybe she should call Todd and cancel tomorrow's outing, but he would be home by now and she didn't know how to reach him. The teakettle whistled, but Jane barely heard it. Alice got up and poured the boiling water into the teapot. Jane carried the desserts to the table.

"That looks wonderful," Alice said. "By the way, Hope Collins asked me if you'd been to talk to that manager of the new hardware store in Potterston. She said to tell you everyone in town is backing you. Nellie asked me about what had happened too. Have you talked to him?"

Jane closed her eyes. No backing out now. She gave her sisters a smile. It felt stiff.

"Yes, I talked to him. He was very nice and sympathetic, but there's nothing he can do to change the chain's advertising or sales methods. That all comes from the corporate offices. I shouldn't have gone."

Alice gave her a gentle pat. "I think it was a very brave thing to do. At least you tried to help, and I know Fred and Vera and all the townspeople appreciate your efforts."

"I've let everyone down."

"You may not have accomplished your goal," Louise said, "but you supported your friends and your community, and no one can fault you for that. I'm sure they all realize the chain stores are a reality and they won't go away just because we wish it."

"If that were all, but there's more. I have a bit of a dilemma. I don't know how to tell you. I don't know what to do." Jane rubbed her fingers against her temples as if massaging a headache.

"Are you ill?" Alice asked with such compassion in her voice and her eyes, Jane wanted to cry.

"Oh no. I'm fine. I . . . I told you I met with the manager of the hardware store. Well, his name is Todd, and I went to dinner with him the other night in Potterston."

"You did what?" Louise asked, both eyebrows raised.

"He's a kind, caring man. He sympathized with Fred's situation and assured me that small local businesses like Fred's usually do all right once the initial grand-opening campaign is over and things settle down. He said small businesses have the advantage of giving personal service, and that's definitely true with Fred. After that, we got to talking about other things and discovered that we have a common interest. He wants to start a garden, but he has always lived in the city, so he needs help. Our conversation was interrupted at the store, so he asked me to meet him for dinner to continue our talk."

"Oh, what a predicament," Louise said.

"Todd's lonely, and I felt sorry for him," Jane continued. "I tried to refuse his dinner invitation, but he just wanted a little more information. I didn't think it would hurt to help him. I figured that I'd meet him one time, suggest some places where he could find help, and that would be the end of it. But somehow I agreed to introduce him to Craig Tracy. I don't intend to see him again after doing that. I'm hoping, since we're meeting at the nursery, that no one will see us together." Jane shook her head. "What a mess."

"You're kindhearted, Jane, and I can see how this happened," Alice said. "Fred would understand, and perhaps no one will know who he is. I'm sure it'll be fine."

"That's what I'm hoping, but everyone in town seems to know I was going to talk to him. I'm going to have to tell people something."

"But you did talk to him," Alice said. "You tried to help Fred. There was mention of a letter-writing campaign and a protest. What are you going to do about that?"

"Nothing. I realized while I was there that it wouldn't work. The Do-It-Yourself Warehouse is very civic-minded. I saw Todd donate a lot of materials for a youth center. It's just too bad the store hurts Fred. I don't know what to do about that. I want to do something. I feel so helpless. What should I do?"

Louise and Alice just looked at her. Neither spoke for a moment.

"That's a difficult question. Do you plan to see this man again?" Louise asked.

"I don't plan to, but I didn't intend to see him again after we met for dinner. I hesitate to make a definite statement one way or the other. If he were not the manager of the Do-It-Yourself Warehouse, I'd enjoy his company."

"I'm sure he's a very nice man," Alice said. "You wouldn't feel drawn to him otherwise."

Alice's reassurance brought Jane a twinge of doubt. Once

she had thought highly of Justin Hinton, so highly, she'd married him. And he turned out to be a first-class heel. But she had changed . . . matured. No, she wasn't being fooled. Todd was a nice man. When she thought back on her marriage, there had been signs, but she'd been too naive to see them. And that had nothing to do with her present dilemma: What to do about Todd Loughlin and Fred Humbert.

"You'll have to make this decision yourself," Louise said. "Secrets have a way of being discovered. If Aunt Ethel should hear about it or see you with him, the whole town will find out, even if no one else in town sees you together."

"I know you're right. I'll have to tell Fred."

"Do you want me to speak to Vera for you?"

"No. I'll do it. Please pray for the right opportunity to open up and for me to say the right thing. I don't want to hurt Fred."

"Of course, dear. We'll pray, won't we, Louise?"

"Yes. This very evening before I go to bed."

Chapter Six

When Jane arrived at the nursery, Todd was already there, talking to Craig Tracy in the shade house. They were so intent on a plant Craig was holding, they didn't look up when she got out of the car and walked toward them.

"Hey, guys." The two men turned. Todd smiled, and her heart beat a little faster. She smiled back and turned her attention to Craig, whose smile made her feel much more comfortable. "Good morning. I see you two have met. Are you enlightening Todd about the native flora?"

"Morning, Jane. Thanks for steering business my way. It sounds like Todd needs a lot of landscaping."

Jane winced inwardly at the mention of business. Somehow, everything had gotten mixed up. Fred was the one who needed the business, and Todd's employer was the cause of Fred's predicament.

"From what I can see, Craig has everything I need. Now I just have to figure out how to arrange it all. I'm going to need a lot of help."

"You found the right person to advise you. Have you seen Jane's gardens?"

"Not yet." Todd gave her a hopeful look.

"She's done a wonderful job of restoring an old garden.

From what you've told me, you have a lot of old, established plants that just need a little TLC."

"I was hoping you could give Todd pointers to help him out," Jane said to Craig.

"I wish I had more time to do consultations, but business is booming, and I don't have the time I need to spend out here as it is. I don't suppose you know of anyone who needs a summer job, Jane?"

Jane winced again. Not all businesses in Acorn Hill were struggling. She glanced at Todd. He gave her a sympathetic smile, and she knew he understood her discomfort. "I can't think of anyone, but I'll keep you in mind, Craig. So, what have you shown Todd so far?"

Craig recited a list of plants, and Jane added a few suggestions. They walked through the rows and loaded four and six-inch starter pots and a few gallon shrubs to the flat wagon Todd pulled along behind him.

"I can see landscaping is going to be a long-term project," Todd said. "With remodeling the old farmhouse, I won't have time to do much to the yard this year. Is there someone in the area who knows the native plants and does yard work? I don't want to hire a landscaping service. They want to tear out the old plants and start from scratch. I don't want that kind of yard."

"There's Joe Morales," Craig said. "He has a gardening service and he'll do whatever you want done."

"He sounds perfect. How do I get a hold of him?"

"Through Fred's Hardware. Fred got him started in the business."

Jane caught the quick glance Todd aimed at her. She interpreted his helpless what-do-I-do-now look. She shrugged and didn't offer any help. Evidently, Todd hadn't told Craig where he worked. That was good, but now what should she do? Joe's business had grown to the point that he worked independently, but he still handled a lot of contract jobs for Fred, so hooking Todd up with Joe seemed like a further betrayal. "I think Joe stays pretty busy with his regular customers," Jane said. "What you need is a strong, willing worker. Maybe you could call the high school for the name of a boy who needs summer work."

"But I wouldn't know what to tell him to dig up and what to leave or prune," Todd said.

"Jane can help you with that. She's become quite the expert," Craig said.

Jane wished Craig had less confidence in her abilities. She wanted to extricate herself from more involvement, not commit to spending more time with Todd. And yet that wasn't quite true either. She felt a rapport with Todd that went beyond friendliness. From the looks he kept giving her, he seemed to intercept her thoughts, or his mind ran along the same track. If it weren't for Fred, she would be volunteering all the help Todd wanted.

"I bet you have plants that need dividing," Craig said. "That would save Todd some money, and he couldn't find better stock. Your plants are in excellent health."

"Sure. I'll give you plants when I thin them," she told Todd.

"Great," he said. Then he gave her a hesitant look. "I hate to impose, though. I'm sure you're busy."

Craig chuckled. "You'd be doing her a favor. Jane hates to throw away anything that is growing."

"True," Jane admitted. "First, I need to help my aunt do some painting in her house. When is your next day off?" she asked Todd.

"I take Sunday and Tuesday off, and I work evenings on Wednesday."

"Next Tuesday, then?" Jane asked, relieved that she had a week before they next met.

"That'll work out great. Well, I'd better get these plants home. I'm going to tackle cleaning up the apple orchard this afternoon."

Relieved, Jane smiled at Todd. "Sounds like you have a busy day ahead of you. Now, I'd better get back to the inn. I'll see you next week. And thanks, Craig." For what, she wasn't sure. Selling plants to Todd was his business, and his helpful suggestions had gotten her in deeper with Todd Loughlin. For that, she wasn't grateful.

She started toward her car. Todd followed her. Before she got in, he stopped her.

"Thanks for suggesting Wild Things. Craig has been a great help, and I feel a lot better about tackling my yard."

She smiled up at him. He had the most beautiful brown eyes. Kind eyes. Interested eyes. Interested in her, if she wasn't mistaken. "You're welcome."

"May I see you before next Tuesday? Would you like to go out to dinner again?"

"Oh, Todd. I don't know." She sighed. She wanted to cry. She wanted to spend more time with this man. But what about Fred and Vera?

He frowned. "Is it my job or me?"

"Your job. I feel like a traitor."

"I was afraid of that. You know I don't want to make you uncomfortable or unhappy, but I want to spend time with you and get to know you better. Can you think of me without associating me with my work?"

"I want to, but it's hard."

"That's because you're a true friend." He smiled. "That's why I am attracted to you, Jane Howard. I appreciate your caring nature and loyalty to your friends. I want your friendship. Will you give me a chance? I'd be honored if you would have dinner with me."

Oh dear. I'm in trouble here. "You really know how to turn a girl's head," she said lightly. But she savored his words like sweet chocolate. "I'll be delighted to have dinner with you, Todd. I'll meet you somewhere in Potterston again."

"Good. You name the place."

She grinned. "Do you like to live dangerously?"

"That depends. I don't do raw fish."

Jane laughed. "There's a new Sichuan restaurant I've wanted to try. It's supposed to be authentic southwestern Chinese food."

"Let me guess. That's the spicy stuff?"

"Yup."

"Well, I'm game if you are." He gave her a smile that nearly melted her sneakers. What was it about this man? She couldn't believe anyone could have that effect on her.

After they arranged to meet Thursday night, Jane started her car and drove away. She glanced in the rearview mirror and saw Todd standing where she left him, watching her leave.

Alice carried a file-size cardboard box filled with fabric scraps and craft supplies down from her room. Then she loaded into the box the New York City guidebooks that she had collected, her Bible and study notes, and a bag of macadamia-nut chocolate-chip cookies that Jane had made. Alice lugged it all over to the church.

It was Wednesday night—Alice's night with the ANGELs. Ashley Moore was just arriving with her parents, and she hurried over to Alice.

"Hi, Miss Howard. Can I carry the box for you?"

The girl had a school pack slung over her shoulder. "It looks like you're loaded down enough already," Alice said.

"I can do it," Ashley said, but her father stepped in.

"Allow me." He took the box from Alice. "Do you want this downstairs?"

"Yes, thank you."

He waited for them to precede him, then followed. "Is this for your trip?"

"Yes, the girls will be making toys for a day care center that we'll be visiting."

"I hope the toys are lighter than this box. Otherwise you'll have to take a porter with you." He grinned.

Alice opened the door and let him go through with the box, which he placed on a table.

"Thank you," Alice said.

Dick Moore pretended to tip an invisible hat to them, then headed up the stairs to the sanctuary.

Jenny Snyder and Linda Farr had arrived before them.

Alice took the cookies out of the box and started unloading her guidebooks and lesson plan.

"Oh yum! Ms. Howard's cookies. What else is in the box?" Ashley asked.

"Our craft project. We'll work on it after our lesson. And we have a special guest tonight. She should be here soon."

In a few minutes, the rest of the girls came down the stairs, escorting Nellie.

"Welcome, Miss Carter," Alice said. She introduced Nellie to the girls, who echoed Alice's welcome as they took seats around a table.

"Everyone is here, so we can get started," Alice said. "Father in heaven, we thank You for bringing us here tonight and we ask Your blessing on our time together. Thank You for bringing Miss Carter to join us. May our lesson and our activities please and glorify You. We especially ask for Your guidance as we prepare for our trip to New York City. In Jesus' name. Amen.

"We have been learning how we can please God. Last week we talked about obedience. God wants us to obey Him in everything we do in our lives. Can anyone recite our memory verse?"

Sissy Matthews raised her hand. "If you love me, you will obey what I command. And I will ask the Father, and he will give you another Counselor to be with you forever—the Spirit of truth. John 14:15–17."

"Excellent. Can someone explain the verse?"

Lisa Masur raised her hand. "If we love God, we should do what He tells us, just like we should obey our parents. And when we obey, God is happy, because we are showing our love and that we respect Him."

"Very good. And that brings us to today's lesson. How can we obey God? What does He want us to do?"

"Love Him," Sarah said.

"Love our neighbor as ourself," Ashley said.

"Yes, and that is what we practice here with our secret projects, isn't it?" Alice asked.

The girls responded "yes" in chorus.

"We make things or plan projects to help people, and then we do them anonymously," Alice explained to Nellie.

"What a marvelous idea," Nellie said. "No wonder you're called angels."

The girls giggled. Their name—ANGELs—was an acronym, but no one other than the girls and Alice knew what it stood for.

"Can you tell me who your neighbor is?" Alice asked.

"Mine is Mrs. Humbert," Sissy said. "She's great."

"Lisa," Jenny said. The two girls were sitting side by side.

"Mrs. Horn and Daisy," Linda said, and everyone laughed. Clara Horn dressed Daisy, her pot-bellied pig, in baby clothes and sometimes wheeled her around in a buggy, as if Daisy were a child.

"I live next door to Mr. Racklin," Kate said with an exaggerated groan, and all the girls echoed her groan. Harvey Racklin was known as a bit of a grouch in Acorn Hill.

"I hope all of you treat your neighbors the way you would

want to be treated," Alice said. "But I think Jesus was talking about more than the people who live next door to you. Who was he talking about?"

"I know," Kate said. "The Good Samaritan."

"That is partly right. The story is in Luke, chapter ten, and that is our lesson tonight. In verses twenty-five through twenty-nine, a man asked Jesus, 'What must I do to inherit eternal life?' 'What is written in the Law?' He replied. 'How do you read it?'—That was Jesus talking. Then the man answered, 'Love the Lord your God with all your heart and with all your soul and with all your strength and with all your mind,' and, 'Love your neighbor as yourself.'

"Jesus told the man he was correct, but then the man asked, 'And who is my neighbor?' So Jesus told him the parable that we call the Good Samaritan. The scripture is in Luke ten, verses thirty through thirty-seven. It tells about a Jewish man who was traveling from Jerusalem to Jericho. Robbers attacked him, stole his clothes and money, beat him up and left him to die. A priest came along, saw the man, but crossed to the other side of the road and kept going. Then a Levite, who worked at the temple, came by and did the same thing, ignoring the wounded man. Then a Samaritan man came by. Usually, the Samaritans and the Jews didn't get along, but this man saw the wounded man and felt sorry for him, so he stopped to help. He took the hurt man to a hotel where he could recover, and he even paid for the man's hotel room and food. In verse thirty-six, Jesus asked, 'Which of these three do you think was a neighbor to the man who fell into the hands of robbers?'"

"The Samaritan," the girls all said.

"Yes," Alice said. "We are neighbors to anyone who needs a friend. That doesn't mean that you girls are to stop and help people. This was a grown man. God wants us to be wise, and you all know that you don't talk to strangers or go to help them. So what could you do?"

"Tell our parents," Kate said.

"Tell our teacher or a policeman," Sissy said.

"Those are all good ideas. There are also ways we can help neighbors who are struggling. We are going to do that tonight. First, here is your memory verse for this week." Alice handed each girl a card with the memory verse printed on it. Nellie asked for one too, and Alice gave her a card.

They discussed the trip to New York and the sights everyone wanted to see.

"I wish I could go with you," Lisa said.

"Me too," Sissy echoed. She and Lisa were the youngest ANGELs.

"I wish I could take all of you," Alice said, "But you girls will go with me next time."

"What are we going to make tonight, Miss Howard?" Linda asked.

Alice opened the box and took out plastic bags filled with brightly colored fabric scraps, yarn, buttons, ribbons and flowers. Then she took two dozen pairs of mittens out of the box.

"We will visit a day-care center for underprivileged families, so we are going to make puppets for the children."

"Cool!" Lisa said.

Alice covered the table with white paper and gave each of the girls a mitten. She put scissors, needles, thread and glue on the table, then showed the girls a puppet Sylvia Songer, the owner of Sylvia's Buttons, had made at her fabric store. The top of the yellow mitten had red yarn hair and blue button eyes with long black eyelashes made from felt. A red heart-shaped button made a perfect mouth. A fringed trim circled the edge of the mitten that covered the wrist.

Alice slipped her hand in the puppet and gave the girls instructions through the puppet, sending all the girls into peals of laughter.

"Oh, the children will love these puppets," Nellie said. "May I make one too?"

"That would be wonderful."

For the next thirty minutes, the girls cut, stitched, glued and giggled as they put together puppets resembling funny animals and whimsical characters. They didn't have time to finish, but they still had three weeks to complete their projects.

Nellie had as much fun as the girls. She made a cat puppet with a big red floppy hat. The girls loved it. Nellie was so pleased with her stylish puppet, she declared that she might have to carry a line of fashion puppets in her store.

Being with the ANGELs already seems to be having a positive effect on Nellie, Alice thought. She hoped that Nellie's enthusiasm would overcome her fears about going to the city.

Chapter Seven

On Thursday morning, because there were no guests in the inn, Alice, Louise and Jane planned to eat a leisurely breakfast at the kitchen table. Jane was slicing fresh strawberries when Alice and Louise came into the kitchen.

"How is Vera this morning?" Jane asked.

"She's fine, although she is furious with Luther Grose," Alice told them. "Vera told me he had the gall to come back and ask Fred to lend him a tool after he bought a lock set at that new store. Can you believe that?"

Louise shook her head. "That man has no common sense. What did Fred do?"

"He let Luther borrow his equipment. You know Fred never refuses to help anyone," Alice said.

"Luther has a lot of nerve taking advantage of Fred's good nature," Jane said.

"Pastor Ken was in the store when Luther came in. After Luther left, Ken praised Fred for his patience and restraint. Then he suggested that Fred start a rental business with some of his equipment, like he did when he set Joe Morales up to use his lawn mowers and garden equipment to maintain people's yards in town."

"That is a great idea," Jane said. "Lots of people go to

Potterston to rent equipment. It would be a lot more convenient to rent from Fred."

"That's what Vera said. But Fred seems to think it would
require too much capital to set it up."

Alice poured coffee for Louise and Jane and a cup of tea
for herself as Jane carried breakfast to the table.

"Have you told Fred and Vera about your friend?" Louise
asked.

"Uh . . . not yet. I just haven't found the right time. But
I will."

Louise said a blessing and added a prayer for the
Humberts and for Jane to find the courage to talk to them.

Jane wanted to talk to Fred and Vera, but she didn't know
what to tell them. She wasn't being disloyal to them, but it
appeared that way.

For breakfast, she served fresh strawberries and blueber-
ries with a new concoction of granola she had made. Louise
and Alice each took some of the cereal, which they topped
with fruit and milk. Jane waited until each sister had taken a
bite.

"Well, how is it?"

Louise looked at her and raised one eyebrow. "Don't you
mean, *what* is it?"

Alice grinned. "It reminds me of the grain mixture Fred
carries for horses. Vera called it MOBC. It has molasses, oats,
barley and corn. An elderly woman from Riverton came in to
buy some and she told Fred it makes great cereal. She cooks
it and serves it to her husband. She said it's cheaper than
cooking oatmeal."

Louise laughed. Jane tried to scowl, but Alice's teasing
hit her funny bone, and she burst out laughing too.

"You made that up," she accused Alice.

"On my honor," Alice said, putting her hand over her
heart. "Truthfully, though, your granola is very good. Just . . .

different. Sweet, but it has a surprising flavor that is tangy and a little sharp. What did you put in it?"

"That would be the ginger and lemon. I found a recipe on the Internet for Lemon-Ginger Granola, and I added a few ingredients of my own, like coconut, sunflower seeds, pecans and dried cranberries. It's very healthful. Do you think our guests would like it?"

"It might be too different for the average person's taste," Louise said.

"Why don't you put out a bowl of it with a place card describing what's in it. Brave people will sample it and appreciate your culinary genius, while the fainthearted will opt for the traditional cereal or eggs."

"Great idea, Alice. I'll do that."

Louise laughed. "I do believe my own sister just called me fainthearted. No one has ever accused me of that before."

"I don't believe you are fainthearted, Louie. In this instance, you just might be lacking good taste," Jane said with a straight face and wide eyes.

"I prefer to think of myself as discerning," Louise said, her expression haughty and an eyebrow raised ever higher.

Jane and Alice laughed in unison. Louise joined them. At that moment, they heard a tap on the kitchen door, and Ethel opened it.

"Good morning," she called out. "Heavens, what's so funny?"

"Good morning, Aunt Ethel," Louise said. "Jane and Alice are impugning my good taste."

"How can they question your taste? You moved in the most cultured circles in Philadelphia."

"Jane is testing her newest granola creation on us," Louise explained. "Have you had breakfast? I'm sure she would love to have your opinion."

Jane turned to their aunt. "May I get you a bowl?"

"No, thank you, dear. I ate earlier."

"How about a cup of tea or coffee?"

"Tea would be lovely," Ethel said as she sat down at the table. "I came to discuss my project with Jane. Can we begin this morning?"

Ethel mentioned her project every time she saw Jane. "I can be ready at nine, if that's all right with you," she told her aunt.

"We need to start as soon as possible. I have a luncheon engagement in Potterston. Lloyd is picking me up at eleven thirty. He must attend a political symposium for rural governments. Of course, he wants me to accompany him."

"Of course," Jane said. "We can get the paint this morning, then I can apply the base coat this afternoon while you're gone, if you don't mind my going ahead without you. Then the walls will be ready for the glaze coat tomorrow."

"That would be wonderful. I'm sure you can paint more efficiently without my interference. I am not proficient at that sort of thing, but I don't want to leave you with all the work."

Jane could easily paint the guest room in an afternoon. It might indeed take longer if Ethel helped. "You can help me apply the faux finish tomorrow, Auntie."

Ethel gave her a concerned look. "I'm not good with a paint brush."

"Don't worry, you won't have to paint. The faux finish is easy, but it goes much faster with two people working," Jane explained. She stood and carried her dish to the sink. She had intended to tell her sisters that she would be helping Todd with his garden the following Tuesday, but that news would have to wait. Ethel didn't need to know about Todd just yet.

On her way home from work that afternoon, Alice stopped at the Potterston pet store for a flea collar for Wendell. When she came out with her purchase, she noticed an equipment-rental store across the street and thought about Pastor Ken's suggestion to Fred. Out of curiosity, she stopped to check it out.

A chain-link fence surrounded the store, enclosing all kinds of equipment, from rototillers, lawn mowers and cement mixers to small tractors and backhoes. Inside the store, one section held power and construction tools. Another area had stacks of folding tables and chairs, outdoor canopies, and a third section held party supplies and equipment like candelabra stands and wicker archways for weddings. Alice wandered through the aisles, marveling at all the equipment available to rent.

"Good afternoon. May I help you find something?"

Alice turned toward the sales clerk who had approached her. "Hello. I'm just looking. I've never been in a rental store before, and I wondered what you carry."

"We have just about anything you could need." He stepped over to the register counter and picked up a brochure. "Here is a complete list of all the items we have. We recommend reserving equipment in advance to make sure it's available. Sometimes we can order extra tables or chafing dishes or other party equipment from our main franchise."

"I live in Acorn Hill. Do you get many customers from there?"

"Oh yes. If we get a large order, we can deliver for a small fee. We also have trailers available to rent for moving the large equipment."

"A friend of mine owns the hardware store in Acorn Hill. He rents out a few things, and someone suggested he should carry more rental equipment. I can see from all of your equipment that it would take a large investment to start something like this."

"Not necessarily. He wouldn't have to carry as much

inventory as we carry here. I own this franchise, and we cater to a much larger population with a variety of needs. Having an outlet in Acorn Hill is something I've considered. What's the name of your friend's business?"

"Fred's Hardware. Fred Humbert owns it. If you don't mind, I'll take your brochure to show him."

"Sure. Tell him to give me a call if he has any questions." The owner handed her a business card.

"Thank you."

Alice got in her car and glanced through the brochure. Fred carried a few party supplies, but not many. Then she came to equipment.

Air compressors, air guns, backhoes, boom lifts, compaction equipment. *Hmm.* He had air compressors and air guns, but not the big equipment. Still, how many times would anyone want to rent a backhoe? Concrete equipment. She knew he had several cement mixers for sale. And lots of electric power tools. He already had a carpet shampooer for rent. Vacuums. She remembered seeing a large tub-like vacuum for outdoor projects, like cleaning up leaves and sawdust. Generators, heaters, ladders, landscape equipment, painting equipment, pressure washers, saws, welders. She thought he might have some of those.

Fred had quite a few items at the store that were on the rental list. Alice agreed with Pastor Ken. Why couldn't he rent out some of his inventory?

Alice stopped at Fred's Hardware before she went home. Vera was wearing rubber gloves and was up to her wrists in soapy cleaning solution. She had removed all the items from a shelf of kitchen gadgets. When she saw Alice, she put down her cleaning rag and pushed back a damp wisp of hair with her forearm. "Hi. What brings you in?" she asked.

Alice smiled. "I thought I might find you here." Alice glanced around at all the dust-free, neatly stocked shelves. "You've been busy."

Vera grinned. "Just thought I'd redd up while I have the time. Now if I could just get the energy to do this at home."

"Your house is fine," Alice told her. "Can you stop for a moment? I have something to show you."

"Let me put these back and we can scoot out for a cup of tea."

"Let me help you." Alice handed items to Vera, and she arranged them on the clean shelf.

When they finished, Vera removed the rubber gloves and put the cleaning supplies in the back room. She ran a comb through her hair, tucking damp tendrils behind her ears. She glanced in a square of mirror over the utility sink by the table where they kept a pot of coffee for the employees. "*Ugh*. Oh well, it will have to do. Let's go to the Good Apple. I heard Clarissa has strawberry tarts this afternoon, and I skipped lunch."

At the bakery, Vera got a tart. Alice meant to pass up the pastries and just get a cup of tea, but she couldn't resist a raspberry turnover. When they sat at a table with their goodies, Alice took the brochure out of her purse and handed it to Vera.

"I stopped at a rental store in Potterston and picked this up. I thought I'd show it to you, rather than Fred. If you think he'd be interested, you can give it to him. I think he already carries some of this equipment in the store. The store owner was very nice and said for Fred to call him if he had any questions."

"Really?" Vera took a bite of her tart and a sip of tea, then opened the brochure. She scanned the contents, turned it over and read the back.

"We do carry a lot of these items," she said to Alice. "Some of them sit on a shelf for months . . . even years, but Fred believes he should have merchandise in stock, because you never know when someone will need that very thing."

"That's the beauty of Fred's store. You know you can find

what you need there when you can't find it anywhere else. Father always told people to go to Fred's first and save themselves a lot of time and energy."

"Your father was one of our best salesmen, and he wouldn't accept a nail or a screw without paying for it. If the rest of our customers were as supportive as Daniel Howard was, we wouldn't be concerned about that new megastore. That reminds me. Jane and Ethel came in this morning for paint for the carriage house. Ethel told me her daughter is coming to visit. I've never seen her appear so anxious. Jane seemed a bit preoccupied too."

"It's been several years since Francine last visited. Aunt Ethel wants everything to be perfect. She asked Jane to help her." Alice smiled. "She wants a change, but she isn't sure what to do. Change is difficult, isn't it?"

Vera nodded her head and chuckled. "It's uncomfortable, but often it's for the best. I know God will provide our needs with this change in our business."

"Honestly, Vera, I can't wait to see what God is going to do with Fred's Hardware."

"Me too. And I will show Fred this brochure. Who knows? This just might be the answer we need."

Jane tried three outfits before she settled on a full-skirted, sleeveless cotton dress for her date with Todd Thursday evening. Large pink hibiscus flowers on a midnight blue background gave the calf-length dress an exotic look. She put her hair up in a French twist, slipped on a pair of jet-and-lapis beaded earrings and applied a bit of mascara to her eyelashes.

She felt a little guilty about meeting Todd again, but at least Louise and Alice knew about him. Facing Fred and Vera had been difficult when she and Ethel bought paint. How could she tell them? They were sure to feel betrayed, and she didn't want to hurt them.

Louise was registering a young couple when Jane came downstairs. The newlyweds, Jane surmised by their loving glances and tightly clasped hands. She and Louise had decorated their room earlier with extra flowers, a basket of fruit and Jane's special chocolate truffles. Their youth surprised her. They looked like teenagers.

Seeing the love in their eyes gave Jane a twinge of sadness. She could remember exchanging such adoring glances with Justin once upon a time. It seemed like a lifetime ago. She tried to remember when the love had faded and the looks turned to something else. She couldn't remember. It happened so gradually, and they had been so busy with their careers, that she hadn't noticed. Jane said a little silent prayer that this couple would keep their love glowing for the rest of their lives.

Jane greeted the couple and said good-bye to Louise. Alice came out of the library and gave her a hug, which took Jane by surprise.

"You look lovely, dear." Alice's smile seemed almost sympathetic, disconcerting Jane even more. "Have a wonderful evening."

"Thank you, Alice. I hope you have a nice evening too."

Alice smiled. "I will. I have a new mystery to read." She went back into the library.

As Jane drove out of town, everyone she knew seemed to be outside enjoying the beautiful weather, and everyone who recognized her waved. She began to feel like a one-woman parade. Finally, she left Acorn Hill behind and drove to the Sichuan restaurant where she was to meet Todd.

Chapter Eight

When Jane pulled into the restaurant parking lot, Todd saw her and came toward her car. Her heart began beating double-time. He looked so handsome. His tailored gray slacks and monogrammed maroon polo shirt accentuated his height and broad shoulders. As she got out of the car to meet him, he reached for her hand to help her and gave her a warm smile. His touch sent shivers up her arm.

"You look lovely tonight."

"So do you," she replied, then, realizing what she had just said, she wanted to sink through the sidewalk.

He smiled. "Shall we?" He held her hand as he led her up the steps to the large red double doors with gold trim and geometric brass handles.

Inside, the soft lighting and Chinese music soothed her nerves. In the center of the restaurant, a wall of water gently cascaded over corrugated copper into a pool of goldfish.

Their waiter brought two small cups and a pot of tea, then left them to read their menus.

Jane opened her menu, but Todd reached over and covered her wrist with his hand. She glanced up and his gaze caught and held her attention. He smiled. Her mouth went dry. She was in big trouble.

"I'm so glad you came. I've been looking forward to seeing you since Tuesday."

"So have I," she said. "I heard that this restaurant is very authentic. This menu is fascinating. I've never heard of some of these dishes." She knew that she was babbling. When the waiter returned for their order, she sighed with relief.

"Ma Yi Shang Shu," Jane read. "Ants Climbing Up a Tree . . . pork and cellophane noodles." She smiled up at the waiter. "I'll have that. That translation is so fascinating, I can't resist."

Todd ordered Bao Chicken with Peanuts.

After the waiter left, Jane said, "I was tempted to order the Pock-marked Mother Chen's Beancurd. What interesting dishes. I'll have to get on the Internet and find some of these recipes."

"You said you are a chef. I'm glad you could get the night off."

"Officially, I prepare breakfasts for our guests. The kitchen is my domain, though, and I fix most of the meals for my sisters. That's when I experiment with different recipes." Jane laughed. "My sisters are very tolerant of my efforts. Once in a while, they even like them."

"I'm sure your cooking is wonderful. Did you enjoy your work as a chef before you moved back to Acorn Hill?"

Jane told him about being the chef at the Blue Fish Grille in San Francisco before moving home. She didn't elaborate about that part of her life, however. She had loved her job, but nothing was worth the heartache that followed. The reminder of that time warned her to move cautiously in this new friendship. Not that she feared relationships. She enjoyed wonderful friendships with Rev. Kenneth Thompson and Craig Tracy, but Todd was different.

After the waiter brought their food, Todd took her hand, bowed his head and asked a simple blessing for the meal.

Then he gave her a gentle smile and picked up his chopsticks. He showed considerable proficiency with the utensils.

"You're a pro. I'm impressed," Jane said. Her own attempt proved equally successful.

He laughed. "Survival," he said. "My, uh, ex-wife loved Chinese food."

"Oh." Jane didn't want to talk about his former relationship any more than she wanted to talk about Justin, so she steered the conversation to a more pleasant topic. "Did you plant everything you bought from Craig?"

"Not yet. I spent Tuesday afternoon clearing brush and weeds and rototilling the garden. I thought I'd better get vegetable seeds in the ground first, so I planted corn, bush beans, pumpkins and seed potatoes."

"Good idea. They need the full season. It takes a long time to restore a garden, but it sounds like you've made a good start."

"A start, yes. But there's so much to do. I hope you will give me some pointers. Craig Tracy bragged about your gardens."

Her smile faltered. She didn't know what to say. She wanted to show Todd her gardens, and yet the thought of having him come to her home made her nervous. She really had to talk to Fred and Vera to explain how she'd become friends with the manager of the Do-It-Yourself Warehouse and to tell them what a nice guy he was. Or she must end the friendship.

His attentive gaze bore a touch of concern. She smiled. His concern disappeared. He smiled back, and tiny creases crinkled around his beautiful brown eyes. She could get lost in those eyes. She chided herself for that silly thought, but she definitely wanted to spend more time with him.

"Craig advised me on my changes and restoration," she said. "He is the real expert, but I'll be glad to help you as much as I can. There's nothing more satisfying than watching life renew itself in a garden."

"I remember my aunt's garden," Todd said. "She grew a true farm garden and sold her produce, but she also had flowers growing throughout it. She told me that different flowers attracted bees or repelled gophers and garden pests. I wish I could remember what she said."

"I have a book that gives advice on various companion plants that are supposed to benefit each other. I'll lend it to you."

"I'd like that. I have so much to learn." He laughed. "Patience, above all. I like projects that show instant improvement. I have a feeling this is going to take a long time."

"You'll be surprised at how quickly plants regenerate. If only a little pruning and watering could restore people," she said and immediately wished she could reclaim those words. She didn't even know why she said them. Perhaps because she'd been thinking about Justin recently.

"I think it depends on who is doing the pruning, us or God."

Jane stared at Todd, astonished. *He is right. Only God can restore people.* Jane didn't know why Todd's observation struck her so intensely, but she felt as if God had spoken directly to her.

As Jane mixed a batch of pale celadon glaze the next morning, she had to smile at the noises coming from her aunt's kitchen. She had given Ethel the task of cutting painter's plastic into eighteen-inch squares. Ethel had gotten out a ruler to make sure her squares were exactly the right size. Now grunts of frustration were coming from the kitchen. Evidently, the plastic wasn't cooperating. Jane debated whether to go help her aunt, then decided against interfering.

She picked up a foam brush and began cutting in at the masked ceiling edge.

Jane was just finishing when Ethel came in carrying a handful of plastic squares.

"This is more difficult than it looks," Ethel said. "Are you certain we can do this? Perhaps Fred can recommend a painter."

"We'll finish the room before you could find a painter who would come right over. Trust me. You'll enjoy this, and we'll be finished before lunchtime."

"I don't know, Jane. I suppose it is too late to change my mind. We could leave the wall without the glaze."

Jane grinned at her aunt. "Definitely too late. And I need you to apply the plastic ragging before the glaze dries. Are you ready?"

Ethel gave Jane a horrified look. "You want me to apply the ragging? I can't. It's not . . . I've never . . . I don't know what to do."

"It's simple." Jane applied the first two roller-widths of glaze, then set the roller on the paint pan. "Do you care if you get paint on your clothes?"

Ethel looked down at her faded blue cotton slacks and blouse. "These old clothes? They are ready for the rag bag."

"Good." Jane held out a pair of rubber gloves. "Put these on and I'll show you what to do."

Ethel wrinkled her nose in distaste, but did as Jane instructed. "All right. Now what?"

"I'll do the top pieces to show you how, then you can take over." Jane took one square of plastic and climbed on the step stool. Holding the square open loosely, she applied it to the top corner of the wall, patting it into place, wrinkles intact. She looked down at her aunt. "See, you want it loose, so when you pull it off, like this . . ." She peeled back the plastic, removing some of the wet glaze with it. "Then the creases will show, leaving a dappled effect on the wall."

"That doesn't look difficult."

"It's not. Here, you try it. Take a fresh piece of plastic and apply it below mine, slightly overlapping the bottom edge. You can reuse the plastic square several times. I'll paint another column, then start the top for you."

Jane got down, set her plastic square aside and moved the stool over. While she got paint on a roller, she watched Ethel. Her aunt carefully placed the plastic on the wall and started patting it into place. As she did so, she smoothed out the wrinkles.

"No, no, Auntie. You want the wrinkles left in place. That's what gives the glaze texture and the marbled effect. Like this." Jane demonstrated the technique again. "Try applying it very loosely just below this."

Jane stepped back and let Ethel apply the plastic square beneath her two applications. Ethel tried to comply, but it was still too smooth.

"Much better. Peel it off and see."

Ethel pulled back the paint-globbed plastic. She dropped the square. It plopped to the ground, paint-side down.

"Oh dear," Ethel said, with a cry of dismay.

"No harm done. That's why I spread plastic sheeting everywhere. And look at the wall. It looks much better."

Ethel peered at the wall. "Do you think it will look all right?" she said, a hint of doubt in her voice.

"It will be beautiful. I promise. Francine is going to love it."

"I do hope so. I want her to enjoy her visit. She doesn't come often enough. It grieves me to admit that I am closer to you girls than to my own daughter."

"Us *girls*? You do realize I am fifty years old. Hardly a girl."

Ethel smiled. "You and Francine are the same age, and you are all girls to me. Forever young."

"Forever young," Jane repeated. "I like that. I think I'll

make a plaque and hang it in my kitchen. Then when I am sore from pulling weeds in the garden, I can look at it and remember that I am young, if only to my dear auntie."

"Oh, go on. You are teasing me," Ethel said. "But I believe you are right. This will look very good in here. Did I tell you all the plans I have made for entertaining Francine?"

"No, you didn't."

"Francine loves fine china and crystal. The Potterston Historical Society is giving a lecture on the history of pottery and porcelain in America. Then the County Horticultural Society has a lecture on caring for orchids."

"Does Francine raise orchids?"

"No, but I hear it's all the rage. Also, I thought I'd take her to tour the various charity institutions in the area. She's very involved in charities. And the preservation society in Potterston is sponsoring a walking tour of the historical buildings. She should find that interesting. Then there's a lecture at the library, a meeting of the quilters' guild that Sylvia Songer mentioned and a reading at Nine Lives Bookstore."

"A reading at Viola's? I thought you disliked the book club events."

"You know very well that I have attended numerous events at the bookstore," Ethel said defensively. "I do think dissecting books after you read them is like conducting an autopsy, but I'm sure Francine will enjoy it. She attends the opera and cultural events, you know."

"That's an awfully full schedule, Aunt Ethel. And what about the Fourth of July festivities? Won't Lloyd want you to attend the celebration with him?"

"The—oh dear, I'd forgotten." Ethel seemed distressed over her memory lapse, but then she frowned. "Lloyd cannot expect to occupy all of my time. I must think of Francine."

Jane thought Aunt Ethel's agenda sounded exhausting and not the sort of activities she'd care to attend. Perhaps

Francine had changed more than she realized. "I didn't know you belonged to the quilters' guild."

"Francine showed an interest in the Amish quilts the last time she visited. Sylvia said we could come as guests."

They had completed one wall and started another while they talked. Ethel's ragging had relaxed as she talked and the effect looked very nice. Jane changed the subject to discuss Ethel's other decorating ideas, and the time flew by. At ten minutes to twelve, Ethel applied the last square of plastic ragging to the glaze.

Jane stepped back to survey their handiwork. "It looks as good as any professional job," she declared.

Ethel stood up and groaned. "I'll never be able to stand straight again," she said.

"Let's clean up, and then we can relax. Your muscles will unkink after you've stretched a bit."

"I hope you're right. I believe I've aged ten years."

Jane pulled the masking off the ceiling, baseboards and windows and wadded it up in a ball. "If you'll roll up the plastic and pick up the trash, I'll clean the brushes and roller. When you're ready, come over to the house and we'll have lunch." Jane took the paint pan and equipment to the utility sink in the garage.

By the time she finished scrubbing the pan and brushes and her arms and hands, Ethel had already changed and was in Jane's kitchen telling Louise about her painting prowess. Louise was putting out the fixings for tuna sandwiches. Jane stifled a grin. From the sound of it, Ethel hadn't needed her help at all.

"Oh, Jane, I was just telling Louise how wonderful the guest room looks. I'm so pleased. Now I want to paint and glaze the living room. I'm thinking of using a different color, though. Perhaps a tan. What do you think?"

Tan? It sounded drab to Jane. But she could probably talk

her aunt into something more lively. Jane looked at her aunt. She seemed a bit pale after the exertion of the morning.

"Are you certain you want to tackle the living room? You seem a bit tired. I know I am."

"Oh yes. I didn't realize how faded and outdated the rooms look until we painted the guest room. Now the rest of the carriage house looks dingy. The living room must have a new coat of paint."

"All right. What shade of tan did you have in mind?" Jane asked. "Perhaps something in a shade of mocha or a hint of rose. You could use a metallic glaze to give it a more formal look, like an overlay of bronze or copper. It's too bad that we gave back the decorating books."

"I'm sure Fred will be happy to let us look through them again. Will you come with me to pick out the color?"

"Certainly, Aunt Ethel. When do you want to go?"

"Today. This very minute. Francine will be here soon." Ethel started to rise. She had barely touched her sandwich.

Jane sighed. There went the time for the new recipe she wanted to try. "All right. We might as well go and get it over with, but let's eat our sandwiches first."

Thirty minutes later, Jane and Ethel walked into Fred's Hardware and went directly to what had been the paint department. Only the dark rectangles on the linoleum floor showed where the shelves of paint had stood. The paint, the brushes and rollers and pans, and even the shelves were gone. A tapping sound came from the back of the store. They followed the sound and found Fred on his knees tapping the base of a shelving unit together and Vera holding a vertical rail in place.

"You are not dismantling the store, are you?" Ethel asked.

Fred gave one more tap and looked up.

"Sorry about the mess," Vera said. "We're moving things around."

"You certainly are. I was hoping to look for another paint and glaze, but that doesn't look possible," Ethel said, surveying the disarray.

"How soon do you need it?" Fred asked. "We'll have this back together by this evening."

"We can wait, can't we, Aunt Ethel? Can you get to the decorating books, Fred? Perhaps we could borrow them again and pick out the colors."

"Certainly. Vera, do you know where the books are?"

"Yes. Hold this a moment," she said to Jane, who stepped over a pile of metal rails and took hold of the upright rail.

"Thanks. I'll be right back." She disappeared through the doorway to the back room.

"What made you decide to do all this, Fred?" Jane asked.

Fred chuckled. "Vera's idea. Alice brought in a brochure from a rental place in Potterston, and Vera convinced me to give it a try. So far, it's a lot of work. I hope it's worth all of this."

"A rental business?" Ethel said. "What will you rent?"

"All kinds of equipment and tools. We'll start with things I have on hand, like paint sprayers and pressure washers— that kind of equipment. If it's successful, we'll acquire additional equipment," Fred said.

"A paint sprayer?" Ethel asked. "Should we use a sprayer, Jane?"

"I think we'd better stick to a brush and roller, Aunt Ethel. We make enough mess without spraying paint all over the room."

"Yes, I suppose so. I just thought we could help Fred by renting his sprayer."

"Thanks for the thought," Fred said. "You've been such loyal customers and friends, I'd lend it to you for nothing."

Jane's face reddened. She knew Fred meant what he said.

She thought about her friendship with Todd and didn't feel like a very good friend to the Humberts. "You can't start lending out your rental equipment for free, Fred. That defeats the purpose."

"I suppose you're right, but I am the boss, so I can do whatever I wish."

Vera came back with two large decorating books. "Is that so?" she said. "You told me this morning that I was the boss."

Fred laughed out loud. "I did say that, didn't I? You've certainly been the bossy one today. Without your . . . uh . . . direction, I wouldn't be doing this," he said, waving his hand in a wide arc, indicating all their mess.

"It's going to be great. You'll see."

"I think we'd better leave them to their work," Ethel said to Jane.

"Do you need some help?" Jane asked.

"Everything is under control," Vera said. She hesitated a moment. "I know you went to talk to the manager of the Do-It-Yourself Warehouse on our behalf. That was such a nice thing for you to do."

"Oh, Vera, I didn't accomplish anything. Really. I didn't help at all."

"You went, and that means a lot. We know there's nothing we can do about the store being in the area, but we appreciate your friendship and loyalty."

Jane sighed. What could she say? This wasn't the time to tell Vera about Todd, but she didn't want them thinking she had done something good. "I just wish I could help. Have you thought about brochures? Fred will need to advertise, and Carlene makes beautiful flyers." As editor of the town's paper, the *Acorn Nutshell*, Carlene Moss loved to promote local interests.

"We haven't gotten that far yet," Vera said. "We just decided to do this last night."

"I'm sure Carlene will want to do a feature story for the paper. Would you mind if I mention your new venture to her?"

"Go right ahead. That would be one less thing to think about."

Chapter Nine

"Aunt Ethel, shall we stop by the *Acorn Nutshell* to talk to Carlene?" Jane asked as they left Fred's Hardware.

"Yes, that's a good idea, but let's go to the town hall first, so I can tell Lloyd," Ethel replied. "As mayor he has a lot of influence. Maybe he can do something to help Fred."

Jane hesitated a moment. She had just provided the opportunity for Ethel to exercise her favorite pastime, spreading the latest news. In this case, Ethel's efforts could be a good thing. She would make sure everyone in town heard about Fred's new venture.

Jane and Ethel stopped at Lloyd's office and told him about Fred's rental business. Lloyd was optimistic about the success of such a service in Acorn Hill and reminded Jane and Ethel that the town had often used the Potterston rental service for equipment for various town functions. That business could now go to Fred.

After they left Lloyd's office, Jane and Ethel stopped at the *Acorn Nutshell*. Carlene was interested to learn about Fred's sideline. She took her notepad and camera and walked with Jane and Ethel back as far as Fred's Hardware. She told Jane she was working on a story about small-town stores going up against corporate giants. She wanted to interview

Jane about her conversation with the hardware-store manager, but Jane declined, telling Carlene she hadn't accomplished anything.

When they got back to Ethel's, Jane plopped down the decorating books on the kitchen table. Ethel started looking through one of them.

Jane sat next to her and said, "I remember seeing a room in one of these books that would be perfect for the carriage house. Let me see if I can find it again." She thumbed through the pages. Not finding it, she opened the other book.

"Here." She slid the book closer to Ethel. "What do you think?"

The room in the book had a soft, warm rosy glow that gave the space a cozy yet elegant appearance. In her artist's eye, Jane could see it bringing new life to Ethel's furnishings.

"Yes, that's lovely. I'm so glad you are helping me with this, Jane."

Her aunt's compliment startled Jane. More often than not, Ethel expressed views that were contrary to Jane's eclectic style. Ethel's agreement spoke volumes about the anxiety her daughter's visit was causing.

"Francine is going to love what you're doing to the house. We'll pick up the paint tomorrow morning, if that works for you."

"I'll be ready at eight thirty, so we can be Fred's first customers."

Jane laughed. "We'd better make it nine thirty. That will give me time to serve breakfast to our guests."

"All right, but we must get started as early as possible.

Alice worked Friday, filling in for a vacationing nurse who had promised to take her shift when Alice went to New York. On her way home from the hospital, Alice went to the

Potterston train station and purchased the tickets for the ANGELs' trip.

She was so excited that she stopped at Nellie's to share the news. Clara Horn's baby buggy was parked outside the shop's door. When Alice entered the store, Clara was purchasing something from Nellie. As Nellie lifted the bright yellow garment, Alice realized it was a child's T-shirt. The neckline had a lace ruffle and the front held a cartoon picture of a chubby pig with angel wings in a blue ballerina outfit. Nellie looked up and smiled. "Hello, Alice. I'll be with you in a moment."

"No hurry. Hello, Clara. Is the T-shirt for Daisy?"

"Yes, isn't it adorable?"

"Yes. I'm sure Daisy'll look very nice in it."

Daisy was Clara's miniature Vietnamese pot-bellied pig. She often dressed the animal in pretty ruffles and frills. Nellie and Alice watched Clara take her package and go outside to show the shirt to Daisy.

Nellie shook her head, then smiled. "Clara had me special order the T-shirt for her. It seems Daisy is gaining weight and outgrowing her clothes. Clara's a bit eccentric, but she loves that pig, and Daisy is kind of cute. I asked Clara how she could lift Daisy into the buggy. Evidently, she has trained Daisy to get up on the couch and climb into the buggy." Nellie shook her head. "Amazing. So what can I do for you, Alice?"

"I bought our train tickets to New York. We leave June twenty-ninth at 9:02 A.M. from the Potterston station." Alice smiled. "Now it's beginning to seem real."

"Wonderful," Nellie said, but she didn't look thrilled. In fact, Alice thought she appeared rather distressed.

"Is something the matter, Nellie?"

"I've been researching New York City and reading the *New York Times* on the Internet. The news isn't good." Nellie shuddered. "I must tell you, Alice, I'm having serious doubts about this trip. If anything happens to the girls, we'll be responsible."

Alice shook her head. Jane loved the Internet and extolled its wonders, but Alice doubted the wisdom of all the instant access. She reached across the counter and patted Nellie's arm. "You can't judge the city by the newspaper headlines, Nellie. If you consider how many people live and work in the city, I think you'll find the statistics of crime are actually relatively low. And we won't take the girls anywhere dangerous."

"No place is safe in the city. Even in broad daylight, things happen. It's not like Acorn Hill, Alice. In the city, people don't stop to help. They don't want to get involved." Nellie shook her head.

"You can always find bad news if you go looking, Nellie. Sensational stories sell newspapers and attract television viewers. Nothing is going to happen. The entire church will be praying for us while we're there. It's been a few years, but I've taken other ANGELs to the city. We had a wonderful time. And don't forget, you have an appointment in the garment district."

"I know, and I really *do* want to go. If we just had some way to ensure the girls' safety. I don't suppose you could cancel now without disappointing them. They're so excited. I envy them. At their age, I wouldn't have hesitated to go."

"And there's no need to worry now. Please don't back out on us. The girls are excited to have you along."

"I won't. I gave you my word. I wish there were time to take a self-defense course."

"We have the best defense there is, Nellie. We have God's protection. We'll be fine. And the girls are looking forward to delivering their puppets to the child-care center."

Nellie drew in a deep breath as if to settle herself. Then her face brightened. "Speaking of the center, I have something to show you," she said. "I got these for the kids there. I found them when I ordered that shirt for Clara." Nellie bent down and picked up a box. She took out a stack of children's tan T-shirts. She unfolded four of them and spread them out on the counter.

"These are adorable, Nellie. The children will love them," Alice said, picking up a shirt with a pink kitten wearing a princess dress and a crown. In large, purple letters over the princess, it said "Precious!" And beneath it were the words, "How precious to me are Thy thoughts, O Lord."

"This is my favorite," Nellie said, holding up a shirt with a teddy-bear ballerina leaping in the air. In variegated pink letters over the bear it said "Jump for Joy," and beneath, the words, "My heart leaps for joy and I give thanks to Him."

Another T-shirt had the same saying, but the picture was a dog on a skateboard with a baseball cap on backward. The fourth style had Noah's ark with animals coming out of the ark and a rainbow overhead.

"I have twenty-four in various sizes. I hope that'll be enough."

"Sister Margaret told me they have from fifteen to twenty children, so you have a few spares. This is a wonderful gift, and it's so special that you'll be able to give them to the children in person."

A sparkle came into Nellie's eyes. "I'm looking forward to that."

At eight thirty Saturday morning, Ethel tapped on the kitchen door, yoo-hooed and stepped into the kitchen. Jane was transferring a hot spinach-and-three-cheese frittata to a platter.

"I know I'm early, but I thought you might be ready to go. *Yum.* That looks delicious."

"Would you like to join us for breakfast, Aunt Ethel?"

"Why thank you, Jane. I spent the morning covering

furniture, so I didn't eat breakfast. May I carry something for you?"

Louise came into the kitchen. "Oh, hello, Aunt Ethel." She picked up a basket of fresh muffins. "Are you joining us? I'll set another place."

"Here, Aunt Ethel." Jane handed her a bowl containing a mixture of fresh and dried fruits. She followed Louise to the dining room.

The table held seven place settings of the Wedgwood Wildflower china. A well-dressed couple about Ethel's age and the honeymooners were seated at the table. Alice was pouring coffee. Jane set the frittata on a trivet in the center of the table.

"I don't believe we've had such an elegant breakfast since we traveled to Paris last fall, have we, dear?" Guinevere Post said.

"Indeed," her husband Robert agreed, smiling at his wife affectionately.

"And the Garden Room is glorious. We will recommend the inn to all our friends."

"Thank you," Louise said as she quickly set another place for Ethel. "I hope you're enjoying your visit as well," she said to the honeymooners.

"Oh, we are," the young man said, glancing at his bride. "We really hate to leave, but we have to get back home. We were just talking this morning about trying to come back here for our first anniversary."

"What a lovely idea," Alice said. "I hope that plan works out for you."

The Posts shared stories of some of the trips they took to celebrate their anniversaries, and Ethel told a very funny story about a surprise anniversary dinner she had once arranged that went terribly awry. The conversation moved on to a variety of other topics with everyone participating in stories and laughter.

After the guests left the table, Jane carried several plates to the kitchen. Louise followed her with more dishes. "Go ahead with Aunt Ethel," she said. "I'll clean up here."

"All right. Thanks. She's anxious about getting her living room painted."

"I know. I haven't seen her so stressed over anything in some time. I hope Francine appreciates all of the preparations Aunt Ethel is making for her visit."

"Yes, I do too."

Ethel came into the kitchen with the leftover fruit. Jane turned to her. "Louise is going to clean up so we can go. Are you ready?"

"I am." Ethel set the bowl down, took her purse from the counter where she'd left it and headed for the door. Jane smiled at Louise and followed her aunt.

Two cars were parked in front of Fred's Hardware when Jane pulled up. Inside, Fred was talking to a man. *A salesman,* Jane assumed when she noticed the color brochure he was showing Fred. She and Ethel went back to the new paint department. Vera came over to talk to Jane while Ethel ordered the paint from a clerk.

"Did you see the man talking to Fred?" Vera asked in a low, conspiratorial voice.

"Yes, who is he?"

"A representative from the big rental company that put out that brochure Alice gave me. The man she talked to in Potterston sent the rep to see us. He wants us to carry some of their equipment as an expansion of his store. He owns the franchise, so we'll go through his business, and he'll get a percentage of every rental. And we can still rent out some of our own equipment too. I think Fred's going to do it. We've already had several people rent the equipment we had on hand, and we haven't even advertised. By the way, Carlene came by and she's doing a front-page article for this week's paper. She said she would send it to the Potterston paper too."

"Great. I hope you don't mind, but Aunt Ethel and I told Lloyd too."

"No, I don't mind, in fact, I appreciate it. Lloyd came to congratulate Fred, and he promised to spread the word. I haven't seen Fred this animated in weeks."

"Wonderful. I hope you realize that everyone in Acorn Hill wants to support you and Fred."

"We are beginning to. Although we can't compete with some of the Do-It-Yourself Warehouse's prices, and I can't blame people for wanting a bargain. So we just have to offer them something else. Like personal service and the rental equipment. I didn't expect to see you back in here so soon. I thought Ethel only intended to paint a bedroom."

Jane was relieved at the change of subject. "Now that the guest room is done, she felt the living room needed a face lift."

"She's keeping you awfully busy. How do you manage everything?"

Jane laughed. "One spoonful at a time. But it's not that bad. Look at what you're tackling. You've done a great job rearranging the store. It looks really good."

"Thank you." Vera grinned. "All those school art projects paid off."

"What art projects?" Ethel asked as she walked up to them. Jane had always thought that her aunt must have superhuman hearing.

"I was complimenting Vera on the way they rearranged the store."

"Yes, it looks very nice," Ethel said.

"I'm eager to see your project too," Vera said, "Jane tells me the guest room turned out lovely and now you're doing the living room. I must stop by and see them when you're finished. I might even take some pictures to show how the glazes look on your walls. People like to see the results in real homes."

Ethel straightened and raised her head, almost preening. "I'd be delighted to have you come take pictures. I'll call you when we finish. Come, Jane. Let's get to work."

Jane carried the two cans of paint to her car and took Ethel home. She lugged the cans into the carriage house and set them on Ethel's newspaper-covered counter.

"I need to change into my painting clothes. I'll be right back," Jane said as she left.

She was only gone a few minutes. When she got back, Ethel had already set out two paint pans, two rollers and several brushes. She had on a painting smock, and she was bending down, applying masking tape to the baseboard trim.

"You are certainly efficient, Aunt Ethel," Jane said.

Ethel stood up straight and rubbed her lower back. "I watched you do this, and it didn't look too difficult. I must admit, though, it looks easier than it is. These old bones aren't used to bending over like this. It's a good thing I took those exercise classes."

Jane laughed. "Bending over and stretching down is hard on any body. Mine included. You've done half the room. Let me finish it up."

"Gladly. I'll get the paint ready."

"You *are* feeling ambitious today, Auntie."

"I just want to get finished. Can you help me do the glaze on Monday?"

"I suppose I can, but not until after we clean the inn. I can't let Louise and Alice do all the work."

Ethel gave Jane a penitent look. "I'm sorry to monopolize your time. I hope you haven't canceled anything on my account."

Jane hugged her aunt. "I'm glad to help you. Goodness, I remember all the time you spent with me when I was growing up. Painting your living room is the least I can do."

Ethel's eyes filled with tears. She took a hankie out of her pocket and dabbed at the corners of her eyes. "I appreciate you so much. You can't know what this means to me. I could never be ready for Francine's visit without you."

"We will have everything finished in plenty of time, and Francine will love what you've done."

"I hope you're right. She's very particular, you know."

Jane didn't know. She no longer felt close to her cousin though they once had been best of friends. They were the same age, and growing up they had been playmates, acting out fanciful roles, like princesses or rodeo queens. As teenagers, they had giggled about the boys from Bob and Ethel's church and planned to marry a particular set of brothers and live next door to each other forever. But that was thirty-five years ago. Now they exchanged greetings at Christmas, and that was about it.

"I see you have two rollers. Are you going to paint?"

"You know painting isn't my favorite pastime," Aunt Ethel said, "but this is for Francine. I count it as a labor of love."

Jane poured paint into the pans. Filling a roller with paint, she started on the wall. Ethel copied her motions, and soon the walls were a lovely, soft shade of mauve.

"Oh, Jane," Ethel said when she stood back to see their work. "This color is lovely. I'm so glad that you talked me out of the tan paint."

After they cleaned up, Jane went home to shower. She met Alice on the stairs.

"Jane, your friend called. I took a message for you." She dug into her pocket and pulled out a folded piece of paper that she handed to Jane.

"Thanks, Alice. I'm going up to shower and change."

Chapter Ten

Jane waited until she reached her room before she looked at Todd's message.

> Todd called. He wants to know if you will go to Longwood Gardens with him tomorrow after church. Call him back.

Longwood Gardens. Jane loved visiting the beautiful gardens. Yes, she wanted to go, but she hoped Todd wasn't planning to go to church with her. She wasn't ready for everyone to see her with him. She didn't know if she'd ever be ready for that, and yet she knew it would happen if she continued seeing him.

After she showered and changed, she went to find Alice. Her sister was in the library. "Did Todd say whether he's coming to our church service tomorrow?"

"Why no, he didn't. Are you expecting him to?"

"I wasn't expecting to see him at all tomorrow. I don't know what to do. I enjoy his company and I want to spend time with him, but I feel awkward because of his job."

Alice gave Jane a gentle smile. "I don't know Todd, but I'm sure he's a very nice person. You need to trust your judgment. I know you aren't doing anything to hurt Fred and

Vera. I think you should tell them about the situation, but I see nothing wrong with you being friends with this man and neither should anyone else."

"But you know people will jump to conclusions."

"Then that's their problem." Alice's expression grew wistful. "I remember having a discussion with Father once when I made friends with a girl most people avoided because she seemed conceited. I discovered that she was just shy. She loved school, but she didn't relate well to the other kids. Father encouraged me to nurture the relationship. He told me God may have put her in my path because she needed a friend. When I said I was concerned about what my other friends would think, he quoted Scripture to me. 'Rejoice with those who rejoice; mourn with those who mourn. Live in harmony with one another. Do not be proud, but be willing to associate with people of low position. Do not be conceited' (Romans 12:15–16). And that is what I would say to you. Don't let what other people think influence you. If you want this friendship, then pursue it."

Jane hugged Alice and smiled. "Thank you. Goodness, I must be having an emotional day today. First I hugged Aunt Ethel and now you."

"You can hug me anytime. I hope I helped."

"Definitely. Now I have a phone call to make."

Jane hurried home from church on Sunday so she could change and be ready when Todd arrived. She considered wearing slacks and a T-shirt but decided on a black-and-white polka-dotted sundress. She let her hair down from its French twist and left it loose about her shoulders. After a quick inspection in the mirror, she took her purse and went downstairs.

Todd was standing in the living room talking to Louise and Alice. Jane had a moment to watch him before she made her presence known. He looked handsome standing in front of the fireplace in crisply creased navy blue slacks and a pale-blue polo shirt. He stood sideways, motioning with one hand as he spoke. She could see the upturned corner of his mouth. Across from him, Alice and Louise were smiling as they listened. Alice chuckled at something he said, and Louise glanced toward her. Jane stepped into the room.

"Hello, Todd."

He turned toward her and his smile grew wider. He stepped closer and held out his hand, not in the manner of a handshake, but in a gesture of affection. The flutter in her stomach reached her heart. His hand enveloped hers, making her feel small and feminine . . . an odd feeling. At slightly over five feet nine inches tall, she wasn't a little person.

"I've been telling your sisters about my old farmhouse. I'm beginning to think I've moved to the funny farm. Last night I heard scratching and scurrying in the attic and realized I have new tenants."

"Squirrels?" Jane asked.

"No, a family of raccoons. The branches of a large willow tree reach up to the attic. The raccoons managed to climb up and tear through the screen to get inside. So now I have to figure out how to evict them." He chuckled. "I must admit, however, I'm rather enjoying the novelty. I don't know what they'll do to the attic, though."

Jane laughed. "You do have a dilemma. As adorable as they are to watch, I think they can be very destructive."

"You're right. I don't know whether to trap them and move them to a different area or block the attic window. I need the ventilation it provides."

"I believe Jack O'Hara, the animal-control officer, handles cases like this. He'll relocate the raccoons to a forested area."

"I'll call him tomorrow."

"I hope the animals don't destroy your house by then," Alice said.

Todd laughed. "Well, it needs a lot of work anyway."

"Yoo-hoo." Ethel came sailing in from the kitchen, still in her church dress. "I knocked on the door. I guess no one heard me, so I came on in. Oh." She stopped in the doorway and stared at Todd for a moment. Then she extended her hand and walked toward him.

"How do you do? I'm Ethel Buckley. I live in the carriage house in back."

"Ethel is our aunt," Louise explained.

Todd took her hand and gave Ethel a charming smile. "Nice to meet you, Mrs. Buckley. Todd Loughlin. I'm a friend of Jane's."

"Oh." She looked at Jane, raising one eyebrow and giving her a speculative look. "How nice," she said. Then she turned back to Todd with a smile. "You must be the *friend* she met for dinner the other night." Her brows lifted.

Todd smiled. "That's possible. Jane's been advising me on my garden."

"I see." The look she gave Jane indicated she saw far more than Todd's explanation implied. Jane had the irrational thought that her aunt had developed ESP and knew all about Todd and about Jane's duplicity in dating the enemy.

"We really must be going if we want to see the gardens," Jane said.

"Where are you off to in such a rush?" Ethel asked. "I haven't even had a chance to talk with your friend."

"Sorry, Auntie, but we're just leaving to drive to Longwood Gardens. Maybe some other time."

"I know." Ethel smiled brightly. "Todd must come to dinner next Sunday. Then we can have a nice chat." She turned to Todd. "We often have Sunday dinner together. Of course, not today, since you're going out. Jane's our chef, you know, and her dinners are excellent. Can you come?"

"Well . . . I . . . I'd love to." He gave Jane a helpless what-can-I-say look.

Louise started to speak, then closed her mouth. Alice looked uncomfortable. Jane shrugged. The fat was in the fire now. So much for keeping Todd away from Ethel and the rumor mill. Everyone in town would know by tomorrow that Jane had a new friend. She had to get Todd out of there before Ethel learned more.

"I'm ready," Jane said, smiling at Todd. She took his elbow and began to lead him out of the room.

Louise quickly stood. "Yes, you must run along. Have a lovely afternoon."

Alice stood too. "Enjoy yourselves," she said. "Aunt Ethel, would you like a cup of tea? I was just going to fix some."

Ethel gave Jane a disproving look as she and Todd walked past her. "I might as well," she said.

Todd opened the car door for Jane. Justin had never opened doors for her. That came of living in San Francisco in the age of women's lib, she supposed, but she liked being pampered. She slid into the car.

He drove out of town. "Your sisters are very nice, but I don't see a strong family resemblance."

"We're very different, but as close as we could be. Do you have brothers or sisters?"

"A brother in Virginia, where we grew up, and a sister in California. We were close when we were young, but we rarely see each other anymore." He sighed. "I envy you. I miss having family around."

"We haven't always been close. I lived in San Francisco as I told you, Louise lived in Philadelphia and Alice stayed at home. We lived very different lives, and we hadn't been together for years. It's sad that it took our father's death to bring us back together, but I know he'd be pleased. Do you have children?"

"No. Unfortunately. I wanted a large family, but it wasn't meant to be, I guess. How about you?"

"No. None." She wondered why she had opened that thread of conversation. Then she answered her own question. *Because I want to know all about Todd.* "My sisters like you," she said out loud.

"I'm glad." He gave her a sideways glance and smiled. "I'm looking forward to getting to know them better. And thanks for coming with me today. I've heard the gardens are spectacular, and I'm hoping to get some ideas and learn more about the plants that do well here. Your yard is beautiful. From what I could see, you are a talented gardener."

Jane laughed. "Hardly. But thanks. I inherited a bit of a green thumb from my mother, but all I did was to restore what she had planted, and for that I had Craig's help. I enjoy spending time in the garden."

They drove the rest of the way in companionable conversation. Todd had never been in the region south of Acorn Hill, and Jane hadn't been to Longwood Gardens for many years. She told him about various points of interest along the way and found herself sharing happy memories. They stopped for a quick bite of lunch, so it was almost midafternoon when they arrived at the gardens. Jane was enjoying Todd's company so much, she couldn't wait to show him this place she'd loved to visit as a child.

They began in the West Gardens, strolling through the Open Air Theater and along the Flower Garden Walk hand in hand. Beautiful beds of annuals brought color to the bucolic setting of placid lakes and rolling lawns. A soft breeze riffled the leaves of the trees and teased wisps of Jane's hair around her face, softly caressing her skin. In the distance, Westminster chimes rang the half hour. Jane smiled, remembering the sound from many years before.

"When I was a girl, they had electronic chimes that played all kinds of music. Sometimes they synchronized the fountains in time to the music. That was one of my favorite things here. I know they shut down the chimes about twenty years ago. That must be a recording. Still, it's lovely."

"I read that they installed a new carillon like the original."

"Really? How wonderful! We will see the Chimes Tower and waterfall later. I hope the chimes play then. That would make today just perfect."

"I don't know that anything could improve on today," Todd said.

Jane didn't respond. What could she say? With the beauty of the gardens and the handsome man beside her, Jane felt as if she'd stepped into a fantasy. She smiled up at Todd. He smiled back.

"A quarter for your thoughts," he said.

"I thought it was a penny."

"Your thoughts are far more valuable than that." His smile mesmerized her.

"You say the nicest things," she said. "I was thinking that this is so lovely, I must have stepped into a fairy tale."

"Which one?"

"Goodness. I don't know. Something with beautiful gardens. I'm afraid I'm not up on my fairy tales."

He laughed. "Neither am I, but walking through the gardens with you is definitely the stuff of dreams."

Jane giggled. "Stuff of dreams? Now that's poetic."

They both laughed. "Definitely not poetic," he said. "I couldn't rhyme if I had to. This seems more like a painting to me. Like a Monet. I always loved his scenes of beautiful gardens and ladies in those old-fashioned dresses and hats and umbrellas."

Jane grinned. "Do you mean Victorian gowns, bonnets and parasols?"

"Yes. That's it."

"I believe you're right. I love his art. I've tried to emulate his style, but my oil paintings are much too bold. I come closer with watercolors, but I never manage that otherworldliness. It'd be fun to come here and spend a day painting. Perhaps I'll do that someday."

He stopped walking and looked at her. "You're an artist too?"

Jane blushed. "I wouldn't make such a lofty claim, but I dabble in art. I studied it in college, hoping to pursue a career in art, but I ended up in a kitchen."

"Another artistic activity. Do you still paint?"

"Yes, when I have time."

"Would you show me some of your paintings?"

"If you're really interested."

"I am. I want to learn all about you, Jane."

Her breath caught in her throat. She couldn't mistake the affection in his gaze. She didn't know if she was ready for affection, but she felt cherished at that moment and it felt nice.

"Where shall we go next?"

"I don't know. I want to see everything," Todd said.

Jane laughed. "Impossible. Not in a few hours. There are over a thousand acres of gardens. And that's just outside. The greenhouse gardens are huge. Let's go through Peirce's Woods. They are lovely. Then we can visit the Italian Water Garden if you want to see something formal, and the Peony and Wisteria Gardens. Or we can head to the Conservatory and the Main Fountain Garden."

"I'd like to see the woods." He opened his map. "According to this, the Idea Garden is near the Conservatory. I want to see that. Let's skip the formal landscapes. We can always come back when we have more time."

"All right."

Todd casually draped his arm around her shoulder as they walked. She liked it.

Every imaginable type of native foliage grew in the woods. Purple creeping phlox contrasted with red columbine, pink azaleas, and purple and white rhododendrons. Flowering trees joined with tall oaks, ash and maples to form canopied woodland rooms. Jane and Todd stood close together, delighting in the wonderful fragrance of mossy woodland, sweet flowers and rich soil.

"I have woods at the back of my property," Todd said. "They're a mess, but I'd love to create a wonderland like this." He dropped his arm and took a little notebook out of his pocket to jot down the name of a plant, and the intimate spell was broken. Jane's disappointment surprised her. She hadn't experienced the closeness of a man's arm around her in a very long time. Even before her divorce, Justin's affection had cooled. She hadn't realized how much she missed that special contact until now. Perhaps it was best that she keep some distance between Todd and her. He seemed unchanged by their closeness, and she didn't want to misinterpret his casually affectionate gestures. She pointed out various plants to him and he made notations in his book.

They sat on a bench in the cool shade, enjoying the quiet beauty. The chimes rang four times for the hour, then rang the notes of a song. After a few chimes, she recognized the song and laughed with delight. "'Tales of the Vienna Woods.' How perfect! Do you suppose someone is spying on us and played that for our benefit?"

Todd grinned. He took her hand and linked their fingers. Her heart skipped a beat. She stared at him and he winked at her. He was teasing her. "We'll pretend they played it just for us. Our own special concert." He rose. "Shall we follow the sound and see if we can find the tower?"

"Oh yes." She rose from the bench and they walked briskly in the direction of the Main Fountain Garden, past the Peirce–Du Pont House and the restaurant. There, on a hillside beyond the dancing water of the fabulous fountains, stood the Chimes Tower. The song had ended, but the tower stood, visible through the trees on the hill above a waterfall, like a majestic medieval bastion overlooking the gardens.

"Isn't it wonderful?" Jane said.

"Breathtaking. You should paint it."

"Perhaps I will someday." And she suddenly wanted to paint a picture for Todd. A reminder of a perfect day.

Chapter Eleven

From the top of the hill, standing by the tower looking over the lake and waterfall, Jane remembered a day forty years before, when she stood near this spot with her father. He had been telling her the history of the tower when he became suddenly quiet. When she asked him what was wrong, he smiled down at her and ruffled her hair and said everything was wonderful. Then he told her how her mother had loved to come to the gardens with a picnic lunch for them.

"You're very quiet. Jane?" Todd tipped her chin up and looked down into her eyes. "You're sad. What's wrong?"

"I was remembering standing here with my father. It's funny, because I asked him the same question. This was a favorite spot of my mother's. She died when I was born, so I never had a chance to stand here with her."

"I'm sorry. I wanted this to be a happy day for you."

"Oh, it is. And I can almost see Mother and Father looking down on the gardens, enjoying them together again." Then she laughed. "I suppose that's pretty silly. They are in a place with gardens created by the Master's hand, not a poor imitation that we humans produce."

"Yes, but these are beautiful, and I think God is pleased when we carefully tend His creation."

Jane smiled. "Yes, I think you're right. Sometimes, when I'm working in the garden, I can almost feel His pleasure shining down on me. That's one reason I love working in the garden. Well, now where shall we go? Down through the Oak and Conifer Knoll to the Eye of Water, or down through Frog Hollow?"

"Definitely Frog Hollow. I have a frog bog of my own. I love to listen to them, but it's a mess. Then we can check out the Idea Garden." He held out the crook of his arm for her and she linked her arm through his. They walked in step, side by side, grinning like a couple of playful children.

As they passed Frog Hollow, the faint sweet, lemony scent of magnolia blossoms filled the air. They spent an hour at the Idea Garden. Todd made copious notes in his little book and seemed to forget that Jane existed. He questioned staff members who were on hand to help the visitors. Jane followed him around and observed his serious interest. She listened intently and was pleased that she was instinctively doing many things right with the Grace Chapel Inn gardens. When Todd finally tucked his notebook into his pocket, he turned to her.

"I'm sorry to be so absorbed in this. I hope you weren't bored. I have so much to learn."

She smiled up at him. "I couldn't possibly be bored. I learned a lot too."

"You're a treasure. You know that?" he asked, smiling down at her with such approval, it warmed her heart.

"Let's go see the Rose Garden before the gardens close, shall we?"

"I'd love to." He took her hand and entwined his fingers with hers.

The roses were in full flower, displaying glorious velvet blooms in every shade of red, pink, coral, yellow, orange and purple. Although the hybrid roses were beautiful, they fell in love with the old-world roses brought from England and

Europe. They reminded Jane of the cabbage roses depicted in old paintings and tapestries. Several of her mother's rose bushes were the old-world variety, and Jane was glad they had survived the years of neglect. She didn't fault Alice or their father. They hadn't had the time or the interest to tend the flowers. How blessed she was that God had picked her to inherit her mother's love for gardening.

"I can't wait for you to see it Tuesday. You can tell me if the previous owners of my place had any talent, and if I should restore it or rip it all out and start over."

"Goodness, I hope not the last. I know it's silly, but I can't bear to tear out plants if they can be saved." She laughed. "Weeds, on the other hand, I can rip out with no problem. I take my frustrations out on them."

Since all of the inn guests had checked out on Sunday, the three sisters ate breakfast in the kitchen Monday morning. Louise was setting the table, and Jane had just poured six small sourdough pancakes on the griddle from a new sponge of sourdough starter. She knew the climate conditions were not as good in Pennsylvania as in San Francisco for perfect sourdough, but she was determined to come up with a great recipe. This one was a German starter made from potatoes. So far, the results looked and smelled the way they should, but the proof would be in the pancake.

Tap, tap, tap. The back door opened and Ethel poked her head in the door. "Yoo-hoo," she called out.

"Come in," Jane said. Ethel was already stepping into the kitchen.

"I just wanted to remind you that we are glazing the living room today. You are so busy, I was afraid you might forget. Oh, I'm interrupting your breakfast."

"I didn't forget. And you know we're always happy to see you. Come have pancakes with us."

Ethel looked at the griddle, then at Jane. "Are you sure you have enough to share?"

"I have more batter."

"I'll set another place," Louise said.

"Thank you, girls. I must confess, I was so eager to get started today, I quite forgot to eat. You always make me feel so welcome." She sat at the table and waited for the rest of them. Alice came in.

"It sure smells good in here. Hello, Aunt Ethel."

Jane carried a plate of pancakes to the table, and Alice gave thanks for their food.

"What brings you out so early, Auntie?" Alice asked. She took two pancakes and a serving of fresh, hot applesauce, and passed the dishes.

"These are wonderful, Jane," Louise said. "The combination of sweet and sourdough is just lovely."

"Thank you." Jane ate a bite and considered the taste and texture. "This is closer to what I want but still not quite right."

"I believe our guests will love them."

Ethel had not taken a bite but was sitting very straight, looking at them with obvious impatience. Jane realized that Alice had asked their aunt a question and that she and Louise had kept on talking.

"I'm sorry, Aunt Ethel. I didn't mean to talk over the top of you."

"I know you didn't mean to be rude," Ethel said. Jane and Louise exchanged repentant looks.

When she had their attention, Ethel said, "Jane is helping me glaze the living room today. When that's finished, we still have wallpaper trim to put up in the bedroom. I ordered a set of bedding yesterday and paid for express shipping, so it should arrive tomorrow. I want to finish the guest-bedroom trim today."

"We do have a lot to do, don't we," Jane said, somewhat alarmed. She wanted to spend time in the garden, weeding, hoeing and reseeding. The lettuce was beginning to bolt and the basil was getting leggy. "I'm not sure we will complete everything today. We have another week, right?"

"Barely a week. I don't want to have to rush at the last minute."

"Can we finish on Wednesday? I have the afternoon free."

"If we cannot finish today, I suppose Wednesday will have to do," Ethel replied, a resigned expression on her face.

"Good. I need to help clean the rooms this morning, Aunt Ethel. I should be finished about ten thirty."

"We can manage without you, Jane," Louise said.

"No, no. You have covered for me several times recently. I will stay and help do up the rooms."

"No later than ten thirty, please," Ethel said, as if Jane were hired help. Jane shook her head. Ethel could be relentless when she wanted something done. Jane didn't mind this time. She wanted everything to be nice for her cousin's visit. She was looking forward to seeing Francine and reestablishing their friendship.

Ethel took a bite of pancake. "This is very good, Jane. Lloyd would like these."

"Then I'll fix them the next time he joins us for breakfast or brunch."

"Perhaps Francine would like them too," Ethel added.

Jane smiled. "Let's have a brunch while she's here and invite a few friends. If you'd like to give me a date and a guest list, Aunt Ethel, I'll be glad to send out invitations."

Ethel clapped her hands together. "That's a lovely idea, Jane. I'll prepare a list tonight and have it for you in the morning."

"Just let me know," Jane said. She knew Ethel had orchestrated this idea, but Jane loved preparing food for groups, and Francine's visit was definitely a special occasion.

∽

Jane started the dishwasher and went upstairs. After she and Louise made up the beds with fresh linen, Jane picked up the laundry. As she walked down the hall, she passed Alice, who was vacuuming. Alice shut off the vacuum.

"Are you going over to Aunt Ethel's now?"

"Yes, if you don't need me. I cleaned the bathrooms, and Louise and I made the beds. She said she would dust, so I think we're done."

Ethel met her at the carriage house door. She was holding the instructions for the wallpaper trim and she gave Jane an impatient look. "Come in, come in. Thank goodness, you're finally here. I thought I'd have to put up the trim by myself."

Jane disliked being chastised when she was going out of her way to help her aunt. She looked at her watch. "Ten twenty-four. Six minutes early."

Ethel's lower chin trembled just slightly, and Jane reminded herself that her aunt was stressed over her daughter's visit. Very few things disturbed Ethel Buckley's confidence. "Aunt Ethel, we'll have everything ready before this weekend, and it's going to be beautiful, I promise."

Ethel dabbed at the corner of her eye with a hankie. "I know, dear. I can't seem to stop worrying. Francine said she's concerned about me. She worries about my health. She wants to discuss it when she gets here. Goodness, you'd think I was getting old or something. I don't know what brought on her concern, but I want her to see that I'm perfectly comfortable and happy here."

"Well, I hope you like what we are doing. After Francine goes home, you'll have to live with it every day."

"I do, Jane. I love what we've done. The rooms are so cheerful and lively. What do you think I should do with the couch and chair?"

Jane studied her aunt's furniture. What could they do in

a week? The couch . . . it was too big and too dark. "You could replace the couch with a smaller, more modern loveseat. That would give you more room in here. I love your chair, though, and you had it recovered a few years ago. We could just add some accent pillows. Let's put the trim up in the bedroom and the glazing on the living room walls. Then we can think about other changes."

A plastic paint cloth covered the floor, and a wallpapering tray filled with water sat on the plastic.

"You have everything ready. I'm impressed."

Ethel smiled. "I read the instructions."

"Great." Jane showed Ethel how to moisten the wallpaper, and then she climbed on the stepladder with the wallpaper brush and a cloth. As Ethel handed her the first strip, Jane let it drip for a moment, then applied the border to the top of the wall. She smoothed it with the brush, pressing all the air bubbles out. Ethel handed her another strip, and they quickly worked their way around the room. When the last strip was in place, Jane climbed down off the ladder and stood back to survey their work.

"It looks great," she told her aunt. "We make a good team."

The glazed walls had the sheen and tint of aged copper with green highlights. A border of pearly magnolia blossoms and violet-blue hydrangea plumes encircled the room at the top of the walls, accenting the tall ceiling.

Satisfied, they moved to the living room. Ethel covered the floor with the plastic tarp while Jane cleaned up their wallpaper mess. A neat pile of plastic squares sat on the kitchen counter.

"You are becoming quite a painter, Aunt Ethel," Jane said, impressed by her aunt's efficiency. "If you need pin money, you can hire out," she teased.

Ethel shuddered. She held the back of her hand to her

forehead. "Perish the thought. I wouldn't do this for anyone other than my children. Or perhaps my nieces," she added.

Jane laughed. "You know I'm teasing you, Auntie. And I'm sure Francine will appreciate your sacrifice." *I hope*, Jane thought. She intended to put a bug in Francine's ear, to let her know how much her mother had done for her.

Jane and Ethel worked well together and finished the living-room walls in no time. After they cleaned up, Ethel got out a catalog. "Let me show you what I've ordered for the guest room." She set the book on the dining-room table and opened it to a tabbed page.

"This one." She pointed to a picture of a bed ensemble. The silk comforter had large stripes in varying shades of greens and blues. The pillow shams were the same fabric, with the stripes running horizontally instead of vertically, finished with gold-trimmed ruffled edges. Three solid-colored throw pillows each matched a stripe and had gold tassels at each corner.

"It's lovely, Aunt Ethel. These will accent the walls beautifully."

Ethel let out a sigh, and Jane realized her aunt had been nervous about her selections. "Thank you," she said. Then her usual confidence slipped back into place. "I know this will put the finishing touch on Francine's room. And look at the sheets. They match perfectly." She flipped the page and pointed out a set of floral percale sheets with delicate hydrangea blooms on an off-white background.

"You're right. Where did you find them?"

"When we picked out the trim, I asked Vera if she had any sources to find linens. It so happens she collects catalogs and goes through them for pictures she can use with school projects, then she throws them away. She gave me a stack to look through, and I found these."

"Now I know where to go next time I need something."

"I need to find a new couch. Can you go shopping with me tomorrow? I'd ask Lloyd, but he is so busy."

"I can't tomorrow. I have plans. But perhaps Wednesday or Thursday."

"You are very busy lately too. It's a wonder you find time to help me." Ethel raised her eyebrows. "I like your young man." She smiled. "So handsome and polite. It's about time you started stepping out, my dear. You are too young to waste away on the shelf."

Jane laughed. "Waste away? Hardly, Aunt Ethel. I have lots of wonderful friends and more activities than I can possibly handle. Todd's restoring an old garden. I am helping him. That's all."

"Jane, you are naive when it comes to men. He could hire Craig Tracy to help him. You are a very attractive young woman." Ethel shook her finger at Jane. "Mark my words . . . he is interested in you, not your gardening abilities."

Jane shook her head. "We're friends, and we have a lot in common. That's all."

"How long have you known him? Where does he come from?"

Jane sighed. She gave her aunt a grin and as little else as possible. "I met him a week ago. He moved here from Baltimore to get out of the city. And now you know nearly as much about him as I do."

"*Tsk, tsk.* I will just have to question him myself. Since your dear father's no longer with us, I feel it's my duty to become acquainted with your beau. I'm concerned about you, Jane. You know, you can't be too careful these days. I don't want you to make another mistake, like your first marriage."

Jane opened her mouth to respond, then closed it. What could she say? Sometimes Ethel said things without thinking. A retort wouldn't solve anything. *Lord, give me patience,* she silently prayed, then she said, "I have to go now. Shall we go shopping Wednesday afternoon?"

Brought back to the topic of her redecorating, Ethel seemed to forget about Todd. "What time Wednesday?"

"I can go at one o'clock."

"I'll be ready. Thank you, Jane."

"You're welcome." Jane left before Ethel could ask her another question.

Chapter Twelve

The closed sign hung on Nellie's door, but a light still burned brightly inside the store when Alice arrived. The door was locked. Alice peered inside but couldn't see Nellie anywhere.

"Hello? Nellie?" Alice called as she knocked on the door. She glanced at her watch. Eight thirty. She was right on time. She wondered where Nellie had gone. As she debated about writing a note and leaving, Nellie came rushing from the back of the store and opened the front door.

"Sorry I wasn't here when you arrived. I hate being late. I went to the bank to make a night deposit and ran into Lloyd Tynan. Not literally. He wanted to talk about Fourth of July plans. With the trip, I'd completely forgotten about the holiday. I usually have a sidewalk sale and order special merchandise for it. Now I suppose it's too late, but I should do something. I'll have to find extra help. So many people come to town for the Fourth of July, I can't expect Lorrie Zell to handle all of the business. I don't know, Alice. I really want to go, but everything seems to be piling up. Maybe God doesn't want me to go on this trip."

Please, Lord, not another obstacle, Alice thought. Could she take the girls without a helper? No. The parents expected two adults to be going. Who could she ask? Her sisters had to run the inn. She couldn't think of anyone else. "Have you ever had Justine Gilmore help out in the store? I know she does a great job for Sylvia."

"Yes, but she's helping Sylvia."

"We'll both have to pray about this, Nellie. I believe God will provide, and I believe He wants you to go to New York with us, so let's wait and see whom He sends to help you."

"I'm praying, but I have a lot more confidence in your prayers."

"God listens to all our prayers, Nellie. Is this problem what you wanted to discuss with me tonight?"

"No." Her frown lines eased. "I want to show you what I found for the trip. Just a moment. I'll bring them out here." She hurried into the back room.

At least she's still thinking in terms of going to New York, Alice thought as she waited.

Nellie came back carrying a box. She set it on the counter, then pulled out a handful of what looked like large beaded necklaces with red, white and blue medallions in various shapes, like stars, flags, bells and flowers. Each medallion had a colorful cord with a clip attached to hang it around the neck. Alice picked up a flag.

"Why, it's a change purse. How cute. It even has a zipper."

"Open it," Nellie said, beaming.

Alice unzipped the little purse and pulled out a card. It was an identification card with a place for a small picture, name, address, phone number and even a list of allergies.

"These are wonderful. Wherever did you find them?"

"The Internet. Great, aren't they? I think the girls will like them, and they can be identified if anything should happen. There's something else here." She pulled out a handful of square cards with lines to fill out and rings like key rings.

"What are those for?"

"These are for you to carry. We'll put on the cards a picture and fingerprint of each girl and her name and ID information, plus a parent's signature for medical emergencies. We'll laminate them and put them on the rings, then on a larger ring, so you can keep them all together." Nellie smiled broadly.

Alice wasn't certain they needed all those precautions, but it couldn't hurt, and she was thrilled to see Nellie's enthusiasm and thoughtfulness. She was even more convinced that Nellie must go with them.

"Can you come Wednesday night to the ANGELs meeting and bring these with you? I'll call the parents and have them send pictures and information with the girls. We can put them together as our project for the evening."

"I'd love to. Your girls are delightful."

"How many of these did you purchase?"

Nellie laughed. "Too many. They're so cute, I couldn't resist. I'll display the rest of them in the store."

"Yes, they would be perfect for the Fourth of July."

Nellie clapped her hands together. "Great idea, Alice. I'll order a few more. We could set up an ID station, so people could fill them out and put them on their children. You know how easily kids wander off and can get lost in a crowd."

Alice nodded her agreement. "Wonderful. With all the out-of-town visitors for the holiday, I know these'll be a hit."

"Now, if I can just find someone to help run the store while we're gone."

Alice smiled knowingly. "Just watch and see. The Lord will provide."

"Thanks, Alice. I hope you're right."

When Alice arrived home, Louise was in the library working on the inn's bookkeeping. Alice poked her head in the doorway. "Would you like a cup of tea?"

Louise looked up over the top of her glasses. "That'd be lovely. I'm almost finished here. Give me five minutes."

"All right. Where's Jane?"

"She went up to her room for the night. I think all this business with helping Aunt Ethel, worrying about Fred's store and the strain of this new relationship is taking its toll on her. She looked exhausted."

Alice shook her head. "This isn't a good time for me to leave on a trip. I should be here to help you and Jane."

"Nonsense. We'll get along just fine without you. Not that you won't be missed," Louise said.

Alice chuckled. She went to the kitchen and started a kettle of water, then placed several of Jane's cinnamon-apple bars on a plate. She was running hot water into the teapot when the kitchen door opened and Jane came in.

"Hi. Making tea? I could use a cup," Jane said.

"Sure. Louise thought you'd turned in for the night." Alice took a third cup out of the cupboard.

"No. Just doing a little reading. My bones are tired enough, but my mind is wide awake."

"That happens to me on days when we've been short-handed at the hospital. It's hard to shift gears."

Louise came through the doorway. "Oh, Jane. I thought you'd gone to bed."

"No. I'm too keyed up to sleep. I thought reading might make me sleepy, but it didn't work."

"That's because you're too busy. Cooking for the inn and keeping the garden tended is enough activity for anyone, but Aunt Ethel's running you ragged with her decorating project. No wonder you're tense."

"Not tense, exactly. But my mind is going in a million directions all at once. I love helping Aunt Ethel redecorate. The carriage house is going to be beautiful when we finish. I'm concerned about her, though. She seems unusually stressed over Francine's visit."

"I noticed that," Alice said. "She's so excited, she forgets to eat breakfast."

"She'd forget lunch, I think, if I didn't remind her," Jane said. "I hope she doesn't make herself sick before Francine arrives."

"Oh dear, that'd be terrible," Louise said. "Let's keep her in our prayers."

"I need you to pray for Nellie too," Alice said.

"What's wrong with Nellie?" Jane asked. "She isn't backing out on your trip, is she?"

"No. At least not yet. This trip is causing some extra pressure in her life, though. She had forgotten about the Fourth of July festivities until Lloyd reminded her. She usually orders special merchandise and has a sale. Now she's worried about leaving the store to Lorrie. She feels that she needs an extra helper during the holiday. I told her we would pray for her to find someone. She doesn't have much time. We leave next week."

"Let's pray right now," Louise said. They sat at the table and joined hands. "Heavenly Father, You hold all of our lives and our activities in Your hands. We know You care about everything that happens to us, and so we commit Nellie's problem to You. Please give her peace of mind about this trip and send her a helper for her shop. Reassure Aunt Ethel, too, so she can relax and stay healthy for this visit with Francine. We ask these things in Jesus' name. Amen."

"Amen," Alice said. "Now, Jane, we never got a chance to hear about Longwood Gardens. I've always loved the gardens, but it's been years since I visited them."

Over tea, Jane told them about her visit with Todd, about the flowers and the new carillon chimes. Louise and Alice declared they would all visit the gardens together later in the summer and have a picnic just like their mother loved to do.

Halfway to Potterston, Jane spotted the newly painted green mailbox shaped like a tractor that Todd had described. She pulled off the road and turned in at a gravel driveway hidden by a large bush. The road wound back through overhanging branches that nearly obscured the way. As she rounded a bend, a farmhouse came into sight. It was surrounded by bushes that looked as if they'd been butchered.

She parked in front. Todd appeared from the side of the house, smiling as he came to greet her.

"Welcome to my humble abode," he said.

"It's charming, Todd."

He followed her gaze as she looked at the house. "I'm going to tear out those bushes, but I wanted to get the house ready to paint, so I hacked them back," Todd explained. The old paint had been scraped off the house. Yet, in spite of the unkempt state of the place, the house, with its wraparound porch and upstairs dormers, held great potential.

Jane handed Todd a picnic basket, which he put in the house, while Jane continued to look over the front yard. When he returned, they walked around the house to the back.

"See what a job I have in front of me?" he asked, waving his hand to encompass the expanse of overgrown vegetation around his yard. A dry, patchy lawn circled the house, ending where the woods had encroached in recent years. The underbrush looked impassable.

"It does need a lot of work."

"That's an understatement. There is more lawn just past the trees, and I've cleared a small pathway to it, but I don't know if I can ever recapture what once must have been a garden. Maybe I should bulldoze and start over."

"Oh no. Let's diagram the yard and mark the plants and trees that you want to save. Then you can design what you want to change. Where shall we start? In front?"

Jane took out the drafting pad she'd brought with her and

put a square in the middle of the page for the house, then drew a double line for the driveway. A circle around the house designated the lawn. They walked slowly around the property, bending down to examine plants, tagging and marking the ones to keep and sketching and labeling significant trees and shrubbery on the diagram.

It was one o'clock when they finished. Todd spread a blanket on the ground under a big old oak tree, and they opened the picnic basket. Jane took out cold roast beef, cream cheese and watercress sandwiches on her homemade pumpernickel bread, potato salad, chips, fruit and strawberry-rhubarb turnovers.

"I never pictured myself eating a gourmet lunch with a lovely lady on this shabby lawn. We'll have to do this again when I get things in shape."

She smiled as she envisioned the restored yard. "A little water and fertilizer and the lawn will bounce back in no time. I see all kinds of potential here, Todd. I can tell from the plants we identified, whoever landscaped this yard loved to garden. With pruning, weeding and nourishment, this yard will spring to life."

"I sure hope you're right. Otherwise, I don't know where I'd start."

Jane put down her half-eaten sandwich and picked up the diagram she'd drawn. "Do you have ideas for changes, or garden areas you want to put in?"

"Not really. Eventually, I'd like to host picnics here for the store employees. After lunch, I'll show you the secluded lawn area. It's big enough for a great game of volleyball or croquet. I thought I'd put a horseshoe pit over there," he said, pointing to an area on the side of the house. "If I make it three pits wide, we could have tournaments. And I need a barbecue area and place for picnic tables, perhaps even under this tree. Or I could clear another area in the woods. Maybe build a deck and a fire pit for evenings."

"What wonderful ideas." Jane looked around, her mind creating images of what it could look like. She sketched in the horseshoe pits. "I think you want the barbecue area close to the house so you have access to the kitchen. Maybe here . . ." She drew a deck on the back of the house in two levels, with a built-in outdoor kitchen area. She drew in several tables under the tree. "Like this?"

"Yes, that looks great. Just what I had in mind."

The artist in Jane pictured an all-season garden around the lawn and a yard filled with laughing, chattering families. This yard would be wonderful for entertaining.

"You need a water feature. Maybe a waterfall and a small pool. That would look beautiful and create that wonderful sound of rushing water. Maybe over there . . ." She pointed to the right, back against the woods. "Dig a pond and push the dirt up to build a mound. Landscape the mound with rocks and a waterfall. You could even stock the pond with goldfish."

"That's a great idea." He gave her a hearty smile. "I knew it was my lucky day when you stormed into the store to see me."

"Stormed? Is that what I did?"

"Like a whirlwind. A beautiful avenging angel."

Jane shook her head. He might be teasing her, but she felt warmed and a little off-kilter from his affectionate comments. She got to her feet and smiled down at him. "Show me the hidden garden," she said.

"All right." He put the leftovers in the basket and secured the lid. "Don't want intruders," he said. He stood and took her hand, leading her into a small break in the woods. They pushed tree branches aside as they went. Jane could see where brush and branches had been cut back, but still the woods seemed to swallow them up. They went about ten yards, then broke through into a clearing.

"It's a secret garden," Jane exclaimed. "I love it!"

Todd grinned. "That was my reaction too. I want to keep it secluded, and yet it needs to be easier to get here. I'll take out a few trees and clear the underbrush to open up the woods. I thought I might put down flagstones for a pathway."

"Leave the bushes bordering the garden. That will make it more private. You could trim it like a hedge."

"Like an English garden. And I'll put benches inside, so people can watch games. I thought I'd clear other paths, too, like Peirce's Woods at Longwood Gardens. I got a lot of ideas from that."

"I can see why. Your woods are wonderful for strolling paths. Is there a spring or a pool on the property?"

"There's a boggy area in the back. It's a mess, but perhaps I could clean it up a little. It has bullfrogs. I can hear them at night. And I thought I heard an owl the other night."

"I wouldn't be surprised. Can we go see it?"

"It's rough going. Lots of berry brambles. We'll get all scratched up."

"I'm game if you are," Jane said. She wanted to see every inch of Todd's wonderful property.

"All right. Wear your gloves." Todd put on a pair of leather work gloves and picked up a machete. He grinned at Jane. "I always wanted to be a woodsman. Here, I get my chance."

They whacked their way through the brambles to the back corner of Todd's property. Underfoot, they stepped on a spongy carpet of green groundcover dotted with tiny yellow flowers, releasing the soothing, pineapple-like scent of wild chamomile.

As she followed, dodging thorny stems, Jane recognized blackberry and serviceberry bushes. "This is fabulous. You have several kinds of wild berries. These bushes need pruning, but wait until after the season. We'll have to go berry picking when they're ripe, and I'll bake a pie and make a batch of jam for you."

"I'll hold you to that. I love blackberry pie."

"We'll have to go to the Coffee Shop in Acorn Hill, then. June is famous for her blackberry pies." Too late, she realized she'd suggested a very public appearance together in Acorn Hill.

The ground grew soggy. Todd stepped on a log, and his foot went through rotten wood with a splash. He stopped and turned to her. "Careful. We're in the water. Here, step up on that log where it's dry." He helped her balance while she stepped up on a higher piece of downed tree trunk. Then he climbed up next to her. From their vantage point, they could see the pond. It was a boggy tangle of dead, fallen trees and overgrown brambles, but Jane saw several species of trees and plants she recognized from around Fairy Pond. Marsh elder, chokeberry, sumac, dogwood, swamp roses, witch hazel, winterberry and several types of viburnum. The high foliage kept much of the sunshine out of Todd's pond, but the filtered light gave the secluded spot an air of enchantment.

"This is wonderful," she said in hushed tones, although there was no one else around to hear her. "It needs a little cleaning out, but not too much. And look at the flowers."

Spots of blue iris and vervain peeked through the underbrush. Along the banks of the bog, yellow, purple and white flowers could be seen.

Jane slapped at something buzzing around her ear. Todd clapped his hands together in front of her face. "Got it," he said triumphantly. "Big mosquito. We'd better get out of here before we get eaten. I was afraid this might be a breeding ground."

They turned and started back through the woods.

"I recently read about natural treatments to eliminate mosquitoes," Jane said. "I'll see if I still have the article."

"Great. I'd much rather clean up the bog than get rid of it. I'll have to get hip waders to get in here, though."

"Get two pair. I'd like to help."

"All right, but let's see if we can control the mosquitoes before we try to work out here. There's plenty else to do."

"That's an understatement. It isn't too late to get started today. Pick an area and let's start weeding."

"I can't do the front yard until I dig out those bushes. How about the backyard, so we can have a nice spot for our picnics?"

Jane was pleased that he wanted to have more picnics. "I think that's a great idea."

Chapter Thirteen

Jane stood at the breadboard punching out biscuits with a cutter. This batch varied slightly from her usual recipe. She had added tiny bits of ham, grated sharp cheddar cheese and fresh snipped thyme. Already in the oven was an experimental breakfast casserole, a mixture of eggs, spinach, potatoes and cream cheese.

"Yoo-hoo." Ethel tapped on the door and walked in. "Oh, you are late with breakfast this morning," she said.

Jane slid the tray of biscuits into the oven. She glanced at the clock. Seven fifty-five. "We're not late. You're early. We don't have any guests this morning, and Alice isn't back from her walk with Vera yet."

"Oh my, I thought it was nine. It seems like the morning is nearly over."

Ethel was dressed in a navy-blue skirt and jacket with a ruffled blouse that she often wore to church. Jane had a sinking feeling her morning was about to be rescheduled. She had hoped to spend an hour on her art before she helped Ethel in the afternoon. "What time did you get up?"

"At six o'clock. I woke up and couldn't go back to sleep. There's so much to do. You said you could go shopping with me today."

Jane sighed. Ethel didn't notice. "Yes, I did say that. I believe I said in the afternoon. I suppose you want to go after breakfast."

"Breakfast?" Ethel blinked. "I ate hours ago. But you go ahead. The stores won't open in Potterston until ten o'clock. I'll have a cup of coffee with you."

"Good. I'll have plenty of time to eat and change clothes," she said with a bit of irony, which her aunt either didn't catch or chose to ignore. Jane never was certain with Ethel. She handed a cup of coffee to her aunt, who took it and sat at the table.

Ethel took a piece of paper out of her pocket and read her to-do list aloud. All the items required Jane's help. It seemed Ethel had scheduled her niece's entire day. There went her morning to start a painting of the carillon tower and falls at Longwood Gardens. She wanted to do it for Todd as a sort of housewarming gift. Jane thought about objecting but held her comments and cleaned off the breadboard instead. The sooner they completed Ethel's project, the sooner she could get on with her own projects. She was taking plates out of the cupboard when Alice came through the door.

"Good morning, Jane, Aunt Ethel. Here, let me set the table." She washed her hands, then took the plates, chatting with Ethel as she worked.

Louise came into the kitchen as the timer buzzed. Jane set the hot casserole and steamy biscuits on the table, and they sat down to eat. They joined hands and Alice prayed, "Dear Lord, we thank You for these provisions. Be with us this day and let us be aware of those in need around us. Relieve our cares and make us a blessing to someone today. Amen."

"Thank you, Alice. I needed that reminder," Jane said. She was sitting between Alice and Louise, and her sisters smiled at her and squeezed her hands. Jane took a deep breath and silently thanked the Lord for such supportive and understanding sisters.

By noon, Ethel and Jane had visited three stores, sat on dozens of loveseats and found nothing that appealed to Ethel. She told the salespeople that she wanted something modern and stylish, but she hated the current styles and fabrics. She also hated the prices. She wanted an old-fashioned sofa like the one in her living room. Jane suggested finding a slipcover, but no. Ethel wanted a new sofa.

Resigned to a wasted day, Jane followed Ethel into another furniture store. This one specialized in living-room furniture. They walked past rows of reclining chairs, rocking chairs and couches. Everything looked like the furniture they'd already seen. They were about to leave when Jane spotted something with a classic tapestry print in the back of the store.

"Wait, Aunt Ethel. Let's look at that furniture in the back."

"I don't think we're going to find anything here, Jane. It all looks the same."

"Let's check it out anyway." She made her way around rows of furniture to the back corner. A small living-room grouping of French country couch, chair and loveseat made a charming seating arrangement. The muted tones of the floral tapestry in greens and mauve would be a perfect complement to the glazed walls in the carriage house. A saleswoman came over to help them.

"This set is brand-new," she said. "And all of the pieces recline."

"Really?" Ethel asked.

"Sit down and see how you like it," the woman invited.

Ethel sat on one side of the loveseat. Jane tried the other. Very roomy and comfortable. She pulled a lever in the side and her seat reclined. She leaned back.

"I like this. It's wonderful." She turned to Ethel. "What do you think?"

"Very nice," Ethel said, but without much enthusiasm. "I suppose it's out of my price range."

The saleswoman picked up the tag, attached to the side. "Our Independence Day sale started today. It will run for ten days. This set is marked down forty percent."

"I don't want the whole set. I only want a loveseat."

"We sell them separately or as a set. Would you like me to write up a quote for you?"

"Yes, please," Jane said before Ethel declined. The woman excused herself, saying she'd be right back.

As soon as she was gone, Jane turned to Ethel. "This would be wonderful in your house, Aunt Ethel. The colors are great and the style is comfortable, yet elegant."

"Do you think so? I get so confused."

"I do. And your rug will look great with it. We can shop for accessories in Acorn Hill. The General Store has wonderful baskets, and Sylvia has a new assortment of lovely handmade pillows. And we might look for something lighter for your windows, like sheers or battenberg lace panels."

"I can't afford battenberg lace," Ethel said.

"You'd be surprised. I saw some in a discount store last week."

"I suppose we could look."

When the saleswoman returned with a very reasonable price quote, Ethel declared that she would take the loveseat. When she inquired about delivery, they learned the store only went to Acorn Hill once a week and charged for delivery.

"I have an idea," Jane said. "I'll ask Craig if I can borrow his van to pick it up." She used her cell phone to call Wild Things. Craig had to deliver flowers to the hospital that afternoon, so he was delighted to pick up the loveseat and deliver it for Ethel.

As they left the store, Jane suggested they stop for lunch.

"Oh no. There isn't time. Take me to that store where you saw the curtains."

"Aunt Ethel, you cannot keep skipping meals. Francine will be more concerned about your eating habits than what your house looks like. You don't want her to worry about you, do you?"

"Heavens no," she said. "She thinks I should move into one of those retirement centers. I'd hate that. I want Francine to see that I'm perfectly healthy and happy where I am."

"Of course you are, but skipping meals won't convince her of that."

"I don't skip meals. At least not usually. I just want to get everything ready for this visit. Then I can relax."

"The redecorating is nearly finished. You can relax now."

Ethel let out a dramatic sigh. "All right. We can stop if you're hungry, but make it somewhere with fast service. We don't want to take all day."

Jane found a small café that served homemade soups, salads and breads. Ethel showed a surprisingly hearty appetite, and the brief stop cheered her. Newly fortified, they found inexpensive floor-length lace panels and valances at a discount department store. Jane helped her select the proper rods to hang them.

When they arrived back at the carriage house, as Jane carried in the packages, Alice came over with a large box.

"This came while you were gone," she said.

"My bedspread!" Ethel said excitedly. "Put it on the table." She took a knife out of a drawer to slit open the box. Alice and Jane stood on either side of her, watching.

One by one, Ethel took plastic covered linens out of the box. When they were all on the table, she opened the comforter. They each took a corner and opened it up.

"This is lovely, Aunt Ethel," Alice said.

Ethel ran her hand over the silky fabric, her pleasure obvious in her careful touch and her smile.

"Let's see how it looks in the room," Jane said.

They carried the comforter into the guest room. Jane opened the Murphy bed and they spread the comforter on the mattress, then they all stepped back.

Ethel studied the bed and the room with a slight frown. "What do you think?" she asked.

"The comforter brings out the subtle hues of the walls beautifully," Alice said.

"I can't wait to see it with the sheets and all the pillows," Jane said. "Francine will love this room."

"Do you think so?"

"Absolutely," Jane said. "When you're ready, I'll help you make up the bed." Ethel's lack of confidence surprised Jane. Francine might have definite ideas about style, but she was coming to see her mother, not the carriage house or the decor. "Let's hang the new curtains in the living room and see how they look."

"I'll help you," Alice offered. "You've made such wonderful changes, I want to see what you picked for the living room."

Jane climbed on the stepladder and held up a rod so Ethel and Alice could help level it. She was glad that she had thought to remove the old rods before painting. She screwed the hooks into the wall while Ethel and Alice threaded the panels on one rod and the valance on another. They handed the rods to Jane, who clipped them onto the hooks. She distributed the gathers evenly, then climbed down and moved the ladder out of the way.

Ethel stood back and looked around the room. Jane held her breath, waiting for her reaction. She turned to Jane.

"That brightens the room. But now the furniture looks shabby. The dark drapes hid that."

Jane wasn't sure if Ethel liked or hated the room. The old furniture did look shabby. In this case, putting more light on the subject didn't help. The maple furniture would look great painted, but she didn't have time before Francine's arrival, so she kept that thought to herself.

There was a knock on the door, and Ethel went to answer it.

"I have your loveseat," Craig Tracy said. His van was parked in front of the carriage house.

Jane went to the door. "I'll help you. We'll have to take the couch out first."

"All right." Craig came in. He took one end, and Jane took the other. With a bit of grunting and groaning, they managed to move the couch outside.

"Where do you want it?"

"I don't know what she wants to do with it. Let's move it into the garage for now."

They picked up their ends again, shuffled to the garage and set it against the wall.

Craig wiped his forehead with his arm. "That old couch is heavier than it looks."

Jane grinned. "They don't make 'em like they used to."

Craig chuckled. "Guess not. Let's get the loveseat."

The loveseat was lighter and easier to move. When they came in with it, Alice was vacuuming the floor where the couch had sat. She turned off the vacuum and moved it aside.

"Set it there," Ethel said, pointing to the spot where the couch had been. She stood back and watched. "No. Move it over there," she said, pointing to the opposite side of the room. She didn't like it there, either. She finally decided on the original position.

"Thank you, Craig. May I get you some lemonade or a drink of water?"

"No thank you. I have to get back to the shop." He headed for the door. Jane followed him.

"Thanks, Craig. Alice and I couldn't have moved it."

"Glad to do it. The living room looks nice." He said good-bye and drove off.

Jane went back inside.

Ethel had placed a throw pillow from the loveseat on her old, overstuffed chair. The tapestry pattern looked nice against the plain tan chair, but it needed something else to make it special.

Jane snapped her fingers. "I know." She turned toward the door. "I'll be right back."

Jane rushed to her room in the inn, dug through the bottom drawer of her dresser, pulled out a large, lightweight wool scarf and hurried back to the carriage house.

She walked in without knocking, crossed to the chair and draped the scarf over the chair at a skewed angle, tucking it at the seat. The bright jade in the scarf brought out small bits of the same color in the loveseat and pillow.

Ethel clapped her hands. "Perfect. Jane, you are a genius."

Alice agreed. Jane beamed. "A few more touches, some flowers and you'll be ready, Aunt Ethel."

"Yes. Thank you, dear. Now I need to plan my menus. What night do you want to have us to dinner?"

"I . . . I don't know. I thought we'd talked about a brunch."

"Well, if it's too much trouble, we can eat out. I just thought you'd want to see your cousin."

"We all want to have a special dinner for Francine," Alice said. "And the family can get together any day that Francine is here."

"Yes, of course that's what I meant," Jane said, giving Alice a grateful smile. Alice wouldn't even be there, but Ethel wasn't thinking about that now. "Any night is fine, Auntie, but let's get it on the calendar so we make sure to keep that evening open." She wanted to make sure she didn't have a date with Todd.

"That'd be lovely. I'll put together a guest list."

"All right. Let me know as soon as possible, so I can plan the menu. Right now, I must get home and get to work."

"I will wash the linens tonight, so we can make up Francine's room tomorrow. And we need to shop for baskets and whatever, as you said."

Jane saw another day slipping away from her. "Why don't you go ahead and pick those out?"

"I suppose I have monopolized enough of your time. Alice, would you go shopping with me?"

Alice raised her hands. "Don't look at me. Jane's the artistic one. I know nothing about decorating."

"Perhaps I'll ask Louise. Don't worry about me. I'll find someone."

Jane refused to let her aunt manipulate her into giving up another day. Making beds wouldn't take long. Shopping would. "See you tomorrow," she said and headed for the door.

"I must go too," Alice said. "The ANGELs meeting is tonight."

"Oh dear me. Is it Wednesday all ready?" Ethel asked. "I don't know if I can make it to church. Lloyd will be expecting me to go. I really *must* go. After all, I'm on the church board."

"Aunt Ethel, you're pushing yourself too hard," Jane said. "No one will mind if you miss one week."

"Jane's right. Stay home and relax this evening."

"No. I'll attend church. You run along now so I can get ready." She shooed them toward the door.

"Come over for a bite of dinner," Jane said.

"No time. I'll make a sandwich here. Go on now."

Jane and Alice found themselves standing on the carriage house porch, the door firmly shut behind them.

"I'm worried about her," Jane said. "She's going to be exhausted before Francine even gets here."

"She won't slow down. You've helped her so much, Jane, and I've noticed you are making sure she eats. Francine'll be here next week, and perhaps things will settle down."

"I certainly hope so. Maybe I'll go shopping with her tomorrow after all, just to get it finished."

Chapter Fourteen

After dinner, Alice walked over to Grace Chapel for the Wednesday night ANGELs meeting. Nellie arrived with the ID cards and an ink pad for fingerprints. She had enough beaded pouches for all the girls to choose the style they wanted. Nellie even provided for those who were not going on this trip. The girls loved the purses.

Alice led the group in a Bible study of the twenty-third Psalm, and they discussed the ways God provided for them. When they finished, Alice said, "Some of you are going to New York with Miss Carter and me, and some of you are going other places this summer. This Psalm assures us that no matter where we are or how big our problems, God is always with us. He knows where we are, even if we think we are lost, and He will provide for us and lead us to safety. Shall we pray?"

"Please add me to your prayers," Nellie said. "I need someone to help in the shop while I'm gone, and I haven't found anyone yet."

"All right." Alice bowed her head. When they finished praying, she raised her head and asked, "Did all of you going to New York bring your pictures and information sheets?"

The girls passed their sheets to Alice, who hand-printed each card. Each girl had brought two wallet-sized photographs.

Nellie then took each girl's fingerprint and attached her picture to the identification card that Alice would carry.

"I almost forgot," Alice said. "My sister wondered if you would like to have another bake sale before we leave? Perhaps on Saturday morning?"

"Sure, Miss Howard," Sarah said. All the girls agreed.

"Where will we hold it?" Ashley asked.

"In front of Fred's Hardware store. Let's say eleven o'clock. Perhaps people will be hungry for lunch and buy our goodies."

Sarah helped Alice and Nellie clean up after the meeting while she waited for her mother, who was attending the service upstairs. Nellie picked up the box of supplies and was about to leave when Sarah's mother came in.

"Hello, Mrs. Roberts," Nellie said.

"Look what Miss Carter gave us, Mom," Sarah said, holding her necklace up so her mom could see it.

"That's adorable. What a wonderful idea. Miss Carter, you come up with the nicest things. I love the clothes you carry. Have you gotten anything new recently?"

"Thank you. Yes, I received a new shipment this week."

"I'll have to come in. And please call me Samantha. Mrs. Roberts sounds so old. It's bad enough that my children are all going off on their own. Our son is off to military boot camp next week, and with Sarah gone, I shall be lost. In fact, I was wondering . . . Sylvia Songer mentioned that you might need some help in the dress shop. If you haven't found someone already, I'd really be interested in the job," she said, looking hopefully at Nellie.

Nellie's eyes widened. She glanced at Alice, then smiled. "As a matter of fact, I do need someone, but just for the time we're in New York. Do you have retail experience?"

"Oh yes. I worked part-time in a department store all through college," Samantha told her.

"Could you come by tomorrow and learn the register?"

"Yes. Oh, thank you. I'm so excited. A week working in your store will be a perfect change of pace for me."

"You are an answer to prayer. I was afraid I would have to cancel going with the ANGELs," Nellie said.

"And I have been praying for something to distract me from worrying about my children. God is so good!"

After the ANGELs meeting, Alice shared her good news with her sisters as they sat at the kitchen table. "God answered Nellie's prayer tonight, right after the ANGELs meeting."

"What happened?" Jane asked.

"Nellie asked us to pray for a helper so she could leave the shop. Right afterward, as we were cleaning up, Samantha Roberts came downstairs. She has been looking for part-time work and Sylvia suggested Nellie's, so she asked Nellie if she still needed any help. Tomorrow Samantha is going to go to the shop to learn what she has to do and how to run the cash register."

"Oh, Alice, that's fabulous," Jane said.

"Yes," Louise said. "The Lord certainly answered your prayers."

"I'm excited to see Nellie's faith grow as God clears the way for this trip," Alice said. "She still has fears about the city, but she's gaining confidence at every step. She plans to come to church this week, so I invited her to Sunday dinner."

"Wonderful," Louise said. "I'm glad you're encouraging her, Alice. She's such a sweet young woman. By the way, Jane, I invited Pastor Kenneth."

"You remember that Aunt Ethel invited Todd?" Jane asked.

"Yes. It'll be nice to visit with him again. Will he be going to church with you?" Alice asked.

"No, thank goodness. He attends church in Potterston."

Louise peered over the top of her glasses. "I gather you haven't told Fred and Vera about him yet."

"I haven't had a chance. Every time I see them, I'm with Aunt Ethel. I suppose Lloyd will be coming too." Jane shook her head. "Sorry," she said. "I'm always happy to have Aunt Ethel and Lloyd join us, but she's determined to grill Todd. I managed to get him away before she could question him last Sunday, but she has tried grilling me."

"You know Aunt Ethel has told people in town about him. Viola asked me about him Friday when I stopped in Nine Lives," Louise said.

"Nellie mentioned hearing about him too. Everyone's curious, but they are happy for you, dear," Alice said.

"I wouldn't worry about Todd," Louise said. "I'm sure he can handle Aunt Ethel."

"You're probably right. I'd prefer that she doesn't discover what he does for a living. I don't want Fred and Vera to hear about him secondhand."

"Jane . . ." Alice covered Jane's hand. "Fred and Vera will understand, but they should hear it from you."

Jane sighed. "I'll talk to them. That isn't my only concern. Aunt Ethel can be so meddlesome, and I'd like to have the chance to let our friendship grow naturally, without any pressure."

"She can be rather forceful. Perhaps we can run interference. What do you think, Louise?"

Louise looked thoughtful for a moment, then she gave Jane a wink. "Aunt Ethel is no match for the Howard sisters. I'll make sure they sit at opposite ends of the table."

The next morning, Jane decided to try to finish her aunt's project early so that she'd have the afternoon free to help at the inn. Two couples were checking in that afternoon. The

Abercrombies were booked through the holiday. In fact, all four rooms were booked for the next three weeks. Jane went over to the carriage house and knocked on the door. Ethel answered, still in her bathrobe and curlers.

"Jane?" Ethel yawned and covered her mouth. She looked at her watch. "Goodness. I overslept. Come in. I'll be ready in a few minutes."

"I brought you some muffins," Jane said as she stepped inside.

"Thank you, dear. I'll make coffee to go with them."

"You go ahead and get dressed. I'll make the coffee."

"All right. I can't imagine why I'm so groggy this morning," Ethel said as she went toward her room.

Jane started a pot of coffee, then went to the guest room. She found the laundered sheets on a chair, so she made the bed. As she folded the top edge of the floral sheet over the top of the blanket, she admired the way it duplicated the wallpaper border. She hated to cover it with the comforter, but the finished bed, with the matching floral pillowcases, and the striped silk comforter and shams created a beautiful ensemble. Ethel came in while Jane was admiring the room.

"You didn't have to do this. Oh. Oh my." Ethel went to the center of the room and slowly pivoted. "This room is fit for a queen." She looked at Jane and smiled. "We did it," she declared, sounding almost surprised.

Jane put her arm around Ethel's shoulders. "Yes, Auntie, we did it."

"Thank you, Jane. I couldn't have done it without you." Ethel straightened her shoulders and held her head high. "Shall we go shopping for the living room?"

"Certainly. Let's have a muffin and coffee, first."

"All right."

When Ethel finished her muffin, Jane drove the few blocks to town so they wouldn't have to carry their purchases home. After they finished and brought their treasures into the carriage house, Jane took the picture frames and stain they had purchased to the inn, promising to return in an hour.

Jane spread newspaper all over the kitchen counter, then she put on rubber gloves and began rubbing stain on the frames.

Louise came in while she was working. "What are you doing?" she asked.

"These are for Aunt Ethel's living room. We're almost done. Come over in an hour and see."

"All right. I think there's just enough time before our guests arrive."

Jane finished and went to the carriage house. Ethel had arranged the pillows on the overstuffed chair and the new loveseat. They looked great. She asked her aunt to help her take all the pictures off the mantel and move all the knick-knacks to the kitchen counter.

"I just dusted and put them back," Ethel objected.

"I know. Just trust me. If you don't like what I do, we can put everything back the way you had them."

"All right." Ethel cleared everything off. "Now what?"

"Could you please roll these skeins of yarn into balls?"

"Now?" Ethel asked, incredulous. "Can't they wait until my living room is finished?"

"They are part of the living room. Trust me. I'll be right back, and Louise is going to pop over to see what you've accomplished. She's in for a happy surprise." Jane winked, put all the pictures in a box and went back to the inn.

The frames were dry. Jane arranged the photographs in the frames, each with a generous mat around the picture. She attached hangers of varying lengths that she'd made out of gold cording to the top of each frame. She gathered the finished pictures, a hammer and nails and went back to the carriage house.

"Okay, Aunt Ethel. I'm ready. Sit and watch while I put these up. I sure hope you're going to like this."

"So do I," Ethel said. "So do I." She watched as Jane climbed the stepladder and attached the picture hangers to the ceiling molding in clusters of five to each side of the mantel. She finished by artfully arranging the small figurines and collectibles on the mantel.

"Well, I declare. Jane, you are a genius. Who would have thought . . . I was so afraid you wanted me to get rid of my little treasures. And my pictures. Why, they look lovely."

Jane set the three baskets on the hearth and arranged the colored yarn balls in one of the baskets. In another, she arranged large pinecones that she had collected in the woods for some future project. "I have to admit, I don't know what to put in the middle basket. Any ideas?"

"My magazines," Ethel suggested. "That would leave the tabletops clear."

"Great idea."

Just then Louise tapped on the door and peeked in. "Are you ready for me?"

"Indeed we are," Ethel said as she went to the door. She took Louise's arm and ushered her into the living room.

"I'll finish up in the kitchen while Aunt Ethel shows you around," Jane said.

As she cleaned up, Jane could hear the pride in Ethel's voice as she told Louise about their decorating. Jane smiled to herself. Louise loved the changes, and so did Aunt Ethel, and that's what mattered.

Saturday morning, Jane wrapped five loaves of apple-rhubarb bread in plastic wrap and labeled them for the ANGELs bake sale. The timer buzzed, and she pulled two strawberry-rhubarb pies out of the oven and set them to cool. Alice had already gone to set up a table outside Fred's Hardware. Jane hoped this bake sale idea worked wonders for the ANGELs and for the Humberts' business.

Louise poked her head in the kitchen. "How are you doing? Need any help?"

"Yes, as a matter of fact. Are you free?"

"For the moment. What can I do?"

"If you could put half a dozen muffins on each paper plate and cover them with plastic, I'll finish making the ham-and-cheese wraps."

"You're making sandwiches?"

"I'm putting together lunch trays. The girls are handing out flyers to all the stores. I'm hoping people will come to get lunch and go into the hardware store while they are there."

"Smart idea. I hope it works. You're going to an awful lot of trouble."

"I really want to do something to help," Jane said. She quickly rolled ham and cheese with fresh greens and spicy mustard inside spinach wraps and tomato wraps. She cut them in half and put them on rectangular Styrofoam trays with a homemade pickle, a scoop of potato salad and a frosted brownie. She covered them in plastic wrap.

"There. Ready to go. Can you help me load my car?"

Louise helped Jane carry a large cooler filled with all her goodies to her car. When Jane got to the hardware store, the girls were already set up and doing a brisk business. Alice helped Jane unload and set out everything except the lunch trays, which they left in the cooler.

"How many did you make?" Alice asked.

"A dozen. I marked them five dollars each. I hope you sell them all. Do you need my help here?"

"No. The girls have everything well in hand."

Bella Paoli, Lloyd's secretary, came hurrying across the street. She stopped in front of the table and took several deep breaths. "Do you have any of the lunches left?" she asked. "I need four to take back to the courthouse."

"Four? It's Saturday. The courthouse isn't open, is it?"

"No. But the Fourth of July committee is meeting. We have a lot left to do before the holiday."

Linda Farr reached for a plastic grocery bag and filled it with the lunches. As Bella hurried away, Vera came out of the hardware store.

"I hope you have two of those lunches left. We are so busy, we can't spare the time for a lunch break." She handed Sarah Roberts a ten-dollar bill.

"You should get the lunches free," Jane said. "After all, you are letting us use your store for our sale."

"No, no. This is wonderful. We haven't been so busy since . . . a long time. Besides, with your brownies included, these lunches are a bargain."

"When you and Fred have a few minutes, I need to talk to you."

"Oh, Jane, I'm sorry. Can it wait? I can't believe how busy we are today." She laughed, "Of course, that's wonderful. Maybe later today . . . oh, no, we're supposed to meet with the rental people after work. I'm sorry. How about after church tomorrow?"

"That won't work for me. I'm cooking dinner for a crowd. Maybe Monday."

Two cars pulled up at the same time that Viola Reed came trotting across the street, a long blue-and-orange scarf sailing along behind her. The girls suddenly were swamped with customers, and it seemed their crowd drew customers into the hardware store too. Or perhaps Todd had been correct that the initial attraction to his big store would fade and that Fred's business would naturally pick up again. Perhaps Fred's crisis was over. Either way, Jane was pleased and relieved.

Chapter Fifteen

The next day when the sisters arrived home from church, they were met by the rich aroma of roast turkey combined with the sweet and pungent scents of honey and ginger. Jane quickly changed and disappeared into the kitchen. Alice was glad all the inn's guests were out for the day. The sisters sometimes included the patrons at their Sunday dinner, but Jane was taking special pains with this meal for Todd. She had gotten up early and put the large turkey in the oven to roast while they attended church.

Lloyd and Ethel arrived first while Alice and Louise were setting the table. Rev. Kenneth Thompson came next, closely followed by Nellie and Todd, who arrived at the same time. Alice welcomed Pastor Ken and Nellie, then introduced Todd.

Lloyd and Ethel joined them, and Ethel managed to stand next to Todd. "I'm so glad you could come," she said. Smiling up at him, she took him by the arm as if to lead him away.

"Jane is in the kitchen, Todd," Alice said. "Would you help me carry things to the table?"

"Todd is a guest, Alice. He shouldn't be asked to help," Ethel said in a disapproving voice. Then she smiled up at

Todd. "You can visit with us while Alice and Jane put dinner on the table."

"But I'm happy to help," he said, giving Ethel a smile. He turned to follow Alice.

"Aunt Ethel, come tell Nellie about your decorating," Louise called.

Alice grinned at Louise, who raised one eyebrow. *So far, so good.* Alice pushed open the kitchen door. "I brought you some help."

Jane turned toward them, and her expression brightened when she saw Todd. Alice glanced at Todd. The tender look he gave Jane reminded her of looks she had once shared with Mark Graves many years ago, when they had dated in college. Jane and Todd might not recognize it yet, but Alice believed they were very close to falling in love.

"Todd," Jane said, smiling. Her cheeks had a rosy glow that could be attributed to the heat in the kitchen or perhaps to Todd's arrival.

"It smells like heaven in here," Todd said. "How may I help?"

"Is everyone here?"

"Yes," Alice said. "Louise is having Aunt Ethel tell Nellie about the carriage-house decorating."

"Great. Alice, if you want to take the salads and iced tea, I'll dish up the rest. Then we're ready."

While Jane and Todd brought the hot dishes into the dining room, Louise called everyone to the table. She seated Lloyd at the head of the table with Ethel on his right. Pastor Ken was directed to sit next to Ethel with Nellie on his right. Louise sat to Lloyd's left, with Alice on her other side. Jane sat next to Alice and Todd was at the end of the table, as far as possible from Ethel's questions.

Pastor Ken gave thanks for the meal and their fellowship, then Jane began passing the food.

"What is this dish, Jane?" Ethel asked. "It looks like stewed fruit."

"That's a papaya, fig and ginger compote for the meat."

"Oh. I thought it was chunky gravy," Lloyd said. His woebegone expression made everyone laugh.

"I think gravy is better suited to a winter meal," Jane said.

"It's delicious," Todd exclaimed.

Lloyd looked doubtful, but he took a spoonful.

"So, Todd, what do you do for a living?" Ethel asked down the length of the table.

As if she had not heard Ethel's question, Louise turned to Nellie and said, "Alice told us about the identification necklaces you gave the ANGELs. That's a wonderful idea. How did you find them?"

"I just surfed the Internet. They're so cute that Alice suggested I sell some of the patriotic designs for the Fourth of July."

"Great idea," Lloyd said. "At least *someone* is interested in the holiday this year." He glanced at Ethel, who blushed and looked down at her plate but didn't respond.

Watching them, Alice realized Francine's visit concerned Lloyd too. Ethel had become such a close part of his life, people in Acorn Hill thought of them as a unit. His comment made Alice realize how much he depended on Ethel's support. She always attended the festivities with Lloyd and stood by his side as he greeted visitors. She sat next to him on the grandstand as he announced the parade participants and as he officiated at the pie-eating contest. Surely she meant to attend with him this year too. Francine would be here for the holiday, but she wouldn't expect her mother to abandon Lloyd.

Alice had known Lloyd since childhood. She had seen his dedication and faithfulness to Grace Chapel and to Acorn Hill. Lloyd lived to serve others. He and Aunt Ethel had been close friends for years, and he counted on her for support and companionship. Francine's visit would pass. The Fourth of July would come and go. Life would settle back to normal and all would be well, but Alice hated to see two of the people she loved go through any distress. She said a silent prayer for them and made a mental note to speak to Jane about them. Perhaps Jane could spend the day with Francine and free up Ethel to be with Lloyd.

When the dishes were cleared, Ethel offered to help Jane serve the dessert.

"It's the least I can do after all the time you spent helping me this past two weeks."

"Thank you, Aunt Ethel. You can scoop the raspberry sorbet," Jane said as they went into the kitchen. She was thankful that Todd would be out of range of Ethel's questions for a bit longer.

Lloyd, Ethel and Pastor Ken left right after dessert. Jane and Todd went out to the garden. Nellie stayed to talk with Alice about their trip. They moved to the living room. Nellie had a copy of their itinerary and a list of items she felt were important to pack. She handed her list to Alice.

Most of the items were also on Alice's list. First-aid kit. Over-the-counter painkiller and an antihistamine in case of an allergic reaction. Extra toothbrush, toothpaste, comb, sunscreen, lip balm and a water bottle. Raincoat. Umbrella.

"This is very complete. Have you traveled a lot?"

"Hardly at all. I found this on the Internet."

Alice chuckled. "I suppose I'll have to learn to use the Internet more. Jane uses it all the time. I don't think we will need jackets. A sweater will be sufficient. And a raincoat is optional. I don't plan to take one."

"I'll pack mine. I believe in being prepared," Nellie answered seriously. "It's just good insurance."

Louise appeared in the doorway. "May I join you?"

"Certainly," Alice said.

When Louise entered the room Alice saw that she was carrying a large bag.

"I have something for you, Alice, for your trip." She handed the bag to Alice, then sat down across from them.

"How thoughtful, Louise. You didn't need to—"

"I know. I wanted to. Open it."

Nellie leaned forward, smiling, making Alice suspect that she was in on this surprise. Alice opened the bag and peered inside. She reached in and pulled out a colorful tote.

"Oh, Louise, this is lovely! It looks like a Monet painting."

"You're right. It's Monet's *Poppy Fields*. You need to retire your old bag. It looks as if the slightest tug would pull it apart. There's more."

Alice laughed. "You might be right." She reached into the bag again and pulled out a folding umbrella. "How did you know I needed a new one?"

Louise chuckled. "I borrowed yours last month. It's worse than your tote bag. And this is smaller. Just push the button to open and close it. Try it."

Alice held it out and pushed the button. It popped open. The pattern matched the floral tote. Alice looked at Louise and Nellie, who were smiling broadly. "I do believe these colors match my new travel outfits."

"I'm certain that they do," Louise said. "I found them at Nellie's."

"I didn't see them when I went in."

"You weren't looking. I got the distinct impression that you don't care much for shopping," Nellie said.

"You're right. I only shop out of dire necessity," Alice admitted. Louise and Nellie laughed. Alice joined in. "It's a good thing my sisters have such wonderful fashion sense," she said.

Nellie set her teacup on the table and stood. "I must be going now. I have to finish packing and make certain the store is in order before I leave. Thank you for a delightful afternoon, and thank Jane for me. The dinner was delicious."

Alice walked Nellie to the door.

"I'm so grateful to you for inviting me on your trip. I'm looking forward to it," Nellie said.

The ANGELs began arriving at seven thirty Monday morning. As Alice lugged her suitcase down the stairs, Linda Farr saw her and rushed to help. Alice relinquished her suitcase to the girl. "Thank you, Linda. Is everyone here already?"

"Miss Carter isn't here yet. All the girls are outside loading their luggage in Mrs. Sherman's and Rev. Thompson's cars. Mine's already loaded."

Alice glanced at her watch. "I'm sure Miss Carter will be here soon. We have plenty of time."

Jane came out of the kitchen carrying a tray. Alice held the front door open for Linda and Jane. "What a gorgeous day for traveling!" Alice said as they stepped out into the bright sunlight.

"The weatherman predicted beautiful weather all week. Not too hot and low humidity," Jane said.

A chorus of "Good morning's" greeted Alice. Then the girls saw Jane's goody plate and they converged on the porch.

Jane poured glasses of juice. "Be sure Mrs. Sherman and Rev. Thompson eat something. There are plenty of doughnuts to go around."

Lisa went to get the adults, insisting they come right away so the girls could have a doughnut. Pauline Sherman took one and accepted a cup of coffee. She sat on one of the porch chairs. "This is delicious."

"It's my mother's recipe. Have another one. I have more in the kitchen."

"I believe I will."

Nellie arrived, parked her car behind the inn and pulled

a large wheeled suitcase around to the front. She loaded it into one of the cars. Panting and looking flustered, she came up on the porch.

"Sorry I'm late. I stopped at the shop. Big mistake. I thought I'd never get out of there." She took a deep breath, stood straight and exhaled. A large grin lit her face. "I never really believed it'd happen, but here I am! I'm going to New York City."

"Yes, you are, and I'm so glad," Alice said. "Help yourself. There's coffee, juice and homemade doughnuts."

"I will, thanks. I didn't take time for breakfast."

Ethel came over from the carriage house dressed in a floral housedress with large pockets. "Goodness, there's enough excitement here to wake the entire town," she said.

The girls giggled.

"Such energy," Ethel said, chuckling. "I wish you'd leave some of that with me. I need it today. Oh, I see Jane made cake doughnuts. How delightful."

"Good morning, Aunt Ethel."

"Good morning, Jane. I can't stay but a moment, but I didn't want to miss Alice's send-off." Ethel went over to the table and took two doughnuts. Alice smiled when she saw her aunt put two more doughnuts in a napkin and put them in her pocket. Then Ethel said good-bye to Alice and left.

"Miss Howard, shouldn't we leave now? We don't want to miss the train," Jenny said.

"Don't worry. We've plenty of time." Alice turned to the group. "Last call for doughnuts and juice. We'll leave in fifteen minutes. Pastor Thompson, would you say a blessing for our trip, please? Then I want to review the rules with all of you girls."

"I'd be delighted," Rev. Thompson said.

They formed a circle, holding hands as they bowed their heads.

"Heavenly Father, we ask your blessing on this day and

upon this group of travelers. We thank You for each and every one of them. Let Your love and glory shine through them so that people may see them as Your ambassadors on the train and in the city, wherever they go. Help them to have a wonderful time and to return to us safely. In Jesus' name I pray. Amen."

"Amen," the others all repeated.

"All right, girls, let me have your attention," Alice said. "We'll use the buddy system. Each of you will have a buddy, and you're not to go anywhere without your buddy—not even to the restroom, unless we are in the hotel. And you are to make sure Miss Carter or I know where you are at all times. If we're in a store or on a tour, you will not go to a different department or room unless you tell me. Is that clear?"

"Yes, Miss Howard," they all echoed enthusiastically.

"Linda and Ashley are team one, Sarah and Briana are team two, and Jenny and Kate are team three. Teams one and two can ride in Mrs. Sherman's SUV. Team three can ride in Rev. Thompson's car."

Bouncing with excitement, the girls moved to stand with their partners. Alice had to raise her voice to be heard. "Does every team have at least one cell phone?"

Linda, Ashley, Briana and Kate raised their hands.

"The cell phone numbers are on your ID cards, and I programmed Miss Howard's number into your phones," Nellie told them.

"Excellent," Alice said. "Does everyone have on her ID necklace?"

The girls all held them up so she could see them.

"Good. All right, time to go."

The girls rushed to the cars, laughing and bouncing up and down.

Jane came out with a bag full of snacks for the group to eat on the train. She handed it to Alice. "We will pray for you every morning and every evening and many times in-between," she said.

"Yes," Louise agreed. "We'll pray for Nellie to forget her fears and to have a grand time."

"Thank you. I hope you have a wonderful holiday too." Alice hugged her sisters as the girls were calling for her to hurry up. She laughed and got into the front seat of the front car. Nellie was in the second car. As soon as they pulled away from the curb, the girls began singing.

Kookaburra sits on the old gum tree
Merry, merry king of the bush is he.
Laugh, Kookaburra! Laugh, Kookaburra!
Gay your life must be.

After four verses, they started over and sang it as a round. Then they changed to a different camp song.

Alice glanced at Pauline, who had joined the singing with as much abandon as any of the girls.

"Do you think you can keep up with this group?" Pauline asked her when the singing stopped.

Alice laughed. "I certainly hope so." She knew she was in for an exhausting week, but she didn't mind. She adored her ANGELs, and the girls kept her young at heart.

The midmorning train wasn't crowded. Alice and Nellie sat together. The girls didn't want to miss anything. They bounced from seat to seat, looking out the windows, check-ing out the dining car, gathering in a group to chat and gig-gle. They hardly sat in their seats during the entire train ride.

"I had forgotten how active girls could be," Nellie said.

Alice grinned. "I'm glad you came along. You're young enough to keep up with them."

"I don't know. I'm feeling older every minute."

Alice laughed out loud. "We're going to have a wonder-ful adventure," she said.

Chapter Sixteen

After the group left for the train station, Jane arranged a bouquet of peonies, snapdragons and fern fronds in a vase and filled a second smaller vase with pale pink and cream peace roses and baby's breath. She tucked the welcome card she and Louise had signed, including Alice's name, into her pocket and carried the bouquets to the carriage house.

Setting one vase on the step, she knocked on the door. Aunt Ethel didn't answer, and Jane thought she heard the vacuum cleaner, so she tried the door. It opened. "Aunt Ethel?" she called out. The sound of vacuuming came from the back of the house, so Jane picked up the vase and went in.

The living room looked as if someone had broken in and taken all of Ethel's precious knickknacks. Then Jane saw everything piled on the floor. The room smelled of lemon oil. Setting the vases on the kitchen counter, she hurried back to Ethel's bedroom.

"Aunt Ethel?"

Startled, Ethel dropped the vacuum wand. It barely missed her slippered foot. She reached down and shut off the vacuum. "Good grief, Jane, you scared me half to death!"

Jane thought her aunt looked dead tired. "I brought over some flowers. Isn't Francine arriving today?"

"This afternoon, and I'm not ready," Ethel said, her voice rising to a squeak.

"You cleaned three days ago."

"I found dust on the mantel. We need a rain shower to settle the dust outside. I'm sorry, dear, but I don't have time to visit. Must get this done."

"I'll help you, Aunt Ethel."

Ethel's eyes filled with tears and her shoulders sagged. "Thank you, dear. I don't know what I'd do without you. Perhaps you could arrange the figurines again. I can't remember how you put them, and they looked so nice."

"I'd be happy to do that. We'll finish straightening up, then you must get ready."

"Yes, all right. I'll just finish here." She flipped the switch, and the vacuum roared to life.

Jane went into the living room and set the knickknacks back in order. She found a pair of lace doilies in a kitchen drawer and set the largest floral arrangement on the living-room coffee table. She carried the roses into the guest room and set them on a doily on the dresser.

The vacuum noise ceased, and she heard the shower running, so Jane left. She soon returned with a plate of doughnuts.

Ethel came into the kitchen a few minutes later, dressed in neat tan linen slacks and a coral-colored knit top. She still looked tired.

"Jane, you are an angel. I was just certain I wouldn't be ready for Francine's arrival. Now I feel much better."

"Did you get any sleep last night?"

"Sleep? I . . . well, I did get up several times. Why?"

"You look tired. I know you want everything to be just right for Francine's visit, but honestly, Auntie, Francine won't expect perfection."

"I'm fine. I just haven't applied my makeup yet. The flowers are lovely, Jane. Thank you."

"You're welcome. I brought you some doughnuts. If you warm them for a few minutes, they'll be good tomorrow, but you're welcome to join us for breakfast."

"I think it'd be better if we eat here in the morning."

"Did you pick an evening for Francine's dinner?"

"Oh my. I've been so busy, I forgot to tell you. Tomorrow night. I invited several people. I have a list." She turned to the kitchen counter. "It's somewhere here."

"I don't need the list right now. How many people did you invite?"

"Let me think." She counted on her fingers. "Seven, I believe. Oh, and Lloyd."

"Does that include you and Francine?"

"No. So that makes ten. Oh dear. And I forgot to include you and Louise. That makes twelve."

"Is that all?"

"Yes. I'm quite sure it is." Ethel's gaze seemed a little dazed.

"Are you sure you're feeling all right."

Ethel stood up straighter, and her eyes snapped into focus. "I said I was, didn't I?"

Jane smiled. "Yes, you did. What else can I do to help you get ready?"

Ethel looked at her watch. "I have three hours before I leave for the airport. That gives me plenty of time. Lloyd is picking me up, bless his heart. He's been so patient. I know he feels neglected, but I told him I need to spend this time with my daughter."

"I'm sure he understands." Jane was relieved to see her aunt sounding more like her normal self. Perhaps she had overreacted to Ethel's appearance. "Do you need any more help?"

"No thank you, dear."

"Then I'll see you later."

Ethel was already busying herself at the sink and didn't answer, so Jane let herself out.

The telephone was ringing when Jane entered the kitchen. She picked it up. "Hello."

"Jane?"

"Hi, Todd. Yes it's me."

"I was wondering if there's a chance you could go to dinner with me tonight."

Jane looked at her watch. Nearly noon. And she had planned to make several batches of yeast dough and bake bread this afternoon. "What time?"

"Seven. This is sort of a business dinner. My regional boss showed up today and his wife is with him. They're great people. I think you'll like them. I know this is short notice, but I think Tom's wife would feel more comfortable if you were there to keep it more social. We talked business enough this morning."

"All right. I can make it by seven. Shall I meet you somewhere?"

"No. I'll pick you up."

"Okay. What shall I wear?"

"Maybe something like you'd wear to church. Thanks, Jane."

"Sure, Todd. Glad to help."

She hung up and burst into a flurry of activity, reaching for her mother's recipe book, pulling out a canister of flour. She slipped on her apron, then went over to the sink and scrubbed her hands and fingernails. She was kneading a ball of dough when Louise entered the kitchen.

"Is everything all right at the carriage house?"

"As much as it can be," Jane answered, frowning. "I hope Aunt Ethel will relax and enjoy Francine's visit."

"What about you? You've been going in so many directions yourself. Have you eaten lunch?"

"No time."

"Haven't I heard you scold Aunt Ethel for neglecting to eat?"

Jane laughed. "Guilty. But I'm eating dinner out tonight. Which is why I'm in such a rush. I just found out."

Louise raised one eyebrow. "I see. Todd, I surmise?"

"Yes. And don't look at me that way. It's a business dinner."

Louise raised her other eyebrow. "Business?"

"His boss came to town and brought his wife. Todd just found out this morning. He wants me to help entertain them at dinner so she won't feel outnumbered."

"Oh my. This sounds like it's becoming serious to me. Have you spoken to Fred and Vera yet?"

Jane shook her head sadly. "I want to talk to them privately, and I haven't found the time. Either they're busy or I am."

"You know waiting only makes it harder."

"Yes, I know."

"If you don't mind a little sisterly advice, make time to tell Fred and Vera. I am certain they'll understand, and that'll ease your mind."

Jane started to reach out and hug her sister. Then she caught sight of her flour-covered hands and stopped. She laughed instead. "I don't suppose you want to be covered with white flour, so I won't give you a hug, but thank you for caring about me, Louie."

"I do care, dear," Louise said, giving Jane a gentle pat on the arm. "Now about lunch, shall I scrounge up something to eat?"

"I'd be obliged. Just something light. I want to save calories for tonight. I'll knead another batch of dough while you fix lunch. By the way, Aunt Ethel has arranged a dinner party here for Francine tomorrow night."

"Tomorrow night? Oh dear. I haven't laundered the tablecloth and napkins from Sunday's dinner. When did she tell you?"

"This morning. And she isn't sure, but she thinks there will be twelve for dinner including us." Jane laughed.

"She isn't sure?"

"Aunt Ethel seemed rather—what's that word?—discombobulated this morning."

Louise shook her head. "Well, she'll snap out of it when Francine arrives."

The clacking commotion of trains reverberated through the underground boarding area at New York's Penn Station. A voice rang out over a loudspeaker, calling out train arrivals and departures. Toting their luggage, Alice, the ANGELs and Nellie made their way through the crowd along the narrow platform. The smell of cleaning fluid mixed with the odors of perfumes, detergents and aftershave. The cacophony of languages fascinated the girls, who tried to see and hear everything while they hurried to keep up with Alice.

Past the waiting room, they came to an area with shops. Beyond that, they took the escalator up to street level. When they got outside, they stood in a line until they finally got two taxis. After a short ride through crowded streets, with cars and taxis rushing and weaving around traffic, their cabs pulled up in front of a narrow, four-story brick building. White columns on either side of the entry supported a curved roof and sheltered steps leading up to an ornately carved double door. Colorful flags and banners decorated the columns.

"It looks very elegant," Nellie said after they got out of the taxis. "But rather small."

Alice smiled. "It's larger than it looks. Wait until you see the lobby."

The drivers unloaded their luggage, and soon they were standing inside an elegantly appointed lobby with a small fountain in the middle of the room, surrounded by clustered seating arrangements. The cream and gold decor set off the polished mahogany reception desk. Only the faded, slightly threadbare carpet and the worn nap on the velvet chairs hinted at the economy of the hotel. While the girls stood looking around, whispering reverently, as if they were in church, Alice checked them in.

"Get your suitcases and bags and come along," she told the girls. She led them down a hallway to an old-fashioned elevator.

The elevator arrived, and the door creaked open. The girls looked at each other as if they were not sure they could trust the old conveyance.

"It's safe," Alice said. "All elevators have to pass regular inspections." Nellie got on last, clearly hesitant, even with Alice's reassurance.

The elevator groaned its way to the third floor. Nellie was nearest the door and escaped as soon as the door opened. Alice led them to the end of a narrow, softly lit hallway. The walls had the smell of fresh paint, but instead of brightening the corridor, the unadorned walls appeared austere. She opened the last doors on either side of the hall and a door at the end.

"Miss Carter and I will take the middle room. Teams one and two will share the room on the left, which is the largest room, and team three will share the room on the right."

The girls stepped into their rooms, and the hushed voices turned to exuberant exclamations.

"Cool!"

"Look at the closet."

"*Ooh!* Look at the bathtub. It has legs with claw-feet and a pull-down shower sprayer."

Nellie grinned. "Sounds like they approve." She opened

the middle door and stepped into their room. Her eyes widened as she looked around. The pale green, high-ceilinged room had a kitchenette in one corner with a sink, a small refrigerator under a counter, a microwave oven and a small table with four chairs. The two double beds, dressers and chairs were good pieces from the thirties or forties, if Alice guessed correctly.

"Why, this is lovely." Nellie ran her hand over a colorful quilt on one of the beds. "I didn't expect such nice furnishings." She laughed. "I hate to admit it, but I was picturing something dark and seedy."

"Oh my. I wouldn't bring the girls to such a place."

"I didn't mean to imply . . . I know you wouldn't knowingly take the girls into a dangerous situation. But the price is so . . . reasonable."

Alice smiled. Poor Nellie. With such misconceptions, it had taken a lot of courage for her to come. "Louise told me about this hotel, and I brought a group of girls here a few years ago. The furnishings are donated and are refurbished by the sisters and volunteers. They do a wonderful job, don't they?"

One door led to the larger of the girls' rooms through a shared bathroom. Alice went through and knocked on the door. Linda opened it.

"Hi, Miss Howard. Are we all connected?"

"Yes, and we will be sharing the bathroom, but there's a bigger bathroom with two showers and several stalls and sinks down the hall. When you finish putting your things away, come into our room."

Nellie peered through the doorway. The compact room held two queen-sized beds, neatly made up with bright flowered comforters, a dresser, an armoire and two chairs. No wasted space, but very neat and cozy.

Another door led from Nellie and Alice's room to the smaller of the girls' rooms on the other side. It looked much the same but had two single beds and one chair, and they had no bathroom.

Alice repeated her instructions to them, then she began unpacking, carefully laying her undergarments in one of the dresser drawers. "You can have the other drawers, and there are a few hangers in the armoire."

"I brought more hangers." Nellie held up two that unfolded to hold multiple pieces of clothing. "One for each of us."

"What great travel hangers. Where did you find these?"

"One of my supplier's catalogs."

Alice stood straight and smiled at her roommate. "You are amazing."

Nellie blushed and looked pleased. "I like to be prepared." She turned and began hanging her skirts, blouses and blazer.

A few moments later, the connecting doors opened, and six girls burst into the room. It suddenly seemed very tiny. The girls sat on the beds and chairs and looked at Alice expectantly.

"Everyone settled?"

"Yes, Miss Howard," they replied in unison.

"We only have a few hours, but I thought we could do some sightseeing this afternoon, then have dinner near the hotel and buy some food for breakfast."

"Yea!" echoed around the small room.

The girls stood and started to move.

"Wait. You will need walking shoes, a light sweater or sweatshirt for later, and your packs and ID necklaces. Also your room keys."

As they rushed for their rooms, Alice added, "Meet back here in ten minutes."

Nellie laughed. "You would think they are excited or something." She grinned broadly. "So am I."

Chapter Seventeen

The ANGELs, with Alice leading the way, descended the stairs from their rooms as a group. Alice started in front but reached the lobby last. As the girls clamored past her, she called out, "We will meet in the lobby."

Shouts of, "Yes, Miss Howard," drifted back to her and the girls disappeared around a turn of the stairs.

"Are you sure we can handle the girls outside? It's a big city," Nellie said.

Alice gave Nellie what she hoped was a reassuring smile. "We'll be fine. We'll take it one block at a time."

Several ladies sat talking in the lobby. They looked up with interest at the excited group of young girls who gathered around Alice and Nellie.

"All right, girls. A little lesson before we go out." Alice got out her guidebook. Nellie opened hers also. The girls listened quietly.

"New York is made up of many neighborhoods and boroughs," Alice said. "We are on the island of Manhattan. The Hudson River borders the west, and the East River is on the east. The rivers come together at New York Bay to the south." She showed them a map of Manhattan Island in her book.

Alice glanced at the group of ladies, who seemed

surprised by the girls' polite attention. She continued her description of the area. "Our hotel is in a charming neighborhood called Chelsea," she said, pointing to the neighborhood on the map. "We'll walk over to see the Chelsea Piers, which have been converted into a sports center. Then we'll have dinner at the Chelsea Market, which is in an old Nabisco factory. If I remember right, they have the best brownies in New York."

"Better than Ms. Howard's brownies?" Linda asked.

"Well, perhaps not better, but just as good."

"Yum!" Ashley said, and everyone laughed.

"We will be walking, so stay together, and remember the buddy system. If we get into a crowded area, I will raise my umbrella so you can see where I am at all times. Ready?"

A chorus of "Yes, ma'am" filled the lobby. Alice headed for the front door, followed closely by a gaggle of chattering, laughing girls.

Totally carefree, the girls talked and laughed as they walked, barely paying attention to their surroundings. Nellie, on the other hand, clung to her purse and looked anxiously from side to side. *Watching for an attacker,* Alice thought. Alice gave her a gentle smile, but Nellie's responding frown and pointed glance from one side to the other let Alice know her companion wouldn't relax her guard.

Alice sighed. What would it take to relieve Nellie's fear? Only the peace of God. Alice could still remember her father's deep, gentle voice reading verses from Matthew:

Look at the birds of the air; they do not sow or reap or store away in barns, and yet your heavenly Father feeds them. Are you not much more valuable than they? . . . See how the lilies of the field grow. They do not labor or spin. Yet I tell you that not even Solomon in all his splendor was dressed like one of these. If that is how God clothes the grass of the field, which is here today and tomorrow is thrown into the fire, will he not much more clothe you, O you of little faith? So do not worry, saying, "What shall we eat?" or "What shall we drink?" or "What shall we wear?" . . . But seek first his kingdom and his righteousness, and all these things will be given to you as well (Matthew 6:26, 28–31, 33).

Alice had taken those verses very seriously, observing the care God showered on His creation. Watching nature and the people around her had opened her eyes to God's deep love. But still it had taken her time to learn to stop worrying and let God have her cares. Undoubtedly, it would take time for Nellie too. Trusting God's constant presence came from walking with Him daily and seeing His hand at work in His creation. That was, in part, why she worked with the ANGELs: to help young girls find their own faith. Perhaps Nellie would see God's hand in her life too.

After several blocks, the piers came into sight. The old piers had been converted into a marvelous sports complex. At the West Roller Rink, a group of young people were practicing roller hockey. The girls watched with rapt attention. When the teams finished, the rink was opened to general skating.

"Can we skate, Miss Howard?" Sarah asked. The others joined her pleas, and Alice agreed that they could skate for one hour.

"Shall we join them?" she asked Nellie.

"I don't know. I haven't skated since I was their age."

Sarah took Nellie's hand. "Come on, Miss Carter. Come skate with us." The girls gathered around their two chaperones, urging them toward the rink.

"I think I'd better stay here and watch all our things," Nellie said.

"That's not necessary," Alice said. "We'll lock everything up in lockers."

"Oh, all right," Nellie said, "but you have to promise not to laugh at me."

"We won't," Briana said. "Besides, I'm not very good, either."

"Then we'll have to stick together."

Briana grinned. "Deal," she said, raising her hand for a high-five. Then she stopped in midair, but Nellie responded by slapping her hand in accord. Briana grinned.

They rented skates and ventured out onto the rink. Alice reminded them to stay where they could see their buddy and the chaperones, and to go in pairs if they went to the restrooms and dressing rooms. The girls readily agreed.

Alice soon lost sight of everyone as they whirled past her. It only took her a few moments to find her balance, and she skated after the girls. Long-ago years of ice skating on Fairy Pond gradually came back to her. She leaned down a bit and pushed off with her in-line skates, going faster and faster. She waved as she passed Jenny and Kate, who took up the challenge and rushed after her. Then Alice skated a circle around Linda, Ashley and Sarah. They tried to follow her. Linda made it. Ashley and Sarah ran into each other and toppled, but they got up quickly. "Where are Briana and Miss Carter?" she asked.

Ashley pointed behind them. It took Alice a few seconds, but she spotted the two, hanging on to each other, stiffly moving their feet forward.

"I'll go check on them." She skated off, deftly avoiding other skaters. She hadn't felt so carefree in ages.

Just before she got to them, Nellie flailed her arms wildly, hunched over to compensate her balance, and fell, pulling Briana down with her.

"Are you all right?" Alice asked, stopping beside them.

Briana was laughing. Nellie's eyes were as wide as those

of a startled child. She looked up at Alice and gave her an embarrassed smile. "I think I'm all right," she said. She tried to get up, but her feet rolled out from under her.

She giggled. "I don't know if I'll ever get off this floor."

Alice grinned. "Let me help you." She reached for Nellie's hand, braced herself, and Nellie managed to stand and stay on her feet. Briana bounded up by herself.

The rest of the girls skated up to them and asked if they were all right.

"My ego is bruised as much as my tail bone, I think. I've never been very athletic. You girls are all naturals. How do you manage to skate so well, Alice?" Nellie asked.

"I was a bit of a tomboy growing up."

"You should see Miss Howard on ice skates. She can do circles and she can glide with her leg in the air," Linda said. "She taught us how to do it."

"Wow. Can you do it on roller skates, Miss Howard?" Briana asked.

"I don't know. And I had my sisters to hang on to."

"You can hang on to us," Sarah offered. "Let's try it."

"First let's help Briana and Miss Carter find their balance.

The girls linked arms, Briana in between Linda and Ashley, and Nellie between Alice and Jenny. They pushed slowly forward, right foot, then left foot, giving the two time to find their balance and rhythm. They made their way slowly around the rink together before they released their arms and struck out on their own.

By the end of the hour, Nellie was gliding smoothly, though slowly, and she even dared to look up, smile and wave at the others.

Afterward, they walked to Chelsea Market. The workday had ended for most people, and the sidewalks were crowded. Nellie clutched her purse and tried to herd the girls along while keeping an eye on everyone around them. Alice held her closed umbrella overhead, so the girls wouldn't lose sight of her, and continued as if they were taking a stroll in downtown Acorn Hill.

A developer had converted the old, five-story Nabisco building into a marketplace. When they entered, they were hit by the mixture of scents—sweet pastries, savory breads, hot Thai cuisine, spicy Mexican food, grilled meat, seafood and pizza. As the girls walked through, their eyes widened at all the choices.

After much discussion, they all agreed on pizza, which they devoured as if they hadn't eaten for days. For lunch, they had eaten Jane's snacks on the train, and skating whetted their appetites.

One store carried a huge array of cooking utensils and supplies. Alice convinced the girls to stop so she could look for a gift for Jane.

Once inside, they discovered the store was the home of a television food network with studios where several popular food shows were taped. None of the girls had watched the shows, but they were awed to see an actual television studio.

The ANGELs all wanted to buy gifts for their mothers, and Alice had to remind them that they had limited space to take extra items home, and they had a week to find gifts. That narrowed their searches. Alice faced a similar dilemma. Jane ran a well-stocked kitchen. Over the years, she had collected many cooking gadgets. Alice didn't even know how some of them were used. After looking at a confusing array of possible gifts, she finally settled on a set of colorful, flexible cutting sheets that would fit in her suitcase.

When the girls finished looking around, Alice gathered them all together. "I want to pick up rolls and cereal for breakfast, then we'll take a bus back to the hotel. Stay together so we can make sure we all get on the same bus. If we become separated, another bus will come by in a few minutes. The hotel is straight up the avenue six blocks from here.

Remember the buddy system. Nellie, will you get on last, to make sure we are all on the bus? I'll go first and pay the fare."

"Sure. Be glad to."

Alice made a few purchases in a market, then they trooped out of the building. As they walked to the bus stop, Nellie looked around, alert to any danger. The bus arrived almost immediately, and they all got on. Within minutes, they were entering the safety of the hotel. Alice thought she heard Nellie breath a sigh of relief.

By the time Todd and Jane left for his business dinner, Lloyd and Ethel had not yet come back from the airport with Francine. As Louise washed up her few supper dishes, she heard Lloyd's car drive up to the carriage house. She quickly dried her hands and went out through the kitchen door and across the lawn.

As they got out of the car, Ethel began issuing orders to Lloyd about the luggage and instructing Francine that she should go rest from her exhausting day and unpack tomorrow. Louise listened to Ethel's nonstop monologue with amazement. She sounded absolutely frazzled. Francine might be exhausted, but probably less from her flight than from dealing with Ethel.

"Hello," Louise called. Francine turned and smiled.

"Louise! How delightful to see you." She stepped forward and they exchanged a hug.

"Welcome to Acorn Hill, dear. We've all been awaiting your visit. It's been too long."

Francine's less-than-enthusiastic, "Yes, it has," made Louise wonder just how excited her cousin was about visiting her mother.

Francine could have stepped out of the pages of a fashion magazine. Taller than her mother, she had the slender figure to wear the tailored gray-and-white striped suit with its fitted skirt that ended at her knees. Her bobbed, auburn hair and perfect makeup, even after a day of travel, gave her a crisp, fresh appearance.

Louise picked up one of the suitcases Lloyd had pulled from the trunk of his car. "I'll carry this," she told Lloyd. She started for the door. "After we deposit your luggage, would you all like to come over for a cup of tea?"

"Not tonight," Ethel said before anyone else could respond. "Francine and I must rest."

"I understand. Travel can be exhausting. Maybe we can visit tomorrow. I want to hear all about what you've been doing."

"Thanks, Louise. We'll catch up tomorrow," Francine said.

Louise followed Lloyd inside and set the suitcase in the guest room.

"Where are Jane and Alice?" Francine asked.

"Alice took her girls' group from church on a trip to New York City," Ethel said. "Where is Jane, Louise? I'm surprised she isn't here to greet her dearest cousin."

"Jane had a dinner engagement."

"She went out with her young man when she knew Francine was arriving tonight?" Ethel's voice grew shrill.

"I believe this was an unexpected business dinner, and her friend asked her to go along as a favor." To Francine, Louise said, "I know she is eager to see you."

"Of course. I understand."

"Well, I don't. To choose him over her cousin, whom she hasn't seen in years. I hope she isn't getting in over her head with this man. You know what happened to her last relationship."

"Mother!"

"Now, Francine. It's true."

"I must be going," Lloyd said. "I'll see you both at dinner tomorrow night."

"Dinner?" Ethel repeated. "Oh yes, Jane is preparing something special for you, dear. She is an accomplished chef, you know."

"I'd better go and let you settle in. Good night," Louise said. She gave her cousin another hug, then followed Lloyd out the door.

Chapter Eighteen

When Todd pulled up to a posh restaurant, Jane was glad she'd chosen to wear her dressy black-and-royal-blue Georgette skirt and black shell. She hadn't worn the outfit since she'd moved from San Francisco.

They were a few minutes early. Todd checked on his reservation to make sure they had a table with a view of the restaurant's lovely garden and waterfall. The maître d' seated them and promised to bring their guests when they arrived.

"Thanks for accepting my last-minute invitation. William Davidson has been my mentor. He recommended me for the Potterston store. His wife Doreen is a wonderful woman. I think you'll like them."

The maître d' returned, ushering a handsome couple in their midsixties to the table. Todd stood and introduced them to Jane. William was at least six inches shorter than Todd and a couple inches shorter than his wife, and slightly balding. Doreen had soft, pleasant features and laugh lines at the corners of her eyes and mouth. Jane liked her at first sight.

"I'm so glad you could take time to join us tonight," Doreen told Jane. "I assured Todd that he didn't need to pamper me, but I must confess, I do tire of endless business conversation, and my William could talk shop all night." She smiled and patted her husband's hand. He gave her an affectionate smile and a wink.

"I bring her along so I don't become too boring," William said.

Doreen laughed and Todd chuckled. "That doesn't happen often," Todd said.

"I'm not sure if that's a compliment or an insult," William said. "I'll assume the former."

Jane enjoyed their banter. These three people obviously liked each other a great deal.

After they ordered, Jane and Doreen talked about their families and homes. Doreen and William had three daughters, all grown and married.

"I always wanted a son, so I've adopted Todd," Doreen confided. "After his wife left him, I wished I had an available daughter, but they are all happily married. Oh dear, that sounds awful. I love my sons-in-law," she added hastily.

Jane laughed. "Todd's a very special man."

"Yes he is. I'm glad you think so." Doreen patted Jane's hand. "I'm so happy Todd has found someone nice and has started dating."

"We're just friends, Mrs.—"

"Doreen, please. I realize you and Todd haven't known each other long, but time isn't important. Caring and sharing are what matter. He told me about your lovely gardens and how you are helping him restore the grounds of his dilapidated place. Goodness, what a job he has ahead of him. So different from his townhouse in Baltimore. But this suits him. And he needed desperately to get away. That . . . his wife hurt him so badly. Such a shame. I liked her very much. I'm glad Todd agreed to take this position. He seems very happy here."

"Potterston is a wonderful town. Not too big, but yet large enough to have all the conveniences you could want."

"I love the wide, tree-lined streets and lovely old homes.

You can tell people care about their town by the neat yards and parks. I told William we should consider retiring here. He laughed and said he didn't plan to retire until they plant him in the ground."

"Does his position require a lot of traveling?"

"Too much. I don't always go with him, but I particularly wanted to see Todd and make sure he's happy. I can see that I don't have to worry about that," she said, giving Jane a wink.

Doreen Davidson seemed to consider Todd and Jane a couple, and Jane didn't know what to do. She hated to leave Doreen with a wrong impression. Was it a wrong impression? How did she feel about Todd? Her heartbeat certainly accelerated when he was around. She wondered if she affected him the same way.

The girls talked and giggled as they got ready for bed. They all gathered in the middle room. As they held hands, Alice led them in a prayer of thanksgiving for their safe travel and for a wonderful day. The girls added their own prayers, then hugged each other when Alice declared lights out. Each girl gave Alice and Nellie a good-night hug, then they trudged off to their beds.

After the girls exited, leaving the connecting doors open just a crack, Alice took out the itinerary and guidebook and sat on her bed while Nellie took her shower. The running water shut out some of the sounds, but the walls were thin, and Alice could hear the girls' muffled talk and laughter.

Nellie came out of the bathroom in her robe. She put away her clothes, then she sat on the side of her bed. "They're still awake. Should we tell them to settle down?"

"Not yet," Alice said. "After the day's activities, they should fall asleep soon. If the noise level rises, we'll quiet them down for the sake of the other guests."

Nellie grinned. "Being with the girls almost makes me feel like a kid again. When I was in high school, our church choir went to another town to sing. The girls slept in sleeping bags in the church fellowship hall. The boys were in the basement of the pastor's house. We talked and laughed for hours." Nellie chuckled softly. "Our poor chaperones. We were a lot noisier than the ANGELs, and some of the girls snuck out and got into the cookies that were supposed to be for church the next day. We all had crumbs in our sleeping bags and unhappy church ladies in the morning."

Alice laughed. "The ANGELs can be creative, but they are good-hearted, and they try to behave."

"They love you," Nellie said.

"Yes, and I love them too."

"I know. That's plain for anyone to see. I feel blessed to be part of this group."

"Oh, Nellie, thank you for coming." Spontaneously Alice got up and gave her young friend a hug. "You've contributed a lot to this trip, and the girls love having you with us. So do I."

Alice thought she saw the start of tears in Nellie's eyes. "I'm going to take a shower now. If the girls are still giggling when I get done, I'll peek in on them."

When Alice came out, the girls' rooms were quiet. Nellie had fallen asleep, and only Alice's bedside lamp cast a faint light around the room. Alice checked the girls, then climbed into her own bed and turned out the light. She snuggled down and was pleased to find the mattress very comfortable. As she turned on her side and closed her eyes, she prayed silently.

Louise rinsed the breakfast dishes and handed them to Jane, who loaded them in the dishwasher.

"Have you heard from Alice?" Jane asked.

"Yes. She called last night. They arrived on schedule and are having a great time." Louise told Jane about the ANGELs first evening in the city. "Speaking of great times, how was your dinner last night?"

"Very enjoyable. Todd's boss and his wife are like family to him. William helped Todd get this position after his divorce, when he needed a change of scenery."

"How nice of him."

"William's wife, Doreen, told me she has adopted Todd as the son she never had, so they've known each other well for some time. She came on this trip so she could see him and make sure he's doing all right."

"Goodness. That must have been uncomfortable for you."

Jane laughed. "Not too bad. I did get the impression that she was checking me out, though. I'm afraid she might have jumped to conclusions. I explained that Todd and I are just friends. I'm not sure she believed me. I lay awake thinking about it last night, wondering what Todd told them about me." Jane frowned. "I'm not sure I want to know."

A rap on the kitchen door made them both turn. Francine stood outside. Jane wiped her hands on a towel and hurried to open the door.

"Francine!" she squealed. She threw her arms around her cousin and hugged her. Francine gave her a weak hug in return, then stepped aside, leaving Jane puzzled and a bit hurt. Then she reminded herself that they were no longer children, and they hadn't seen each other in many years.

"Come in, come in. It's so great to see you. You look fantastic." And she did. She had on white linen slacks and a soft blue and white knit top.

"Good morning," Louise said. "Did you sleep well?"

"Not very. But that's the price one pays for traveling, isn't it? No bed is ever as comfortable as your own."

"That's true," Louise said. "Aunt Ethel isn't with you?"

"No. She's expecting me to return shortly."

"Would you like a cup of coffee?" Jane offered.

"No, thank you. I had my one cup for today. I wonder if you have noticed anything unusual about my mother's health or behavior recently. She seems anxious."

Jane and Louise exchanged a glance. "She has been busy and wanted everything to be perfect for your visit," Jane said. "She's very healthy. Don't you agree, Louise?"

"Yes. Your mother's in excellent health."

Francine seemed to relax. "I'm pleased to hear that. Do you know if she has had a good physical recently?"

"Not that I am aware of," Louise said, "however, she is careful about eating healthy food and exercising regularly. She's very active."

Francine nodded her head thoughtfully. "That's a relief. Well, I must be going." She sighed. "Mother has our day planned, beginning with a trip to Potterston to hear a lecture at the historical society."

"Oh yes, she mentioned something about a presentation on the pottery and porcelain," Jane said. "She thought you'd be interested."

"I understand we'll be dining with you tonight. I hope you're not serving red meat." She offered a half smile. "I must watch my cholesterol."

"In that case, we'll have a chicken dish. Thanks for letting me know."

"Of course. I'll see you tonight."

Francine was through the door and gone before the sisters could respond.

"Francine has changed," Jane said as they watched their cousin cross the lawn and disappear into the carriage house.

"Perhaps she feels ill at ease with us because of the years since we've seen her," Louise surmised. "I'm sorry, Jane."

Jane turned to look at Louise, surprised. "For what?"

"You were once very close."

"Yes, but that was a long time ago. Francine has changed, and so have I."

"Yes, you have become a beautiful woman, inside and out." Louise surprised Jane with a heartfelt embrace that eased the hurt Jane had felt at Francine's cold greeting.

A knot formed in Jane's throat. The ringing of the telephone broke the spell and saved her from showing her feelings. She hadn't realized how close to the surface her emotions were this morning. Seeing Francine had set them off, but her relationship with Todd had her riding a rollercoaster. Thrilling, but also upsetting.

Louise answered the telephone, giving Jane a moment to take a drink of water and ease the lump in her throat.

Louise covered the mouthpiece with her hand. "It's Todd for you," she said quietly. She extended the phone to Jane and left the kitchen.

"Hi," Jane said brightly. She leaned back against the counter.

"Good morning. I wanted to thank you for coming to dinner last night. William and Doreen think you're wonderful. So do I," he added in a husky tone.

"I liked them too."

"I'm glad," Todd said. "Doreen said I should grab you before you get away."

Jane didn't know what to say. Fortunately, Todd kept talking, so she didn't have to respond.

"I'll be tied up with William all day, then they leave tonight after dinner. I don't suppose you could join us again?"

"Sorry. I'm hosting a dinner for my cousin tonight. She's visiting from Minneapolis. Perhaps Thursday night?"

"I can't." There was silence for a moment, then she heard Todd exhale. "I . . . have a complication. My ex-wife called. She wants to talk, so she's driving up."

"Oh." Jane felt disappointment.

"I don't know what she wants that couldn't be settled by a phone call." He sounded unhappy, which Jane understood. Though she had forgiven Justin, she had no desire to see him or talk to him. That would just dredge up old pain.

"I'll say a prayer for you," Jane said.

"Thanks. Enjoy your family. I'll call you next week."

After she hung up the phone, Jane started the dishwasher, then took a basket and went outside to the vegetable garden.

She bent down to pull a weed, then stood and looked to the sky. "Dear Father, I am so confused," she whispered. "I don't know what to think of this relationship. Am I jumping to conclusions? I don't want to hurt Todd, and I don't want to be hurt. I'm not looking for love. Did You bring Todd into my life for a reason? Give me some kind of sign, Lord, so I'll know what to do. And bless Todd. Please don't let his ex-wife hurt him more. Fill him with Your peace and happiness. Please, Lord. Amen."

I'm not looking for love . . . When Jane realized that she had prayed those words, she wondered where they had come from. *Am I in love?* she asked herself. Her heart was beating fast and she felt shaky. She knew she was standing at the edge of a precipice, and one tiny step would put her over the cliff. She took a step back, realized what she'd done and laughed.

Taking the gardening clippers from the shed, Jane snipped fresh parsley and chives, then went to the flower garden to pick a fresh bouquet for the table.

"Good morning," she said to the Abercrombies, guests who were enjoying a stroll in the garden.

"Indeed it is," Neil Abercrombie responded.

Jane had learned when they registered that the English couple were making a pilgrimage across America.

"I do believe your garden rivals the finest cottage gardens in England," he said.

"Thank you. That is high praise. My mother put it in many years ago, and we've restored it."

"Apparently your mother chose good root stock. That is so important," Neil said.

"I get the impression that you love gardens. You should see Longwood Gardens, less than an hour from here. I was there recently, and they're in full bloom. They are well worth a visit."

Neil looked at Delphine. "Perhaps we should take a day trip there."

"I would like that," his wife said.

Jane excused herself and cut a generous bouquet of roses, iris and daisies. Wendell was sunning himself on a bench. She scratched his head, and he purred loudly and stretched so she could scratch his belly.

She called, "Enjoy your day" to her guests and headed back to the kitchen. Her heart felt lighter. She smiled and bounced a little with each step, not quite breaking into a skip but almost. She laughed. She could imagine the Abercrombies watching and wondering if she'd scrambled her brains this morning along with the eggs.

Chapter Nineteen

After a quick breakfast in Alice and Nellie's room, the ANGELs gathered their gifts and took a bus to a neighborhood in midtown Manhattan where the nuns ran a daycare center for low-income families. The center occupied part of an old brick building that had once been a grocery store.

The children were shy at first, then the girls opened the bag that held their handmade puppets. Within minutes, the ANGELs were surrounded by happy, excited children. The girls sat on the floor and showed the children how to make the mitten puppets talk and bow and move. The girls acted out a little play they had rehearsed about a lost sheep and the shepherd who went to find him and bring him safely home. Sarah narrated the play, telling the children about Jesus, the Good Shepherd. The children sat, enraptured by the simple toys and little play. They giggled and clapped as the puppets bobbed and chattered. They cheered as the shepherd returned with the lost lamb.

When they finished, the girls gave each child a puppet, and Nellie opened her bag and passed out the T-shirts she'd brought.

Sister Margaret, who was in charge of the center, brought out cookies and juice for the children and their guests. Nellie sat in a rocking chair in earnest conversation with a darling dark-haired, dark-eyed little girl who was on her lap. When Nellie looked up at Alice, she had a look of subdued amazement on her face.

By the time the ANGELs left the day care, Nellie was besotted.

"I was tempted to tell you to go on without me. I could spend the entire week with those children," Nellie told Alice as they walked along the sidewalk. She seemed more relaxed than she'd been since their arrival in the city. She'd forgotten to hang onto her purse. She wasn't even looking where they were going.

"Your T-shirts were a hit," Alice said, "and you captured the heart of that little girl."

"Oh, Alice, I thought my heart would break when she hung on to me and didn't want me to leave. She told me about her family. Her daddy is dead, and she told me the names of four brothers and two sisters. I don't know how her mother can manage. I asked Sister Margaret if there's some way that I can help. I gave her my address. I hope she contacts me. She told me there are millions of children who need help."

"God brings people and situations into our lives so we can bring His light and hope to the world. There's a verse that says, 'Religion that God our Father accepts as pure and faultless is this: to look after orphans and widows in their distress' (James 1:27). I'm sure you'll find a way to help."

"Where are we going?" Nellie asked, suddenly looking around.

"To take the subway to Times Square. It isn't far," Alice said.

Nellie tightened her hold on her purse. "Shouldn't we take a bus?"

"This is faster, and I want the girls to experience the subway. It's really quite safe."

They reached the entrance to the subway, and team one started into the corridor.

"Wait!" Nellie called out. "We must stay together."

The girls stopped and looked back.

"Yes, girls, let's stay together, so we can be sure to get on the same train." Alice went ahead to purchase MetroCards, which they could use on buses and subways in the city. Then they filed through to the trains. Nellie held on to her purse with one hand and Kate Waller with her other hand. As the train came to a stop in front of them, and passengers streamed off, Nellie glanced around nervously.

"This is our train," Alice announced, and they moved forward as one, crowding through the open doors into one of the cars. The girls had to stand, holding on to the overhead bars. Nellie clung to a post and her purse.

Alice thought Nellie looked uneasy, but she didn't say anything to Nellie. Instead, she said a brief prayer for her.

The subway train stopped so abruptly, Nellie nearly lost her balance. She stood rigidly and hung on tightly. Just before the next stop, Alice stood, grabbing a rail to keep her balance.

"This is where we get off," she said. The girls surged for the door as it opened, piling out as a unit. Nellie and Alice followed them. New passengers pushed forward and around them to get on before the doors shut.

"Is everyone here?" Alice counted the girls. Nellie was right beside her. "All right. Let's go to street level."

"Hang on to your backpacks, girls," Nellie warned.

They emerged onto a crowded sidewalk and got swept along in the stream of foot traffic. Alice raised her unopened umbrella and called to the girls to stay together. They made their way to a less crowded spot in front of a store window.

"Is everyone here?" Alice did a quick head count.

"Does everyone still have her belongings?" Nellie asked.

The girls all nodded and voiced assent.

"Good," Alice said. "I think we can see most of the square from here."

"But it isn't square," Briana said.

Alice chuckled. "That's true. It's more pie-shaped. The square is named for that tall, skinny building, down at the end. It was built originally to house the *New York Times* newspaper. That was a long time ago." Alice thumbed through her guidebook. "When this was first built, it was one of the tallest buildings around here. Now, all the tall buildings dwarf it, but they use it as a rolling billboard, with lights all up and down it flashing the latest news and advertisements."

"Isn't that the building where they drop a crystal ball at midnight on New Year's Eve?" Ashley asked.

"That's right."

"Mom let me stay up last year to watch it. It was kind of cool, but not very exciting. I like fireworks better."

Alice laughed. "I suspect it's a lot more exciting in person."

"Oh, look." Jenny Snyder pointed to a brightly lit, multistory toy store. "Can we go there, Miss Howard?"

"Oh yes, please, please, please?" five other girls chorused.

"We still have the Empire State Building on our agenda for today, but I suppose an hour wouldn't hurt."

"Yea!" "Cool!" "Yippee!" rang out around her.

"However . . . no one leaves a floor until we all meet and go together. Understood?"

"Yes, ma'am," the girls echoed.

"And don't spend all your money there. We have a week and a lot of places to visit. I'm sure that anything you find in this store, you can find in Acorn Hill or Potterston."

"Have you been there before?" Nellie asked Alice.

"I was railroaded into going there the last time I brought a group here. It's fascinating, but be warned. We'll have our hands full keeping track of everyone."

Nellie straightened her shoulders.

"Ready?"

The girls all nodded their heads.

Alice grinned. "March." And she led the charge up the street to the store.

A sixty-foot-tall, brightly colored Ferris wheel dominated the store. Each of its seats was formed into the likeness of a toy, from fashion dolls to trucks. The girls all wanted a seat in their favorite toy character.

When Kate Waller decided not to go on the ride, Nellie turned to Alice. Her eyes sparkled with delight. "I think I'll take her place."

After their ride, the girls checked out every display in the store, from a walk-in playhouse to a life-size board game and a twenty-foot-tall, animated T-Rex. The creature's head, elbows, wrists and tail moved, its jaws opened and closed, and it roared quite terribly and convincingly.

The girls wanted to see everything at once, and there was much to see. Every imaginable toy occupied the huge, flagship store. The hour turned into an hour and a half before Alice rounded up her group and they left. They decided to take a bus down Fifth Avenue on their way to the Empire State Building. As they walked east on Forty-second Street toward Fifth Avenue, Nellie confided to Alice that she hadn't had so much fun shopping since she was a child. Her enthusiasm tickled Alice.

When they reached Fifth, they came to Bryant Park where they bought hot dogs for lunch and found a place to sit. The girls dived into their hot dogs. Alice started to take a bite, then noticed that Nellie was about to spill hers in her lap.

"Nellie, your mustard is going to drip."

"Oh." She put a napkin beneath the hot dog. "Thanks."

Nellie took a bite but paid scant attention to what she was doing. She was too busy peering from side to side, trying not to look obvious.

Alice watched her expression go from wary to puzzled to astonished. She turned and looked at Alice.

"Do you know what all those people are doing?"

Alice looked around. She saw people on benches, chairs, the grass, anywhere they could find to sit, working on portable laptop computers while they ate their lunches in the sunshine. "What a shame that they have to work during their lunch hour, but at least they can bring their portable computers outdoors, so they can get some fresh air."

"I wonder if they're all working," Nellie said. "Most seem to be logged on to the Internet."

Alice looked around, thinking Nellie must be imagining things. "Without telephone lines?"

Nellie grinned. "Amazing, isn't it? Wireless Internet. We don't have it in Acorn Hill, but it's available in most cities." She shook her head in wonder. "It seems this entire park is set up for wireless Internet connections. Wow!"

Alice chuckled. "I've seen a lot of things in my time, but this is like stepping into the Twilight Zone. At least it looks harmless."

At lunchtime, Jane called Fred's Hardware and learned that the Humberts had gone home for lunch. She wrapped a tea towel around apricot scones fresh out of the oven, put them in a basket and hurried out the back door. As she power-walked to the Humberts' house, her ponytail flipped back and forth and her dangling silver-and-turquoise earrings tapped against her neck with each step. She was breathing hard as she knocked on their kitchen door.

Fred opened the door. "Jane? This is a surprise. What brings you here?"

"I must talk to you and Vera. Could I . . . is this a bad time?"

"Not at all. Come in." He held the door open and stood back. "Vera, we have company," he called over his shoulder.

"Who? Jane? How lovely. Come in. Have a cup of tea with us," Vera said, smiling graciously.

"I brought you some fresh scones." She handed the basket to Vera.

Vera opened the tea towel and sniffed the sweet aroma. "Yum. Thank you, Jane. Fred, would you like one?"

"Sure would. I was just getting ready to leave, but I can take a few more minutes."

Vera offered Jane a chair, poured a cup of tea for her, set the scones on the table and sat down herself. "It's nice to see you."

Fred downed his scone in three bites and took another.

Jane shifted in her chair. "I must talk to you both. I don't know where to start."

Vera and Fred gave her their full attention. That made Jane even more uncomfortable.

"You know that I went to that hardware store in Potterston to talk to the manager," Jane began. "I should think before I leap, but I saw a flyer from that store and I wanted to do something to keep them from hurting your business."

Vera nodded. "We heard about it. Florence was quite taken by your enthusiasm."

Jane sighed. "From what I hear, she told everyone in town about it. Well, I went to the store."

"What happened?" Fred asked.

"I met the manager and talked to him."

"I bet he was impressed with your concern." Fred chuckled at his own sarcasm.

"Actually, he was very nice. He listened, and of course, he can't do anything about the company's advertising policy, but he said the management had done a lot of market studies before the Potterston store was approved. He said that the results of those studies showed that there's plenty of business for both of you. I don't know about that, but I sure hope he's right."

Fred shrugged. "They put a crunch on my sales for a bit, but it looks like the rental business will help a lot." Fred grinned. "Then we have friends who put on bake sales."

"I'm afraid that you may feel I haven't been a very loyal friend to you."

"Whatever do you mean?" Vera asked. "We're touched and grateful that you tried on our behalf, aren't we, Fred?"

"Yes, indeed. I wish I had more friends like you."

Jane sighed. "No, you don't."

"Why not?" Vera asked.

"I'm afraid I went out with the enemy. Well, he isn't really the enemy. I . . . *uh* . . . had dinner with Todd Loughlin, the manager of the Do-It-Yourself Warehouse."

Vera looked stunned. "*He* is your new gentleman friend?" Vera asked. Her wide-eyed, open-mouthed stare made Jane want to disappear.

"The manager of the Do-It-Yourself Warehouse is a friend of yours?" Fred asked uncertainly.

Jane leaned on the table with her elbows and cradled her head in her hands for a moment. How could she explain what she didn't understand herself? She looked up at Fred and Vera. "Not exactly."

"Then what, exactly?" Vera asked, her voice a shade cooler.

"I went to the store to complain about their advertisements being delivered to Acorn Hill. Before I was able to talk to him, I saw him donate materials to a youth center in Potterston and offer to help them, like you do so often, Fred. When I told him his store was having a negative effect on small local businesses, he was genuinely concerned, although there's nothing he could do about it. We began talking. He moved here from the city and he loves living in a small town.

I told him I was from Acorn Hill. He bought an old place between here and Potterston, and he wants to restore the garden and add to it."

"*Ahhh*. Now I understand," Fred said.

"Well I don't," Vera said.

"I am so sorry. I know it looks like I was disloyal. I wouldn't hurt you for anything in the world."

"Of course not," Fred said. "And I can see how you got involved, Jane. You're one of Acorn Hill's best gardeners. This man is lucky to have met you. He can learn a lot about local gardening from you. And you haven't done anything wrong. Potterston was due for a large hardware store. We'll do fine, won't we Vera?"

"Certainly. And I'm sure your new friend is very nice. You have every right to see whomever you wish, Jane, so don't give it another thought." Vera smiled, but her generosity seemed a little strained, and Jane couldn't blame her.

"After I introduced him to Craig, I didn't intend to see him again, but one thing led to another, and . . . well, we've been out several times."

"Everyone in town knows you have a new beau," Vera said. "You know nothing stays secret in Acorn Hill." Then her smile softened. "I'm glad you let us know about him."

"I really did try to tell you before, but it was never the right time. Your friendship means a lot to me, and I didn't want you to think that I'd betrayed you."

"We know that, Jane, and we don't think anything of the kind." Fred said.

Jane stood. "Thank you both for being so understanding. I still want to help you. I'll take flyers door to door if that would help. Anything."

Fred stood and smiled. "Thanks, Jane. And now I'd better get back to the store. Thanks for the scones. They're great." Fred kissed Vera good-bye and left.

As the door shut, Jane turned to Vera. "I'm so sorry about this. I know how it looks."

"No, no. You just startled me for a moment. I know you didn't set out to become friends with this man. What did you say his name is?"

"Todd. Todd Loughlin."

"That's a nice name. You know, God has an interesting way of putting people in our paths. And the Lord knows you have a special compassion for people, Jane. It seems He has put you in an awkward position this time, but I'm sure God has a purpose. Everything'll work out just fine."

Chapter Twenty

A s Alice, Nellie and the ANGELs got off the bus on Fifth Avenue near the Empire State Building, the girls gathered around Alice. She took out her guidebook and explained, "We will be going up to the observation deck on the eighty-sixth floor. There is an inner, glass-enclosed room, and an outside walkway around the building, so you can really see the sights. The Empire State Building was finished in 1931 and is the oldest of the world's tallest skyscrapers."

Nellie had a printout from the Internet and picked up where Alice left off. "With one hundred and three floors, the Empire State Building is the ninth tallest skyscraper in the world at 1,454 feet tall."

"Way cool," Jenny said.

Alice noticed Kate Waller lean against the building behind them. She looked pale. Alice moved to stand next to her.

"Are you all right, Kate?"

She looked up, then quickly looked down. "Yes, Miss Howard. I felt a little dizzy for a minute, but I'm fine now." She looked down at the sidewalk.

Alice took a small bottle of water out of her tote bag. "Take a little drink. You may be dehydrated. Sometimes that happens when you travel."

Kate took a drink, then started to hand it back.

"Keep it in your pack, in case you need it again." Alice turned to the girls. "This will be our last stop today before we have dinner and return to the hotel."

"Stay together, girls," Nellie said.

They entered the building and took their places in line. Finally, they reached the observation-deck elevators. Nellie made sure they all got on the same car.

As they stepped out of the car and went to look at the view, Alice realized all the girls hadn't come forward. She looked back. Kate and Jenny were standing by the elevator. Nellie stood watching them. They were her team to chaperone. Alice saw that the other girls were captivated by the amazing panorama, so she went back to Nellie.

"Is something wrong?"

"Kate's afraid of heights. That's why she chose not to ride the Ferris wheel. I feel so bad. I had to quote all those figures about the height of the building. Poor kid."

Alice looked at Kate. Her face looked white. Her eyes were closed as she leaned against the wall. Alice started to go to her, but Nellie stopped her.

"Wait. Jenny is talking to her. If she wants to go back down, I'll go with her and wait for everyone."

Jenny took Kate's hand. After a moment, Kate pushed away from the wall and hesitantly walked forward with Jenny. A wall topped by a safety grate surrounded the observation deck, but still the sight was awesome and terrible to someone who feared heights. Clinging tightly to Jenny's hand, her feet planted firmly and her stance stiff, Kate reached out her free hand and tentatively touched the wall. She looked out for a long time. Alice and Nellie approached the girls.

"Are you all right, Kate?" Alice asked in a soft, gentle voice.

The girl turned to look at Alice and Nellie. There were tears in her eyes, but the radiance on her face stunned Alice.

"I did it, Miss Howard. I didn't think I could. I was so scared, I almost chickened out, but Jenny helped me. She told me she wouldn't let me fall." She turned and smiled at her friend, and Alice knew a deep bond had just formed between the two girls. Alice had noticed Jenny's compassion before. God had given Jenny a special gift of insight and gentleness to encourage others.

Kate turned to look out again. "I feel like I can see the whole world."

Nellie laughed. "Pretty close. It's so clear today, I bet that we can see eighty miles. That's the direction toward Pennsylvania. Over on that side"—she pointed—"is Connecticut."

"Wow. Wait till I tell my dad. He won't believe me." She looked at Jenny, Alice and Nellie. "Will you vouch for me?"

"You bet," Jenny said.

"I'll do you one better. I'll take a picture of you." Nellie took out her camera and backed up a few feet. "Look at me and smile." She clicked the camera. "Now when you get home, you can look at this picture and remember how brave you were."

"I'm not brave, Miss Carter. I'm still scared. My legs are shaking and I have a knot in my stomach."

"Well, I feel that way when we are walking on the sidewalk," Nellie said. "Aren't we something?"

"Really? I didn't know you were afraid of anything. You seem so . . . in control."

"Don't tell anybody. It's all a ruse." Nellie smiled. "Silly, isn't it?"

"No," Jenny said. "I'm scared of bugs. Everyone is afraid of something. I try to remember that verse you told us, Miss Howard. 'Perfect love casts out fear.' So when I'm afraid, I sing 'Jesus Loves Me,' because I know God is love."

"Very wise, Jenny. I will remember that next time I feel afraid." Alice said.

Jenny and Kate looked at Alice as if they couldn't believe she would ever fear anything. Alice just smiled.

"Why don't you girls make your way around to the other side, so you can see the full view. We'll stay a few more minutes, then we'll go down and have some dinner."

"Okay, Miss Howard. Thanks," Kate said.

"I'll stay with the girls," Alice told Nellie. "Go ahead and take some photos."

"Thanks." Nellie went along the promenade, aiming her camera at the tall buildings hundreds of feet below.

Louise had spread the best white linen tablecloth on the dining-room table and was setting out twelve place settings of their mother's Wedgwood china when Ethel came to the inn to decide on the seating for dinner. Jane had arranged two low baskets of fresh flowers, one of which was placed at each end of the table.

"This will do nicely," Ethel said.

"Your place cards are lovely," Louise said as Ethel put a small, formal card with gold borders and a neatly lettered name above each plate.

"I want to make sure everything is perfect," she said. "You girls did a poor job of arranging the seating last Sunday. I couldn't even converse with Jane's young man."

Louise suppressed a smile.

"Lloyd will sit at the head of the table, and you may sit at the foot," Ethel said. "I'll place Francine in the center of this side." She set a card above the middle plate, with cards for Rev. Thompson on one side and Nia Komonos on the other.

"The Simpsons will sit across the table, with Carlene next to Lloyd," she said as she walked around the table to place their name cards. She stood back and studied the table. "No, that's not right."

Louise watched Ethel scurry around the table as if she were playing musical chairs. Louise almost laughed, then sobered. This wasn't humorous. Of course, Ethel wanted everything just right for Francine.

"Viola can sit next to Florence. Yes, I believe that'll do. I'll sit between Lloyd and Rev. Thompson, and Carlene may sit next to Nia. Now, who's missing?"

"You haven't placed Jane or Sylvia."

"Oh, of course. Jane. I have their cards here somewhere." Ethel fished into her deep pocket and pulled two more place cards. "Jane should sit next to you on the side of the table nearest the kitchen. That way you both can serve. Since Sylvia and Jane are such good friends, Sylvia may sit next to her, so she can help. Now, is that everyone?" She walked around the table, checking place cards.

"Were the Leys unable to come? They've known Francine for many years."

"I didn't invite them." Ethel rung her hands together. "I do hope they won't be offended. I couldn't invite everyone, you know. I did invite the Holzmanns, but they had a previous engagement. I want Francine to feel comfortable with people who share her interests and lifestyle."

Louise raised one eyebrow, but Ethel, intent on making her point, didn't notice. "Not that anyone in Acorn Hill moves in the society that Francine enjoys," she continued. "However, Rev. Thompson and Nia Komonos are educated and conversant with metropolitan society, and Florence and Ronald are prominent in the community. Of course, Lloyd is a leading political figure, and the others are good conversationalists."

Ethel stopped and smiled smugly. "I believe I've gathered the cream of Acorn Hill society."

Louise shook her head at Ethel's reasoning. Louise loved that most people in Acorn Hill didn't value some residents above others. *Cream of society, indeed.* "If you'd like to include anyone else, Jane and I could eat in the kitchen," Louise couldn't resist saying.

"Oh no," Ethel replied, not getting Louise's humor. "You're family. Besides, you're an accomplished classical musician, and Jane has achieved some success in the culinary field."

Well, thank you for that recognition, Louise thought.

"If you can handle the preparations, I'll go change for dinner," Ethel said.

"Don't worry," Louise assured her aunt. "Jane and I have everything in hand. It's just half past five. Come back with Francine at six thirty. We will serve at six forty-five. That'll allow time for introductions and appetizers."

"Excellent." Ethel sailed toward the kitchen door, and Louise followed, just in case Jane needed reinforcements.

"Don't stop your preparations," she told Jane. "I just want to make sure you have dinner under control."

Jane looked up and smiled. "Good evening, Auntie. Everything's right on schedule. Would you like to sample an hors d'oeuvre?" Jane offered a tray of delectable tidbits that she'd been preparing.

Ethel popped a bite-size bruschetta topped with cream cheese, prosciutto and melon into her mouth. "Very good." She licked her fingers delicately and picked up a bacon-wrapped scallop and popped it into her mouth. "Lovely."

"I also have little quiches and pot-stickers."

"Pot what?" Ethel's eyes widened and she wrinkled her nose. "That sounds awful."

Jane laughed. "You'll be pleasantly surprised," she said.

"Aunt Ethel, you should be getting home. Francine will wonder where you've gone, and you still must get ready."

Ethel looked at her watch. "Oh dear. You're right. I must run. I trust you'll make sure everything is perfect?" she said, looking from Jane to Louise and back.

"Absolutely. Now run along."

Louise finally coaxed Ethel out the door and shut it behind her. She leaned back against the door as if to bar Ethel from returning. *"Phew."* She shook her head. "Aunt Ethel is turning this into a big production. She seems determined to impress Francine. She made quite a business of arranging the seating. You and I are at the end nearest the kitchen so we can serve her guests."

Jane grinned. "Well, that's convenient, since I let all the hired help have the day off." She laughed, and Louise joined her.

"You're so calm and tolerant. I must confess, Aunt Ethel's motives behind her guest list bother me. While I like and admire everyone on the list, she neglected to invite people who have known Francine for years. Aunt Ethel thinks that they don't measure up to Francine's standards. I don't believe our cousin's so particular, and I need a dose of your good disposition."

"I keep reminding myself that Aunt Ethel's doing her best to please Francine, and we'll have a delightful time with this wonderful group of our friends."

"Well said. And right now I'll finish setting the table and leave you to finish the dinner."

Louise began humming part of a symphony as she left the kitchen.

When the guests arrived, Jane put the bite-size hot quiches on the tray of appetizers and carried it into the living room where everyone had gathered. Ethel had Francine by the arm, leading her from one person to another, introducing her to those she didn't know. Jane walked up to Sylvia Songer and Viola Reed, who were discussing their marketing plans for the Fourth of July holiday.

"Hors d'oeuvre?" Jane asked, holding the tray in front of them.

"Those look delicious," Viola said, taking one. "In fact,

everything looks wonderful, and Ethel positively sparkles tonight."

"Yes, she does," Sylvia said, "but poor Francine looks a bit subdued. I hope she doesn't feel intimidated by all these new faces. She knows a few of us. Lloyd and, of course, you and Louise and me. You've met her before, haven't you, Viola?"

"No. I don't know what I was doing last time she visited, but I missed her. She must know Carlene and Florence and Ronald. Perhaps you should have made name tags for us, Jane, so she wouldn't get confused."

Jane laughed. Then she realized Viola was serious. "I'm sure my cousin can hold her own. She's quite active in charitable circles in Minneapolis, and she and her husband entertain a lot. Perhaps she's tired rather than subdued."

Just then, Ethel approached them, Francine in tow.

"Hello, ladies. Have you all met my daughter?"

"Hi, Cousin. You look lovely tonight," Jane said. "Would you like an hors d'oeuvre?"

"Thank you, Jane. I'd love one," Francine said. She made her selection, then she greeted Sylvia and turned to Viola. "I don't believe we've met."

"This is Viola Reed, our bookstore owner," Ethel said, introducing the two. "She carries classical literature," Ethel added, as if that were the only type of book she read, whereas Ethel generally dismissed what she called "musty old tomes" in favor of current romance novels. "Viola started a cat-rescue center here in Acorn Hill." To Viola, she said, "Francine is involved in many charities, so you have something in common."

"Welcome to Acorn Hill, Francine," Viola said. "I'm delighted to meet you."

Florence bustled over to greet Francine. Her husband, Ronald, followed and helped himself to the hors d'oeuvres, giving Jane a nod and muttering, "Thanks."

"It's lovely to see you again," Florence said, opening her arms wide and giving Francine a dramatic embrace. Florence was wearing a green designer wrap dress that was a bit too snug, and a dazzling array of gold jewelry.

Francine seemed taken aback.

"I need to circulate with these," Jane said. "I hope we get a chance to talk later, Francine, but I'll leave you to chat."

"Do you need help?" Sylvia offered. She reached out and took the tray from Jane. "I can pass these. I'm sure you have more to do in the kitchen."

Jane glanced at her watch. "Thanks. There are just a few minutes until dinner. I could use the time." She shared a smile with Sylvia before she left the room.

Louise was coming out of the kitchen with a tray of water-filled glasses as Jane went in.

"How are you coming?" she asked Jane.

"Good. Everything is ready. I just need to serve it."

Louise nodded. "Good. Ethel will be ushering everyone to the table in a couple of minutes. Hardly time for everyone to have appetizers. You'd think this was her dinner party."

Jane smiled. "I suppose it is. We're just catering it. I'll get the salad course ready."

"Good idea. I'll be back in a moment to help carry things out."

Jane arranged assorted baby greens from her garden on iced salad plates. On top of the greens, she arranged diced oranges, thinly sliced red onion, slivered toasted almonds and blue-cheese crumbles. She sprinkled the salads with balsamic vinaigrette, then tucked a crisp, homemade sesame cracker into each one and carried the filled plates on a tray to the dining room. Louise brought out a second tray of salads, and they were ready to serve when Ethel led everyone to the table and seated them.

Ethel invited Jane and Louise to sit with them while

Rev. Thompson said a blessing. When the blessing was finished, she told them that they could now get the rest of the meal. At that instruction, Louise raised one eyebrow. Francine's eyes widened. Jane coughed into her napkin, which drew her cousin's attention. Jane winked at her, and Francine drew a deep breath, then smiled back. Jane thought her smile was strained, but for the moment, the tension had eased.

Chapter Twenty-One

"What is going on between Aunt Ethel and Francine?" Jane asked as she and Louise put hot grilled asparagus bundles, rice pilaf and ginger-peach chicken on each plate.

"I don't know. Aunt Ethel appears to be a little too effervescent, and Francine seems ready to boil over. I'm afraid the visit isn't going as either of them had hoped."

"I'm afraid you're right." Jane frowned. "I wonder if there's something we can do to help."

"We need Alice. She can bring calm to any situation. She'd probably be glad she isn't here to run interference, though. I hope she and the girls are having a good time."

Jane and Louise each carried two plates to the table, then went back for more. As they arrived with the last plates and sat down, Ethel said, "Tell Rev. Thompson about the residence that you started for families of cancer patients, Francine. Rev. Thompson visits the Potterston Hospital every week as part of his ministry."

"Really, Mother, I don't think anyone is interested."

"Francine practically built it single-handedly," Ethel continued.

Francine laughed, although her expression held no

amusement. "Hardly. I helped. That's all." She gave her mother a narrow-eyed look.

Rev. Thompson smiled gently at Francine. "I'd love to hear about this home."

Francine shrugged and took a deep breath. "We have a research center that's making remarkable advances in treating cancer. A family who came for treatment for their daughter began attending our church. After a few weeks, we learned that they were living in a shabby hotel and cooking on a single burner in their room. One of our families invited them to stay in their guesthouse. We learned of other families who needed housing, so several churches joined together to purchase a big old home near the medical center. We remodeled it to create small apartments where families can stay during treatment."

"What a wonderful ministry," Rev. Thompson said. "I'm sure the Lord has blessed your efforts."

Ethel had a satisfied smile on her face. Francine turned the conversation. "I love all the changes you've made to the inn," she said to Jane and Louise. "I hope I can get a peek at all the rooms before I leave."

"I'm sure we can arrange that," Louise said. "Let us know when you have a little free time."

Francine pursed her lips. "Mother has scheduled every minute, but I'll find a way to get out of something."

"Did you address me?" Ethel asked.

"No, Mother," Francine answered. She turned to Nia Komonos on her other side. "How do you like living in Acorn Hill?"

"Very much. Everyone is so friendly and so supportive. Your mother tells me you are part of the Friends of the Library. Speaking on behalf of all librarians, we appreciate all you do to promote libraries and reading."

Francine shook her head. "I'm a member, but not very

active. I give them my used books and make a donation every year, so I hardly count myself as a supporter."

"Oh no. Every contribution helps. What do you like to read?"

"Just about everything. My mother made sure we visited the library every week." She glanced at her mother. "For that, I am thankful. Are you familiar with Elizabeth Goudge? She is a favorite of mine, but her books are hard to find."

"I love her writing. We have a few of her works in the library. I try to keep a stock of out-of-print books. Come by and I'll show you what I have. Perhaps there's something you haven't read."

"Wonderful, although I don't know if I'll have time to do any reading. But I believe a presentation at the library is on Mother's list of activities."

"Excellent. Come early and I'll show you what we have."

"I have several books by that author," Viola said. "Are you a collector?"

"Only of a few favorite authors," Francine said. "I can't say that I have an extensive library, but I do love to find a treasure."

"Well, I specialize in treasures," Viola said. "Stop in and see what I have."

"I believe you are on Mother's list too."

"What list would that be?"

"Scheduled activities. You are giving a reading of Emily Dickinson's poems, I believe."

Viola's eyes widened. "Your mother's coming to that? She seldom attends my readings."

"Really?" Francine glanced at her mother, who was in conversation with Lloyd and Rev. Thompson, then gave Viola a smile. "I'll make a point to stop by and see your books."

∽

"I have two things on the agenda for today," Alice said as the group ate cereal and muffins in her room Wednesday morning. She spread a map of Manhattan on her bed.

"This afternoon, we will attend the theater. This morning, I thought we could visit Pier Seventeen and the South Street Seaport."

After Alice told them a bit about the seaport, the girls cleaned up their breakfast dishes and collected their packs. Alice reminded everyone to take a light sweater, as it might be cool by the water. She wore the geranium-colored outfit that she bought at Nellie's and put the jacket in her tote bag.

They rode the subway to the South Street Seaport and walked out to the pier. From the open deck at the end, the girls looked out at the long, high expanse of the Brooklyn Bridge stretching across the East River to Brooklyn.

"Wow. Can we go across it?" Briana asked.

"It's really tall," Linda said, shading her eyes as she looked at the bridge that towered above the river. She turned to Alice. "Is that Brooklyn?" she asked, pointing across the river.

Alice smiled at the wide-eyed awe on all the girls' faces. "Yes. And it is a long way across. I'm afraid that we don't have time to cross it."

Briana and Sarah voiced disappointment. "What if we hurry through the seaport?" Sarah asked.

"We can't possibly see all the sights of New York City in one week," Nellie said. "I doubt if people who've lived here all their lives have seen everything. That's why Miss Howard prepared an itinerary . . . so we can see some of the most interesting sights. I know I want to visit again."

"Me too!" six young voices echoed.

Alice applauded Nellie's insight and thoughtful response. "Miss Carter is right. There's so much to see here, we may

run out of time as it is. Right now, let's go look at those beautiful old ships at the seaport."

Kate let out a deep breath and looked relieved. Jenny
briefly squeezed Kate's hand, and they walked together to the
seaport pier.

Nellie gave Alice a smile brimming with affection. The
girls had accepted Nellie wholeheartedly, which pleased
Alice. If she ever decided that she had to retire from leading
the ANGELs—though Alice certainly didn't see that in
the near future—Nellie would be a good choice for her
successor. Perhaps Nellie could become an assistant in the
meantime.

Alice noticed that Nellie seemed more relaxed today. She
still hung on to her purse, but she looked around at the sights
more than at the people around them. She gave due attention
to her responsibilities, trailing after the girls and keeping
them always in sight; however, she smiled more and truly
seemed to be enjoying herself.

Perhaps it was the old-time museum atmosphere.
Walking through the seaport was a journey back to the days
of tall-masted ships and street vendors. The beautifully
restored wooden ships, the Nineteenth Century Print Shop,
the boat-building shop and the maritime crafts center, and
even the street mime, juggler and fiddler, added to the old-
world atmosphere. Alice found her mind wandering too. The
modern, bustling city was only yards away, yet seemed non-
existent for those few hours.

Then they left the old ships and entered Pier Seventeen.
Stepping into the three-story glass-and-steel building,
they made a quick one-hundred-year transition forward.
Modern shops and restaurants abounded. The girls were
hungry and decided to eat lunch in a hamburger restaurant.
Alice was happy to sit down. Nellie plopped down beside
her.

"Tell me we don't have time to walk the bridge today. I've had enough walking this morning to last all day."

Alice laughed. "I was just thinking the same thing. Having fun is hard work."

Nellie laughed out loud, and the girls all wanted to know the joke.

"Let's just say my feet feel like they've run a marathon," Alice said.

The girls all laughed and agreed that they'd had their fill of walking for the day. By the time they ate lunch, they barely had time to take the subway back to the hotel and get ready for the show.

Jane jogged longer than usual, and as a result, her calves ached and she had a stitch in her side. She walked the last few steps to the driveway of Grace Chapel Inn bent over, breathing hard.

Jane thanked the Lord for Louise. Her sister had shooed her off on her much-needed run, promising to serve the breakfast menu that Jane had prepared: assorted rolls, muffins, fresh-fruit parfaits, granola and yogurt, hot ham-and-egg casserole, juices and coffee.

Jane mopped at her forehead with a handkerchief from the pocket of her shorts. A door slammed and she saw her cousin walking toward her, looking irritated.

"Hi, Francine."

"Hi, Jane. If I'd known you were going jogging, I'd have joined you."

"I'll let you know next time I go."

"It's been a while since I've jogged, but I must get out of the house."

"Starting to feel cooped up?"

"Stifled is more like it. Mother's driving me nuts. I don't

know how you and Louise and Alice put up with her. She's a bossy busybody. Always has been, but I'd hoped she'd mellowed. I should've known better. She'll never change. In fact, I believe she's worse. Gloria warned me."

"Gloria?"

"Oh, a friend. She just went through this with her mother. She said all of her mother's irritating traits became more pronounced as she got older. I can see what she meant. *Argh*. I shouldn't have come."

"Your mother's a bit opinionated, but . . ."

"Opinionated? That's the understatement of the year. And stubborn. I can't even talk to her."

Two ladies passed the inn on their morning walk. They waved and said hi. Jane waved back. To Francine, she said, "Come on inside where we can talk. There's fresh coffee and rolls. Have you had breakfast?"

"No. Mother and I had words, and I stomped out."

Louise was cleaning up in the kitchen. "Good morning, Francine. Would you two like some coffee and rolls?"

"If you'll give Francine something, I'll run upstairs to shower and change. Won't take me but a few minutes." Jane said as she headed out of the kitchen.

"Thanks, Louise. We didn't get much chance to talk last night." Louise poured a cup for Francine and one for herself and set a plate of breakfast rolls in front of Francine.

"You're out early this morning," Louise said. "How did you manage to sneak away from your mother?"

Francine grimaced. "Don't get me started."

"Uh-oh. I gather the visit isn't going as well as you'd hoped."

"That's putting it mildly. I refuse to go to another one of mother's meetings so she can show me how important and popular she is. You'd think she's the only person in Acorn Hill who can do anything."

"From a mother's perspective, I have a hunch she wants everyone in Acorn Hill to see what a wonderful daughter she has. Your mother's very proud of you."

"I wish that were the case."

"What makes you think it isn't?"

"If she were truly proud of me, she'd treat me like an adult. Instead, she acts as if I don't have any brains or common sense. She tells me what to do, how to do it and when. She has a schedule of all the things we have to do, and there's no flexibility. And if I try to talk to her, she won't listen. She just changes the subject. I told Jane I don't know how you put up with her. You must be saints."

"I'll admit your mother can be strong-minded, but we're certainly not saints." Louise wasn't certain she understood, but she had a sudden image of herself and Cynthia. Did she treat her grown-up daughter like a child? Cynthia hadn't complained, but that didn't mean she didn't feel overmothered from time to time. Louise knew she wanted to protect her daughter, to be the advisor she turned to, to help her avoid the ruts in life and make her pathway smooth. All mothers felt that way. Didn't they?

"I worry about Mother," Francine confided.

"Really? Why?"

"She gets in such a dither over inconsequential things, and she's so impulsive. She's getting to an age when things can happen. She could fall and break a hip or have a heart attack. Or someone could come along and take advantage of her. Why, she has gotten three phone solicitations since I've been here. People her age are vulnerable to fraud, you know. I've watched my friends go through problems with their aging parents. I know Mother has you nearby, but my brothers and I don't expect you all to take care of her. Since my brothers don't want to face that she's aging, the responsibility falls on me, but I'm so far away. I'd thought about asking her to move in with Geoffrey and me. Now that the boys are grown, I have extra room. After two days with her, however, I believe living together would be impossible."

"Your mother is blessed that she has a daughter who cares so much about her well-being. I understand your concern, but she's in good health."

"Yes, her health is good so far, but that can change in an instant. I saw it happen to my friend's mother. She recently had a stroke, and my friend's going through a terrible time trying to take care of her."

Louise reached out and put her hand over Francine's hand. "Anything could happen to any of us. Jesus told us not to worry about what tomorrow might bring. Today has enough cares of its own. Your mother has made her home here. She has many friends and responsibilities. As long as she's able to help people, she has purpose, and that's more important than being comfortable, believe me. Eliot's planning and preparations left me comfortable, but after he died, I had no purpose. Coming home to Acorn Hill and my sisters has given me new purpose and happiness."

Francine sighed. "I wish Mother and I could talk like this."

"Could we pray about that?"

Francine nodded. The tears in her eyes revealed her emotions before she bowed her head.

Louise took both of Francine's hands. "Heavenly Father, You are the great Healer and Peacemaker. You created families and You want us to have loving, understanding relationships. Please help Francine and her mother talk and find a deeper relationship while Francine is here visiting. Give them patience and understanding. Ease their fears about the future and let them see that You are here with them. In Jesus' name. Amen."

Francine looked up. "Thank you, Louise. I'd forgotten how wonderful it is to share with my cousins." She smiled.

"My husband's a dear, but you know how men are. He's so logical and practical. He wants to fix things, but he doesn't have a lot of tolerance for emotions." Francine glanced at her watch, then stood. "It's later than I realized. I was hoping to visit with Jane, but I'd better go back before Mother gets worried. Please tell Jane that I'll see her later."

As the kitchen door shut, the door from the dining room opened, and Jane entered the kitchen.

"Beautifully handled. You gave her a lot to think about."

"How long were you outside the door?" Louise asked.

"Long enough to hear some very good advice. I hope Francine learns from it."

Louise laughed. "Well, I know I learned something," Louise said.

"And what's that?"

"To let Cynthia be an adult and to listen when she tries to talk to me."

Jane grinned. "That goes for younger sisters too."

"You have my attention."

"I'll just keep an 'attention credit' for later, when I need it."

Louise looked at the kitchen clock. "It's almost time for me to listen to Jason Ransom. He'll be here for his piano lesson in ten minutes."

Jane knew that the ten-year-old pianist required lots of patient correction. "Your ears are getting a workout today," Jane said, laughing.

Louise agreed with a sigh and a smile.

Chapter Twenty-Two

J ason Ransom's fingers raced through his piano piece. He hit the final note rather hard and looked up at Louise.

"You played that well. When it says 'militaristic,' though, it does not mean a race to the finish. It means a marching tempo with crisp notes. More precise. The ending's like a sergeant yelling, 'Attention!' not firing a cannon. I sense that you're in a hurry."

"I have a game today." He was dressed in his Little League uniform.

"Yes. That's why we switched your lesson to morning. I believe you have an hour before your game begins."

Jason looked alarmed. Louise smiled. "Because your time's up for today, we'll begin your next lesson with this piece. Work on the tempo and accents."

Jason grabbed his music book and got up from the bench. "Thanks, Mrs. Smith."

"Oh, Jason," Louise called as he ran for the front door.

He stopped and turned, frowning. "Yes, ma'am?"

"Have a good game."

A smile lit his face. "Yes, ma'am."

The front door slammed shut. Shaking her head, Louise put away her lesson material and went to the kitchen. Jane was unloading the dishwasher.

Jane glanced up. "You look like you need a cup of tea. I just made a fresh pot. Come sit down. I'll have a cup with you before I head to the garden."

"Wonderful." Louise sat at the table while Jane got out cups.

Jane suddenly laughed. "I automatically took out three cups. I miss Alice. I hope they're having a great time."

"I talked to her while you were jogging. She was in a hurry, so she didn't say much, but it sounds as if they are having a grand time. I miss her too. Interesting how close we have become after living apart for so many years. Francine noticed it too."

"Closer than sisters," Jane said. "Best friends. How fortunate we are. I hope Francine and Aunt Ethel can work out their differences."

"Speaking of Aunt Ethel," Louise said, responding to a familiar tap on the door. It opened and their aunt stepped into the kitchen.

"Hell-o," she said in a singsong voice, although her tone lacked its usual lilt.

"Good morning. Come in. Where's Francine?"

"She's reading a book. She went out this morning in a huff, came back, borrowed my library card and left again. She returned with two books, planted herself in a chair and she's been reading ever since. I don't think she knows that I left. I don't know why she wants to waste her time reading while she's visiting me."

"Vacations are for relaxing, Auntie. Perhaps she can't find time to relax at home. That's often the case, you know."

Ethel sighed. "She does keep a busy schedule. Too busy, if you ask me. I told her that too. She needs to slow down or she'll burn out. Stress is a killer, you know. Of course, Francine's young, but she needs to begin taking care of herself now."

"At least you two are on the same page," Jane said. "She is concerned about your health also."

"Fiddle-dee-dee. My health is excellent. And I told her that. She seems to think I'm ready for the grave."

Jane brought the third cup to the table. "This must be for you. Sit down and rest a bit." She poured tea into Ethel's cup.

"I might as well." Ethel sat down. "As long as Francine's nose is buried in that book, I don't have anything better to do."

Louise and Jane shared a concerned look. Jane stood and carried her cup to the sink. "I hear the spinach and rhubarb calling. I'll be back in a few minutes." She grabbed an empty basket and went outside.

"I hope I didn't interrupt anything," Ethel said.

"Not at all. My morning piano lesson just finished and I needed a break. I'm sorry your plans aren't working out, but I'm glad to have your company."

"I don't know what to do," Ethel said. "I put my normal schedule on hold so I could spend time with Francine. I lined up activities that would interest her, but here she is, reading a book. I don't understand her."

"Have you asked Francine what she wants to do?"

Ethel looked surprised. "Of course not. How could she know what's available? It's the duty of a hostess to entertain her guests."

"Entertaining is one thing. Imposing a schedule is quite another. You could make suggestions and let her choose the things that interest her. Perhaps she just wants to visit with you. That's why she came, after all."

"She came to tell me what to do. She starts talking about my health and my future as if I belong in a nursing home. I don't need my children running my life and planning my future. I can take care of myself."

"Of course, and I'm sure she can see that."

"I don't think she's paying attention. She has her mind made up."

Louise smiled gently. "Francine's a lot like her mother, isn't she?"

Ethel looked startled. "What do you mean by that?"

"You are both strong, independent women. You raised Francine to think for herself and to care about the welfare of those around her, just as you try to help others."

"Well, yes. She does a great deal of charity work. But she's so critical of me. I don't understand it. I've tried to please her. You know how hard I worked to prepare for her visit, so everything would be nice. When I make a suggestion, she snaps at me." Ethel dabbed at her eyes with a hankie. "I'm beginning to think my own daughter despises me. I don't know what to do. You and Cynthia have such a loving relationship. What am I doing wrong?"

"You know, sometimes we get so busy doing things that we just need to step back and take a few moments to breathe. From what you've just told me, it's clear that you and Francine love each other deeply."

"It isn't clear to me."

"Perhaps, because I'm an observer, I can see you both more objectively. You worked hard to prepare for Francine's visit, so naturally you want her approval."

"I just wanted to please her and make her comfortable."

"I heard her tell Sylvia that she loves the changes you made to the carriage house."

"She did?"

"Yes. You say Francine is concerned about your health. Didn't I hear you say you are concerned about her health?"

"Yes. She works too hard."

Louise chuckled. "I believe that runs in the family."

Ethel smiled. "I suppose you're right. She's a lot like me, isn't she?"

"Yes. Francine's a fine, lovely woman. You have every right to be proud of her."

Ethel beamed. Then her face fell. "That doesn't solve my problem. How do I make her see that?"

Louise said a quick prayer for guidance. Ethel rarely listened to the advice of others. Would she listen now?

"What if you were to turn the tables on her?"

Ethel looked puzzled. "Explain what you mean."

"Ask her to share her concerns with you."

"I don't want to hear about retirement villages and long-term-care planning."

"Do you know why she wants to discuss this right now?"

"I suppose she thinks I'm getting old."

"Or perhaps she has seen someone go through problems and she loves you so much, she wants to make sure you are prepared, for your sake."

Ethel's eyebrows rose. "I don't know. I really don't want to talk about it."

"Couldn't you listen and assure her that you'll think about it? Then you could move on to enjoy your time together."

"I don't see how that's possible, when she doesn't want to do anything."

Louise reached over and patted Ethel's hand. "When Cynthia comes to visit, I try to clear my calendar so we can spend time together. I can't avoid all of my obligations, but I can postpone or cancel most things. We're a little selfish with our time together, and we do whatever she wants to do. Sometimes she wants to rest and catch up on her reading or letter writing, and that's fine. At least we're together."

"Oh my. I've been telling Francine to rest, then I get upset when she takes my advice." Ethel grimaced. "No wonder she gets irritated with me. My poor daughter."

"Surprise her. Tear up your list of plans and ask her what she'd like to do. She might surprise you."

Ethel stared at Louise. "When did you get to be so wise?" She shook her head. "I keep thinking that you girls are still young, but time has played a trick on me."

Louise chuckled. "It's tricked us all, but we're very fortunate, you and I, to have such lovely daughters. I think I'll call Cynthia today and tell her so."

Ethel stood. "You're right. I'll do it," she said. Standing tall and taking a deep breath, she went out the back door like a woman on a mission. Ethel could be so dramatic. Louise hoped her advice wouldn't backfire. Francine might wonder at her mother's sudden change.

Alice stood in line in front of the New Amsterdam Theatre with great anticipation. Today they would see the stage version of *The Lion King*, but for Alice, the play was less important than the beautifully restored art nouveau theater. One of her favorite childhood memories was the summer her father had taken them to Chicago. As a special treat, they attended the theater to see Shakespeare's *A Midsummer Night's Dream*. She enjoyed the play, but she especially loved the wonderful classical frescoes on the walls, the crystal chandeliers and gilded archways, like the cathedrals in one of her father's art books.

As they walked through the lobby into the foyer, the girls oohed and ahhed over the marble walls and intricate carvings. The promenade brought to mind a fabulous Italian palace with curved gold ceilings. They made their way up a curved stairway to the balcony, where they had front-row seats.

"I thought this would be like going to the movies. I've never seen a theater like this before," Sarah said, and all the girls agreed.

"You are in for a special treat. This won't be anything like the movie."

"I was in a play at school," Briana said.

"Several of you have been in plays and have done wonderfully well. I think you'll appreciate this even more, because you know what it's like to perform in front of an audience."

"I don't think I've ever been in a more beautiful building," Nellie said. The lights dimmed, and the crowd settled down.

Once the play began, the girls were captivated. When the intermission came, they could hardly wait for the play to start again. The time whizzed by until the final curtain, and the girls jumped to their feet to join the standing ovation.

"That was incredible," Sarah said.

"I want to be an actress," Linda said.

"Me too," Ashley chimed in, and they all agreed that they loved the musical.

"It's so much better than the movie," Nellie said. "Such vitality and involvement that you just don't get from a film. I loved it."

Alice smiled at the enchantment in Nellie's eyes. All of the girls had the same dreamy looks. Alice had enjoyed the play and loved coming to the theater, but the real joy for her was seeing the delighted reactions of Nellie and the ANGELs.

The sidewalk was jammed with theatergoers and New Yorkers on their way home from work. Alice raised her umbrella. "Follow me, girls, and stay together."

As they began winding their way through the crowd, Alice counted at least a dozen umbrellas raised by tour guides leading their groups through the streets. She was glad Louise had given her a new, patterned umbrella for the girls to follow. She looked back, and all of the girls were close behind, with Nellie bringing up the rear. A crowd waited at the bus stop, so it took two buses before they could all get on. A young man in a T-shirt and baggy jeans gave up his seat so Alice could sit down, but the girls had to stand. At the next stop, a large group got on. The girls shuffled their packs, trying to make more room. A lady almost fell trying to get through the crowded aisle. Linda scooted in as far as she could, shoving her pack under the seat.

They stayed on the bus until Alice passed the word that they would get off at the next stop. She stood before the bus came to a stop. Linda stepped out into the aisle and pulled her pack out from under the seat. It caught. She tugged, and it came flying out, spilling contents all over the floor and nearby passengers. Alice leaned down to help pick up the contents. The other girls scrambled to help, too, and they stuffed everything back in and hurried to get off before the bus shut the doors. People were trying to get on as they got off.

After a struggle, they all made it off the bus, just as the doors shut and the bus pulled back into traffic.

"*Phew.* That was tight," Nellie said.

"Rush hour. I should have planned that more carefully," Alice said. "We could have stayed in the theater district for dinner, but I thought we'd have a better chance finding a table near the hotel."

They walked two blocks to a neighborhood café that served home-style cooking. Three of the girls ordered spaghetti and meatballs. Alice and Nellie ordered meatloaf and the rest of the girls ordered macaroni and cheese. The food was hot and tasty. They were discussing the play when Alice reached down to get her wallet out of her tote bag to pay for the meal. It wasn't next to her chair.

Unperturbed, she looked down, then under her chair, then under the table. No bag.

"Has anyone seen my tote bag?" she asked.

They all looked around them.

Nellie frowned. "When did you last have it?"

"On the bus. I distinctly remember holding it on my lap. I had it when I stood to leave."

"When Linda's bag spilled?"

"Yes." Realization dawned. Alice's eyes opened wide. "I must have put it down when I leaned over to pick up Linda's water bottle. Oh my. It must be on the bus."

"Oh no," Nellie said, greatly distressed.

"It's all my fault," Linda cried. "If I hadn't been so clumsy . . ."

Alice put an arm around Linda's shoulder. "The bus was

so crowded. It isn't your fault. I wasn't paying attention. Unfortunately, our cash and my credit card are in the tote."

"What about our tour tickets and train tickets?" Nellie asked.

"Our train tickets are at the hotel in my suitcase. Right now I'm more concerned with paying for our meal."

The girls all reached for their packs. The dismay on their faces made Alice feel terrible. They had worked hard to earn the money for this trip, and she had just left much of it on a bus. She shook her head. *Lord, how could I be so forgetful?*

"I'll pay for tonight's dinner," Nellie said. "You girls can put your money away."

"Thank you, Miss Carter," the girls each told her.

"Can we call the bus company?" Jenny suggested.

"They won't find it," Nellie said. "Someone has taken that bag and you'll be lucky if they don't charge up a fortune on your credit card."

"What are we going to do?" Sarah asked.

"We are going to say a prayer right now. That's what we'll do," Alice said.

Jenny reached out and took Kate's hand on one side of her and Sarah's on the other. One by one, the girls clasped hands until they reached Nellie and Alice and completed the circle. They all bowed their heads.

"Dearest Lord, we have had such a wonderful trip so far, and we thank You for watching over us and keeping us safe. Forgive me for being so forgetful, Lord, and for letting these girls down. Please, help us retrieve my bag. I know that might not be possible, Lord, but we trust You, and we know that You will work all things for our good, just as You promised us in Your Word. Please continue to watch over us and keep us safe. In Jesus' name. Amen."

Chapter Twenty-Three

With the loss of the tote bag, the magic of the theater faded, leaving behind a group of weary, dejected travelers.

"Cheer up, girls," Alice said. "This isn't such a tragedy. We claim to have faith. Let's act like it. The Lord will provide, and we will still have a great time here."

Nellie shot Alice a doubtful look. "At least we still have our tickets to get home," Nellie said. Her voice lacked enthusiasm, but she was trying to be upbeat. Alice gave Nellie an approving smile.

They walked to the hotel in silence. In the lobby, Alice said, "I don't have our room key."

"Whoever has your bag has our key," Nellie said anxiously.

"The hotel is securely locked after curfew. A security guard screens anyone coming in late, so we will be perfectly safe. I need to report the missing key to the management, though." Alice walked over to the reception desk. Nellie and the girls followed her.

"Miss Howard, I'm glad you stopped before you went to your room," the woman behind the desk said. "I have something that belongs to you."

"Really?" Alice's hopes rose.

"Yes. A young man came by with this." She reached down behind the desk and picked up the missing tote bag.

Nellie looked stunned. Alice smiled and said a soft, "Thank You, Lord." And the girls cheered.

"I can't believe it," Nellie said.

"Who is he? Did he leave his name?" Alice asked.

"No. He said he didn't need any thanks."

"More likely he didn't want you to trace him, because he took your money and credit card," Nellie muttered.

The receptionist shot a reproving glance at Nellie and went on with her story. "The young man told me one of your girls had a mishap on the bus with her backpack, and your bag got left behind in the confusion. He picked it up and got off at the next stop and went back to find you, but you were already gone. He was going to take it to the police station, but he was worried that you wouldn't know where to look for it, so he looked inside and found the hotel key. Then he brought it here." The receptionist smiled, as if personally proud of the young New Yorker. "He said you remind him of his grandmother, and he'd want someone to take care of her. And"—looking straight at Nellie—"he said to assure you nothing is missing."

"I'm sure it's all there. Thank you, Lord. And bless that young man. Now we can continue with all our plans."

"Amazing," Nellie said. She looked at Alice and shook her head. "Simply amazing."

When Alice, Nellie and the ANGELs boarded the train for Battery Park at the tip of Manhattan, New York was just gearing up for the day. The girls were still sleepy and dozed most of the way, but Nellie sat wide-eyed, looking around at all the passengers. The wariness in her gaze had been replaced by a new sparkle. By contrast, most of the other passengers snoozed, read or looked down, oblivious to those around them. Nellie looked over at Alice and smiled.

"I'm so excited about seeing the Statue of Liberty."

"I never tire of seeing it," Alice answered. "There is something inspiring about it that makes me more thankful for all my blessings. Most of the time, I think we forget what an amazing country we live in."

"Truly amazing. Acorn Hill is such a peaceful, close-knit community, I tend to forget how diverse America is. I guess I've been through culture shock leaving there."

Alice chuckled softly. "The city can be intimidating. But people are the same, deep down inside. Some envy our small town life, but others thrive on the fast pace and energy of the city."

Nellie laughed. "The pace here wears me out. Give me Acorn Hill any day, but I'm glad I came. I'm embarrassed about some of my misconceptions about the city."

The loudspeaker announced their destination station, so Alice and Nellie roused the girls and made sure everyone had her possessions, which were few today. Backpacks weren't allowed in the Statue of Liberty, so the girls carried their spending money in their small coin-purse necklaces that held their identification. Several of the girls had cameras and cell phones. Alice carried her tote bag with sunscreen, a few first-aid items, the girls' identifications and medical permission slips, guidebooks, camera and cell phone. She would lock her bag in a locker at the monument.

As they walked from their stop to Battery Park, Nellie suddenly said, "Look!" She pointed ahead. "There's Castle Clinton. I read in the guidebook that it was built in 1811 to defend against British attacks, but it never was used as a fort. In 1824 it became an entertainment center, and today they have concerts here."

"This is where we buy our tickets," Alice said as they walked inside the circular fortification. "Nellie, you and the girls can look around while I stand in line. Fortunately, we're early enough that the line isn't too long, so we should be able to catch the first boat."

"All right." Nellie got out her guidebook. As they moved away, she read, "'Dutch settlers landed here in 1623 and established New Amsterdam.'" She looked up. "That's also the name of the theater we attended last night. 'Then in 1855 the building became an immigration depot.'"

Alice had to chuckle. Nellie was so busy reading the guidebook, the girls had to lead her along. Nellie seemed to have forgotten to watch out for muggers and pickpockets.

On board the boat, the girls ran from side to side to see the views from the water. Nellie posed the girls as a group, then as teams, snapping their pictures against the background of New York's skyline. As the boat got close to the Statue of Liberty, a friendly tourist spent several minutes snapping pictures of the entire group with each of their cameras. The girls thanked him profusely, and Nellie took pictures of the man and his wife with their camera.

Before they disembarked, Alice gathered the group for instructions.

"I have reservations for the Observatory Tour. That includes a trip to the tenth floor. If anyone would rather not go up to the observatory, I'll stay with them and we can wait for the others at the base."

Alice expected Kate would want to stay at the base, but the girl surprised her.

"I want to go up to the observatory," she said. "I don't want to miss anything."

"Cool," Jenny said, giving Kate a high-five. "Come on. Let's go." Kate smiled proudly at Alice.

A park ranger led them up to the pedestal observatory, where they had a full circle view of New York Harbor, with New York City on one side and New Jersey on the other. The boat looked like a tiny toy on the water. More impressive, they got a close-up view of Lady Liberty.

Back downstairs, in the center of the pedestal base, the original torch was on display. The base also housed a museum, and the ranger told them the history of the statue and about the major renovation in the 1980s. The full-scale replica of Lady Liberty's toes really fascinated the girls. The height from the bottom of her sandal to the top of her foot measured almost as tall as Kate, who was the shortest of the ANGELs, but the toe configuration caught their attention. Their guide explained that the lady's toes showed a condition common in Roman and Greek statuary, an irregularity that actually occurred in about one in twenty people. The second toe was longer than the big toe, a condition called Morton's Toe. All the girls had to check their feet, but none had Morton's Toe.

Back on the boat, Nellie read to them from her guide-book as they crossed the harbor to Ellis Island. "'The first immigrant to arrive at Ellis Island was a fifteen-year-old girl from Ireland named Annie Moore, who came to join her parents in America.'"

"Maybe she's one of your ancestors, Ashley," Sarah said.

"Wow, can you imagine coming all that way by yourself?" Jenny said.

"On a ship like the ones we saw yesterday? No way," Linda said. "I'd stay in Ireland."

"Not me," Sarah said. "I bet it was exciting."

The girls soon realized that the voyages and the cramped conditions of the immigrants on the ships were far from exciting. They were more like frightening, miserable and cold.

They saw where immigrants first entered the baggage room to find their belongings, but the people had to leave their things there to begin the long, slow process of medical and legal examinations.

"Is that like going through customs with a passport?" Briana wanted to know.

"They didn't have passports in those days, and many of the immigrants had left their homes because of famine or oppression," Alice explained.

"'After the luggage room, the immigrants had to climb the stairs to the Great Hall,'" Nellie told them as she read from the guidebook. "'Doctors would stand at the top of the stairs and watch them to see if they had trouble climbing the stairs. If they had trouble, they got a chalk mark and had to go for a physical exam. Otherwise, they could go to the Great Hall to wait.'"

"Wait for what?" Ashley asked.

"They had to be interviewed by legal inspectors. Oh, this says by 1917, everyone had to be examined by the doctors. If they had a disease that was curable, they were sent to the island's hospital. If not, they were sent back home."

"That's awful," Jenny said.

"Sometimes families would stay here for weeks or even months if someone in the family was sick and had to be in the hospital. There were other requirements, like being able to read and write and having at least twenty dollars. Otherwise, they couldn't come into the country."

"Did Annie Moore have to go through all that?" Ashley wanted to know.

"She came early enough that most of those restrictions weren't in place yet," Nellie said.

"I bet she was scared," Linda said, and she took Ashley's hand. The other girls held their partners' hands, and they went through the buildings and exhibits with a new awareness. Alice thanked God for an immigrant girl who shared Ashley's surname and brought their heritage alive for six modern-day ANGELs.

◠◡

Friday morning, the girls were up early. This was Nellie's special day, and they were all eager to get started.

Nellie wore a white silk jacket with royal-blue ribbon trim and covered buttons over a matching blue-and-white dotted georgette skirt. With navy low-heeled shoes and matching purse, she looked pretty and sophisticated. The girls pronounced her outfit perfect.

They all accompanied Nellie to Macy's, where the buyer had arranged to meet her. Rebekah Goldberg arrived at the same time and whisked Nellie away after they arranged to meet back there at two o'clock.

After exploring every floor of Macy's, spritzing themselves with perfume samples and moisturizing with lotions and taking pictures of each other in various hats, Alice led the ANGELs up Seventh Avenue to see the sights of the garment district.

While they ate lunch in a delicatessen, the girls watched the activity outside the window with fascination. Models hurried along the street. Men in business suits talked on cell phones as they walked. Workers rushed by pushing racks of clothing. Everyone seemed to be in a hurry.

After lunch, they returned to Macy's and did some more looking around. By the time Nellie joined them, looking exhilarated and as fresh as she had when they started, Alice understood what it meant to shop till you drop. She was ready to soak her feet in the bathtub, but they still had much more to see, and only the rest of this day and all of the next were left of their trip. The itinerary for the next day included a trip to Central Park and a quick visit to the Metropolitan Museum of Art before they went to view the Macy's Fourth of July Fireworks extravaganza. As they headed on an uptown bus for Rockefeller Center, then St. Patrick's Cathedral, Alice hoped her feet would hold out.

⚯

The last stanza of "God Bless America" rang through the downstairs of Grace Chapel Inn. Louise's piano lessons were finished for the day and she was practicing for church. Jane waited for another song, but the piano was silent. She went to the open door of the parlor and peeked inside. Louise looked up over the rim of her glasses and smiled.

"That was beautiful," Jane said. "Are you finished?"

"Yes. Come on in." She was putting away music.

Jane closed the door behind her and leaned against it. "I just wanted to let you know I may not be here for dinner. Todd called. He wants me to meet him at Jacob's Mill Park."

"Maybe I'll call Viola and talk her into going out for dinner." Louise put her music in the piano bench. Then she looked at Jane. "It sounds to me like Todd is becoming serious."

Jane tilted her head, considering the comment. "I don't know. We agreed to be friends and take it one step at a time, but he has hinted at us having a future. I think we may be at a crossroads."

"How do you feel about that?"

Jane laughed. "Unsure. A little frightened. This relationship is moving too fast."

"You talked to Fred and Vera, didn't you?"

"Yes. And they reacted just as you said they would. They're not upset. I'm relieved, but now I'm faced with Todd and the direction of our relationship. I like him a great deal, but I also like my life, and I don't want that to change. I suppose I can't have it both ways, can I?"

"Have you prayed about it?"

"Oh yes. Constantly. I haven't heard an answer. Sometimes I feel that I'm not a very good listener. I need God to shake me and tell me what He wants me to do."

Louise smiled. "That would make it easier, wouldn't it? Just keep listening. God will let you know."

"Yes, I know He will. I'd better go change now." Jane went up the stairs to her room.

She wore her favorite green linen skirt with an embroidered peasant blouse and turquoise squash-blossom necklace and earrings. She curled her hair and left it loose, then applied a bit of makeup. A quick check in the mirror satisfied her. She picked up her purse and went down the stairs.

Louise was sitting on the porch, visiting with Viola Reed. Jane went out to say good-bye before she left.

"You look lovely," Louise said.

"Special date?" Viola asked.

"Yes." And for once, Jane wasn't ashamed to admit it. Talking with Fred and Vera had freed her to pursue this relationship. "Gotta run. See you later, Louise."

Chapter Twenty-Four

As Jane drove to Potterston, her anticipation grew. Was she ready to commit to a deeper relationship? She thought the answer was yes. She cared for Todd. Perhaps a special friendship like the one Ethel and Lloyd shared would work for them too.

She pulled in next to Todd's car in the parking lot, and he got out and came over to open her door. She thought that he looked especially handsome. She wondered what it was that he had to say. It was way too early for professions of love.

"Hi," he said. His smile held warmth and affection, but his eyes had a twinge of something else. Sadness, she thought, which seemed odd.

"Hi yourself." She was just sure he could see her nervousness.

He handed her a small bouquet of wildflowers. "I picked these in the woods by my house."

"They're lovely. Thank you." She smelled the sweet fragrance and remembered the day they'd forged their way through the thick undergrowth to his bog. She held the flowers as they walked along a garden path to the mill pond. The quarried stone remains of a mill stood beside the pond. The pond garden was deserted except for a family of ducks with a string of ducklings paddling along after their mother. Off in the farthest part of the park, a string quartet was giving a concert. The distant laughter of children could be heard from the picnic area. The air had cooled from the heat of the day, and a slight breeze ruffled Jane's hair. The serenity of the scene soothed her nerves. She sat on a large, squared-stone wall and gazed across the pond.

"I love it here," she said. It reminded her of their afternoon at Longwood Gardens and the closeness they'd discovered that day.

For several moments, Todd stood looking at the pond in silence. Then he sat next to her.

"Jane." He turned to her and looked into her eyes, and she saw pain. She reached for his hand.

"What's wrong, Todd?"

"I . . . I don't know how to tell you this." He clasped her hand. "You know I care about you a great deal. I think . . . I feel . . . I haven't felt this way about any woman since . . ." His voice trailed off. He gave her an awkward smile.

Jane closed her eyes for a moment, then she looked into his eyes. "I'm afraid to verbalize my feelings. We haven't known each other very long, but . . ."

"Wait. Don't say anything."

Jane stared at him, wondering why he cut her off so abruptly. He squeezed her hand, then let it go.

"I told you my ex-wife was coming to talk to me. Well, she came. She wants . . ." He slowly shook his head.

"What, Todd?"

"She wants to get back together. She wants us to be married again."

"She does?" Jane couldn't believe what she was hearing. Todd nodded his head.

"What did you tell her? Does she know about us?" Suddenly, Jane felt as if she were the other woman in a triangle. But that was ridiculous. That woman had divorced Todd. She had hurt him. How could he even consider taking her back?

Then the thought came to her, *How could he* not? *Todd is a Christian. He believes in the sanctity of marriage, just as I believe. Being divorced doesn't change that.* Jane sighed. She had begun thinking she and Todd were a couple.

"I didn't tell her about us, Jane. I'm sorry. Our relationship is none of her business. She left me. I don't want to taint what we have by telling her. Does that make sense?" He gazed at her with such bleakness, she wanted to cry.

"How can she just waltz back into your life and expect you to accept her back? That's not fair to you. But then, she hasn't been fair, has she?" Jane wanted to lash out at this woman. She wanted to drive her away.

"She . . . Brenda was hurting when she left. She says now that she knows she made a mistake. She asked me to forgive her. I know I must forgive her, and I believe that she means what she says. She quit her job in the city, sold the house and is moving to Potterston. She said that she intends to stay here and make me understand no matter how long it takes." He looked at Jane with real sorrow in his eyes. "I feel so torn. I don't want to lose you, Jane."

"I . . . I don't want to lose you either, but you must pray about it. Ask God what you should do." That was the right answer, she was sure, but it sounded so shallow. Besides, right now, all Jane wanted was for that woman to go away. She doubted that was how God wanted her to pray, but it wasn't fair. She didn't want to lose Todd.

"I've been praying all day," Todd said. "I don't have an answer. Brenda was very young when we married, and she worked to help me finish college. She started working as a secretary in a large corporation, and she stayed there all these years, working her way up but never breaking out of that mold. She said she felt stifled and she needed to find something more for her life. She included me in her dissatisfaction, as if I had held her back. She says she has discovered that happiness has to come from God first, then from each other. She wants us to try again."

"What if it doesn't work, Todd?"

"That question is burning a hole in my stomach, but I can't turn my back on her. I still have feelings for her."

His face showed such pain that Jane's heart ached for him. She hugged him. He put his arms around her, and they clung to each other. Finally, Todd let her go.

"I'm sorry that you got involved in all of this. I haven't given her my answer yet. I'm still not certain she and I have a chance. Besides, I wanted to talk to you first. Would you pray for me, for us?"

"Yes. Yes, I definitely will."

"Thank you. I know I can count on you." He ran his hands through his hair and sighed. There wasn't anything more to say.

After a few minutes of silence, Jane said. "I'd better go now."

"All right. I'll walk you to your car."

They rose from the wall and walked side by side, but they didn't talk and they didn't touch. Todd waited for her to leave before he pulled out of the parking lot and followed her as far as his driveway. As she drove home, Jane tried to pray, but the words wouldn't form in her thoughts. Her emotions churned—grief, anger, disbelief. Todd had not betrayed her. His wife had turned his life upside down once again, only this time, Jane was caught in the turmoil.

A light was on in the study when she got home. Ignoring it, she went upstairs.

She plopped down on the small couch in her room and hugged a pillow to her chest. Her paintings of the seasons of her life that decorated the walls failed to bring her comfort. She wanted to pray, to find God's comfort, but her thoughts were too jumbled and unclear.

At that moment, she missed her father more than she had since the day of his funeral. He always knew what to say and how to help her figure out what to do. Then she remembered her father telling her, "It is not so much what we pray as *that* we pray and reach out to God with our hearts. Our Father in heaven knows our needs without telling Him, but He loves to hear our voices."

Finally, she whispered, "Dear Lord, I hope you are reading my heart, because I don't know what to say or what to ask for. Help me and Todd. Amen."

It rained during the night. Restless, Jane listened to the patter on the roof. The sound usually lulled her to sleep, but this night, the drumming emphasized her misery. It seemed she had just fallen asleep when the jangling of the alarm clock woke her. She opened her eyes and squinted against the brightness. July fourth—Independence Day—and she had guests to feed.

With little enthusiasm, she showered and dressed and made her way downstairs to the kitchen. She had planned to fix their Fourth of July picnic, a tradition that her mother had started and that she had revived. She looked out the back window. The sun was peeking over the horizon, sending rays of light to lift dew from the grass. A few fluffy clouds drifted in the sky.

She started a pot of coffee, then began to pull food from the refrigerator: ham, crepe pockets with cream-cheese filling, savory cheese-and-sausage custard cups and hard-boiled eggs that she'd cooked the day before. She also had made granola breakfast cookies and cheese polenta to slice and toast.

She prepared the batter for a berry clafouti, poured it

into a quiche pan and slid it into the oven, then mixed up a batch of cranberry-orange scones.

Pouring a cup of coffee, Jane sat at the table and checked her menu. She had invited the inn guests to join their picnic; however, she would set the buffet in the dining room for anyone who opted for the comfort of the indoors.

Thoughts of Todd pushed their way to the forefront of her mind. She wondered if he would see his ex-wife today, and a feeling of jealousy surprised her. *Dear Lord, what am I going to do? I don't want to lose him. I really care for him. Just as I thought we might have a future, why did his ex-wife come back into his life? What is Your will, Lord?"*

Even as she asked the question, she knew God had established the marriage relationship and desired to keep it pure and whole. *But Todd's wife had rejected him once. Will she hurt him again? I only want to protect him. Or am I being selfish?* Her questions only increased her heartache, so she set her half-full coffee cup in the sink and went about her preparations.

At eight o'clock, Louise escorted the Abercrombies and the Larkins to the backyard, where Jane had spread a red-and-white checkered tablecloth on a table. Jane came out carrying trays of food.

"Oh, Jane," Millie Larkin said, "What a delightful way to start the day."

"I'm glad you could come," Jane said. The retired couple had stayed at the inn before. Jane greeted the Abercrombies.

"Please, help yourselves. Who would like coffee?" Jane asked. She poured coffee from a carafe and passed cups around as everyone settled at the table for their alfresco breakfast. Then she turned to Louise. "Where are Aunt Ethel and Francine?"

"You won't believe it, but they left town last night while you were gone."

"Really?" Jane said as she set the platters of food. "Where did they go?"

"To Hershey. Francine said she was dying for some chocolate."

"Aunt Ethel deserted Lloyd on the Fourth of July weekend so Francine could have chocolate in Hershey?"

Louise shrugged. "I promised Aunt Ethel we would take care of Lloyd today. He declined to join us for breakfast but said he'd be happy for our company later this morning. He didn't say so, but I gathered we're poor substitutes in his eyes."

Jane laughed. "Well, good for Aunt Ethel and Francine. And our other guests?"

"They decided in favor of the buffet in the dining room, so we are all here."

Looking around the yard of Grace Chapel Inn, sharing a breakfast picnic with her sister and their guests, Jane realized the rich blessings in her life. She had no doubt God had guided her to return to their family home, to reunite with her sisters and find the faith that she had forgotten for a time. Whatever else happened in her life, she could rejoice in the love and happiness she had in this home, with her sisters in Acorn Hill, and today she'd choose to do just that.

After breakfast, Jane and Louise enjoyed a rare day of leisure together. For once, they didn't play active roles in the holiday plans.

Fred took advantage of the festivities to launch his rental business. Dressed up as a minuteman, he drove a small orange yard tractor in the parade and tossed candy to the crowd. A sign on the back of it read Rent Me at Fred's Hardware.

They ate lunch in the park with Lloyd, then the sisters walked through town, talking with friends and admiring all the arts and crafts for sale in the booths set up along the sidewalks. At Nellie's, Lorrie Zell and Samantha Roberts were swamped with customers, but the two were smiling and seemed to be handling everything smoothly. Samantha told Jane that her jewelry had sold out right away.

"What a crowd," Louise said when they turned up Chapel Road toward the inn. "Lloyd must be pleased, although it was obvious he misses Aunt Ethel. I hope she and Francine are having a great time."

"After the strain between them at dinner the other night, I was amazed that they took off like that. They must have taken your advice to heart."

"I hope the advice I gave them helped. I prayed about it, and tried to think what Jesus would say."

"I wish God would give me some answers."

"I saw you come in last night. You seemed upset." They had reached the inn. As they climbed the steps to the front porch, Louise said, "Do you want to talk about it?"

"Yes, please, if you have time."

Louise gave Jane a loving smile. "I always have time for you. With all the activities in town, I doubt any of our guests will return until later. Shall we sit on the porch?"

"Good idea."

They sat on the wicker chairs, and Jane stared at one of the hanging baskets overflowing with flowers. Louise sat quietly next to her.

"I knew Todd had something important to tell me when he called yesterday," Jane said. She let out a short, humorless laugh. "I know he cares about me, so I expected him to ask for some kind of commitment, and I was worried about how to respond. I care about him more than I realized. That's what makes this so hard."

"Are you worried about leaving the inn and us? We'd miss you terribly, you know, but we want your happiness. If that means a new life for you, then you have my blessing. I'm sure Alice would tell you the same thing."

"Thank you, but he didn't ask." Jane shook her head.

"Todd's ex-wife came to see him. She wants to get back together."

"Ah. And what does Todd want?"

"He doesn't want to end our relationship, but he wants to do what's right. So what's that? I mean, I know God wants marriage to work, but are we supposed to stay with someone who hurts us?"

Louise was silent for a moment. "God knows that we are imperfect people, and He loves us and forgives us anyway. I think He wants to be first in our lives and in our marriages, and if people put God first, they would try to work out their problems together and with God's help. But it takes two people. Both partners. Unfortunately, that doesn't always happen."

"Todd's wife left him because she felt unfulfilled in her life, and she blamed him for part of that. She hurt him terribly when she left him. If one spouse betrays the relationship, should the other person be obligated to take her back? What guarantee does he have that she won't do it again?"

"You know better than anyone that no relationship is guaranteed to work out."

"I certainly expected my marriage to Justin to last forever," Jane responded.

"We all believe that when we're in love. When I think back on my marriage to Eliot, I can see how much we grew together." Louise smiled. "We weathered our share of misunderstandings and hard times. Being married doesn't mean we'll always be happy, but a marriage centered in God will teach us about real love and holiness. When we put ourselves first, we have problems. When we put our spouse first and choose to love him, even when we don't feel like it, we're exercising godliness. After all, Jesus told us to serve each other with gladness. When I didn't feel loving, I'd pray for Eliot. Now that I think back, I believe the times I prayed were the times I came to love him the most. He must have known, because he'd love me back. Those were the times I received a tiny glimpse of God's love."

"But what if one person stops loving the other?"

"We can't make someone love us, but we can exercise love. Jesus commanded us to love, so choosing to love is obeying God."

"Even when love isn't returned," Jane said, realizing the enormity of the command. "God loves us, even when we don't love Him back."

"Yes."

"I still loved Justin for a long time after our divorce, even though he hurt me. Now, I don't think about him very often. I suppose Todd felt that way about his wife."

"Very likely."

"Thank you, Louise."

"I'm afraid I didn't give you any advice."

"I didn't need advice, I needed insight." Jane got up. "Thank you. I certainly have a lot to think about."

"I suppose that means you'll be cooking this afternoon."

"You know me so well. Any requests?"

"Surprise me, but make it something light and cool. It's too hot to bake."

"Will do."

Jane decided on stained-glass dessert as her surprise "light and cool" dish. It required an angel-food cake. Fortunately, she had one in the freezer. She took out the cake to defrost. Then she made the three flavors of gelatin dessert that the recipe called for. As she cut up a fresh pineapple, she thought about her marriage to Justin Hinton. Justin had refused to try to salvage their marriage. Although his betrayal had hurt her deeply, she didn't hate her ex-husband, nor did she love him.

Justin didn't want her love, but God wanted her to give love. She remembered another verse: "Bless those who curse you, pray for those who mistreat you" (Luke 6:28).

"Heavenly Father, I can't change what has happened, but I want Justin to know Your peace and love. I've forgiven him for hurting me. Forgive me for not caring enough to pray for him. Wherever he is, whatever he's doing, watch over him and let him see Your love. In Jesus' name. Amen."

A little knot of resentment unraveled and began to disintegrate. She had thought forgiveness was enough, but now she knew the freedom of release.

What about Todd and his ex-wife? What if his wife had discovered God's command to love? What if she truly resolved to love Todd? God had designed marriage to unify two people. How could Jane stand in the way? She couldn't.

Chapter Twenty-Five

When Jane got home from church, she found a letter addressed to her on the kitchen counter. As she picked it up, her hand began to shake. It was from Todd. She slid the single sheet of paper out of the envelope, unfolded it and read the hand-printed words.

Dear Jane,

I'm sorry to tell you this in a letter. It seems too impersonal, and yet I think I can form my thoughts better this way. Brenda and I talked yesterday, and I know she is sincere in wanting to start over. She knows it won't be easy to overcome the hurt we've both felt, but she is determined to make a new life together. When we got married, I made a promise to love her, and I know God wants me to fulfill that promise with His help.

I value the friendship you gave to me, a stranger who stood as an obstacle to people you love. Your example of loyalty, your understanding and your prayers have helped me find the courage to recommit to my marriage. I will be forever grateful for the times we spent together.

Good-bye, my friend. May God bless you.

Todd

A tear worked its way down Jane's cheek as she refolded the letter and tucked it into her recipe book. She sat at the table and bowed her head. Todd's letter put an end to this brief chapter in her life. She felt a deep sadness, and yet she was glad for the short time they had spent together. She was sorry she couldn't say good-bye in person, but meeting again would only make it harder for both of them.

Dear God, I know this is the right answer. Please help Todd and his wife to find happiness together. Help them to work out all their differences. And help me be happy for them. Amen.

Jane dabbed at her eyes and put on her apron. Alice would be home soon, and she had dinner to prepare. She was glad to be making a welcome-home dinner for Alice, Nellie, Ethel and Francine. She had missed Alice. Grace Chapel Inn did not seem complete without all three sisters. Jane had even missed Ethel.

Cooking always served as a panacea for Jane's problems. This Sunday was no different. She knew she had done the right thing, but the loss of Todd's friendship and of what might have been left a tender spot in her heart.

She went out back and put a pork-tenderloin roast on the barbecue rotisserie, then went to the garden. Louise came out to find her.

"Could you use some help with dinner?" Louise asked.

Jane stood and lifted the basket of greens she'd just picked. She shielded her eyes so she could see her sister. "Sure. I'm just finished here."

They went inside and Louise went to work, washing salad greens while Jane chopped an onion.

"You're awfully quiet. Are you all right?" Louise asked.

Jane turned to her sister. Her emotions still felt raw, but she knew that would get better. She offered Louise a half-hearted smile. "I got a letter from Todd. He must've dropped it off while we were at church. I'm sure he planned it that way to save us both from an awkward good-bye. He's going back to his wife. It's what I expected."

Louise sighed. "I'm sorry. I know that this hurts."

"Yes, it does, but I'm going to be fine." She gave Louise a sad smile. "Pastor Ken has the most amazing ability to preach the perfect sermon for whatever ails me. He could have been talking directly to me this morning. I know I did the right thing, encouraging Todd to work things out with his wife, but my heart wasn't in it. But God can change our hearts. I don't know what will happen, but Todd's willing to let God help him love his ex-wife, and that's what God wants from us."

"Kenneth's Bible reference really hit home, didn't it?" Louise asked. "'Dear children, let us not love with words or tongue but with actions and in truth'" (1 John 3:18).

"Yes, it did. And it's true. All the turmoil I felt is gone, and I believe God will take away the pain of losing a good friend too." Jane blinked back a tear that threatened to spill down her cheek. She smiled at her sister. "Besides, I love my life here with you and Alice. I wouldn't change that for anything in the world."

"At least not right now," Louise added. "Who knows what God has in store for any of us?"

Jane laughed and wiped away another tear with her sleeve. "Boy, these are strong onions. Yes, for right now. If God wants me to move, He will have to change my heart."

Alice poked her head in the kitchen. "Hello."

"Alice!" Jane went to her sister and gave her an enthusiastic hug. "I'm so glad you're home."

As soon as Jane released Alice, Louise hugged her too.

"With such a warm welcome, perhaps I should leave more often."

"No. We missed you terribly."

"Thank you. I am happy to be home."

"Yoo-hoo!" The back door opened and Ethel sailed in, looking radiant. Francine followed her through the door. She smiled, and Jane sensed none of the earlier tension.

Alice and Francine hugged, then Francine gave Jane a hug, surprising Jane with her show of affection. Something had changed. Francine's reserve had disappeared.

"Okay, everyone out of the kitchen now, or I won't get dinner finished," Jane said, shooing them all out.

By the time Jane and Louise carried dinner to the table, Nellie had arrived. Louise asked a blessing, giving thanks for bringing everyone home safely. Jane said a hearty, "Amen," and everyone laughed.

"Aunt Ethel and Francine, I'm dying to know what made you decide to sneak away to Hershey," Jane said.

Ethel and Francine exchanged an amused look. "We decided to take a stroll down memory lane," Ethel said.

"Mom asked me what I'd like to do with our last few days together. I hadn't thought about it before, but a trip popped into my mind. When I was about six years old, Daddy took us to Hershey to see the chocolate factory and the zoo. I've never forgotten it. So I suggested it, and mother said, 'All right. Let's go.' She called the hotel, and they had a cancellation, so we threw a few things in a suitcase and went."

"Did the factory and the zoo live up to your memories?" Nellie asked.

"We never went to see them."

"What did you do?" Louise asked.

"We talked a lot," Ethel said. And everyone chuckled. Ethel loved to talk.

"We agreed on one thing: We both adore chocolate," Francine said. "From there, we just talked about all the things we love, and we discovered our tastes are amazingly alike."

"Louise, you remember how Francine and I were concerned about each other's health?" Ethel said. "Well, we promised we'll tell each other if something is wrong, and we'll make a conscious effort not to be worrywarts."

"That's right," Francine said. "Unfortunately, that's something else we share. Not worrying will be hard, but we're determined to stop."

"When we were raising our children, my dear Bob used to tell me I worried too much, but I always said somebody had to do it, and that someone was me." Ethel shook her head. "Unfortunately, I guess I passed that bad habit on to my daughter."

"But we're not going to worry anymore. And we practiced not worrying, too, didn't we mother?" Francine said. "We ate chocolate at every meal and spent most of our time relaxing at the spa."

"That's right. I had a whipped-cocoa bath and chocolate-bean polish," Ethel said.

"And I had a chocolate hydrotherapy and a chocolate fondue wrap," Francine added.

"Wow. It sounds like you overdosed on chocolate. I'm glad I didn't make chocolate mousse for dessert."

"I don't know, Jane. All this talk about chocolate has my mouth watering," Louise said.

"I have something chocolate for you," Ethel said, "but you cannot eat it." She took a gift bag out of her purse and gave each of them a cocoa-latte bath bar.

Louise held it to her nose and sniffed. "It smells good enough to eat."

"Quick, pass Louise some food," Jane said, then turned to Alice. "How about you and Nellie? Tell us all about New York."

Alice began, but Nellie jumped in to embellish the tale, and Alice settled back in her chair with a smile while Nellie gave them an amusing account of all their travels. Nellie had quite a flair for the dramatic, and she had them all in stitches.

"To hear you talk, I'd never know you had any misgivings about traveling to the city," Louise remarked.

"Alice can tell you, I was terrified. I can just imagine what the New Yorkers thought when they saw me walking down the sidewalk, clinging to my purse and anxiously glancing around." Nellie laughed.

"You did look a bit . . . stiff," Alice said. "But you relaxed after a couple of days."

"After you lost your tote bag," Nellie said.

"The new bag I gave you?" Louise asked.

"Temporarily misplaced," Alice said. "A nice young man returned it to the hotel, so all was well."

"You were lucky to get it back," Jane said.

"The Lord was watching over us," Nellie said.

Jane shot Alice a surprised glance. That sounded like something Alice would say, not Nellie. Alice just smiled.

"Where'd you go?" Francine asked.

"We went down to Chelsea Piers the first night, then to Chelsea Market."

Jane perked up. "Did you shop at that fabulous kitchen store?"

"Indeed, we did," Alice said. "And I brought you a present. But you have to wait until after I unpack."

Jane gave Alice a little pouty look that made everyone laugh.

"You look just like you did when Father would come home from a trip. He always brought you something special but made you wait to open it," Louise said.

"I remember. The anticipation drove me crazy."

Alice laughed. "Consequently, you drove the rest of us crazy."

"Did you skate at the pier?" Louise asked.

"Yes," Nellie said, "or I should say, they skated and I fell down a lot. You should see Alice skate. She had us all gliding around in a line with our arms linked together. Well, the girls and Alice did, and I just hung on for dear life. But I made it all the way around without falling."

"You'll have to try ice skating on Fairy Pond next winter," Jane said.

Nellie's eyes widened in alarm, and then she giggled. "Only if I'm surrounded by the ANGELs. They can keep me on my feet. And that was only the first day. I can't believe we rode the subway all over Manhattan. Of course, we took the boat to the Statue of Liberty and Ellis Island. We went to the theater. That was fabulous! And I saw two celebrities coming out of the elevator at Rockefeller Center—oh, and I expected to see Eloise come bouncing out of the Plaza Hotel—what a fabulous building! I must read those books again. I loved them when I was a child."

"I'm getting exhausted just listening to all the places you visited in a week," Ethel said. "I'll stick to Hershey and the spa."

"But there is so much we missed. We did make it to"— Nellie put her hand over her heart and gave an exaggerated shudder—"Central Park. I was certain a mugger hid behind every bush, but we made it through unscathed."

Alice laughed at Nellie's shenanigans. "Nellie led the way through the park. In fact, she became our tour guide the last few days of the trip, giving us the history of all the things we saw. Remember the wonderful musical clock near the zoo, Louise? Did you know it was a gift of publisher George Delacorte?"

"Yes," Louise said. "He was a philanthropist too."

"I love the mechanical animals," Nellie said. "Especially the monkeys perched on top of the clock. They bang hammers against a large bell. And the bear with the tambourine, oh, and the elephant playing the accordion . . ."

"We had a hard time dragging Nellie away from the

clock," Alice said, grinning. "She wanted to hear all thirty-two nursery-rhyme tunes, but the girls finally convinced her to leave so we could visit the zoo."

Nellie laughed. "I figured out that we'd have to stand there for sixteen hours. We'd have missed the fireworks that night. Seriously, Alice, I'm so grateful to you for urging me to go along on your trip. If you ever want to get over a fear, take a trip with Alice's ANGELs."

"I sense a story behind that. What happened?" Jane urged.

"Well, poor Kate Waller was afraid of heights. We didn't realize that until we went up to the observation floor of the Empire State Building. That dear child went up the elevator with us, thinking she'd brave it and be all right. She stepped off the elevator and saw the view of the city, and I thought she was going to pass out on us."

"I felt terrible," Alice said.

"Jenny Snyder helped her, bless her heart. She took Kate's hand and held onto it. With Jenny's support, they managed to go near the wall, but Kate looked like a scared rabbit the whole time," Nellie said.

"After that incident, I expected to stay at the base with Kate at the Statue of Liberty, but she went upstairs with the rest of the group," Alice added.

"Then she insisted on riding the aerial tram that went from Manhattan across the East River to Roosevelt Island. I was amazed at her determination to overcome her fear."

"And that's why you set aside your misgivings?" Francine asked.

"Partly. But it was something Kate said about the tram. She said the Bible says God holds the world together by the power of His hands. If He can do that, then He can hold a tram in the sky and keep her from falling. I suddenly realized I have nothing to fear. Even if something happens, God will be there to help me through it."

"Hallelujah. What a wonderful discovery," Jane said. "And did you enjoy your tour of the garment district?"

"Fabulous," Nellie said. "I ordered some terrific winter styles, and I've decided to take another buying trip next year."

"You're going back to New York City on your own?"

Nellie got a twinkle in her eyes. "Who knows? Next time I might just go all the way to Paris, France."

"I am amazed at the change in Nellie," Jane said as the three sisters relaxed on the front porch later, enjoying the coolness of the summer twilight.

"A trip to New York with the ANGELs seems to have had a profound effect on her," Louise commented.

"I was happy to see her relax and enjoy the trip, but I didn't realize until this afternoon how much the ANGELs influenced her. The girls love her. I wouldn't be at all surprised if she gets more involved with the young people at church. And her plans to go to Paris took me completely by surprise."

"It sounds to me as if Nellie's future holds something special. I hope she doesn't decide to leave us for a city. That'd be a real loss for Acorn Hill," Louise said.

"She told me she was glad to get home," Alice said as she petted Wendell who was happily esconced in her lap. "She loves being part of a small town, and she feels like she contributes to it. She did mention doing more promotions on the Internet, and she is very savvy."

"Good for her," Jane said. "She has such a flair for fashion, I know she'll do well."

Jane leaned back in her chair and looked out at the lawn. In the softening light, a tiny glow appeared, flickering faintly. As she watched another appeared, and then another. She smiled contentedly.

"The fireflies are out. I love seeing them. Summer just doesn't seem complete without them. I was just thinking about all the things that have happened this past month. Remember when we sat here talking about the feeling of anticipation in the air?"

"Indeed. It has been an eventful time," Louise said.

Alice took a deep breath. "Not to mention exhausting. I'm sure glad I don't have to go back to work tomorrow. I can't wait to walk with Vera and find out how the rental business is going."

"We stopped in yesterday and they were swamped with customers," Jane said. She smiled, thinking about Fred's new venture. "You should have seen Fred in the parade. He was just beaming as he drove a small, shiny orange tractor. I'm sure it's very useful, but it looks like a big toy. I bet every man in Acorn Hill wants a chance to rent it."

"Vera's thrilled. After their discouragement over that new superstore, she said this opportunity has given Fred a new focus," Louise said.

"And what about you, Jane?" Alice asked, giving her a sympathetic smile. "Louise said you aren't seeing Todd anymore."

"No. Todd's having his own fresh start. He and his ex-wife have decided to get back together."

"I'm sorry. I know you were very fond of him."

"It's hard to believe we only knew each other for about a month. He became a very good friend, and yet I'm not sorry. He made the right choice, committing to restore their vows, and I believe it's renewed my faith in marriage." Jane shook her head to clear away the sudden cloud of sorrow that marred the beautiful evening. "And I had the fun of helping Aunt Ethel redecorate for Francine's visit."

"I'm sorry I didn't get to spend more time with her," Alice said. "She and Aunt Ethel seem to have had a grand time together."

"A grand finale, anyway," Jane said. "They had a couple of rocky days, but our wise sister set them straight."

"Oh?" Alice looked at Louise and raised her eyebrow, imitating their older sister. Jane couldn't be certain, but she thought she detected a faint blush on Louise's cheeks.

"I didn't do anything special. I just reminded them how blessed they are and how much they have in common," Louise said.

"I see. You did this together or individually?" Alice asked.

"Individually," Louise responded. "At that point, they were not together on anything, I'm afraid."

"Well, they're very much together now," Jane observed. "For two very independent women, I'd say they've had a meeting of their hearts."

Alice smiled. "I'm so glad. Family relationships are something to be cherished." She sighed. "And right now, after all the excitement, I intend to cherish this blessed peace and quiet."

Alice closed her eyes. Jane and Louise laughed softly. Then Louise sat back and closed her eyes. Wendell purred contentedly. A firefly winked at Jane a couple times from a butterfly bush before it flew off.

Jane sighed. Alice was right. Although she loved a challenge, Jane was perfectly pleased to enjoy a peaceful evening with her sisters on the porch of Grace Chapel Inn.

Ginger Peach Chicken

SERVES FOUR

4 boneless, skinless chicken breast halves
2 tablespoons olive oil
2 fresh peaches, peeled and sliced into thin wedges
   (canned peaches may be substituted)
4 thin slices of prosciutto ham
4 slices Havarti cheese
   (provolone may be substituted)

FOR THE MARINADE:

½ cup frozen orange juice concentrate
1 tablespoon grated fresh ginger root
1 tablespoon orange zest
⅛ cup soy sauce

Marinate the chicken three to six hours or overnight.
Drain chicken and discard marinade. Brown breasts on both sides in olive oil in nonstick pan to seal in juices. Continue cooking five minutes on each side. Arrange breasts in 9" x 13" baking dish. Cover each breast with thin slice of ham, add on the peach slices and top with cheese. Bake at 350 degrees until cheese is melted and bubbly (about fifteen minutes). Serve hot.

About the Author

Award-winning author Sunni Jeffers grew up in a town much like Acorn Hill. After raising their children and running a business in a large city, Sunni and her husband moved to a small farm in northeast Washington state where deer, moose and elk graze in the hay fields, and hawks and eagles soar overhead.

Sunni began writing after her children left home. Her novels reflect the inspiration and hope she has found through faith and a relationship with Jesus Christ. Sunni served on the national board and the Faith, Hope & Love Chapter of Romance Writers of America. When she isn't writing, she loves to entertain and spend time with her children and four granddaughters. Tea parties with all the trimmings, cooking and reading are favorite pastimes.

Sunni loves to hear from readers. E-mail her at sunnij@sunnijeffers.com and check her Web site www.sunnijeffers.com.